THE WISE VIRGINS

By Leonard Woolf

*

HISTORY AND POLITICS
International Government
Empire and Commerce in Africa
Co-operation and the Future of Industry
Socialism and Co-operation
Fear and Politics
Imperialism and Civilization
After the Deluge, Vols. I and II
Quack, Quack!
Principia Politica
Barbarians at the Gate
The War for Peace

CRITICISM
Hunting the Highbrow
Essays on Literature, History and Politics

FICTION
The Village in the Jungle
Stories of the East
The Wise Virgins

DRAMA
The Hotel

AUTOBIOGRAPHY
Sowing: An Autobiography of the Years 1880 to 1904
Growing: An Autobiography of the Years 1904 to 1911
Beginning Again: An Autobiography of the Years 1911 to 1918
Downhill All the Way: An Autobiography of the Years 1910 to 1939
The Journey Not the Arrival Matters:
An Autobiography of the Years 1939 to 1969

A Calendar of Consolation: A Comforting
Thought for Every Day in the Year

THE
WISE VIRGINS

*A Story of Words, Opinions
and a few Emotions*

BY

LEONARD WOOLF

With an Introduction

by

IAN PARSONS

HARCOURT BRACE JOVANOVICH
NEW YORK AND LONDON

Requests for permission to make copies of
any part of the work should be mailed to:
Permissions, Harcourt Brace Jovanovich, Inc.,
757 Third Avenue, New York, N. Y. 10017

Printed in the United States of America

Library of Congress Cataloging in Publication Data

Woolf, Leonard Sidney, 1880–1969.
The wise virgins.
I. Title.
PZ3.W8834Wi   1979b   [PR6045.068]   823′.9′12   79-1861
ISBN 0-15-197511-6

First American edition

B C D E

To

Desmond MacCarthy

CONTENTS

*

INTRODUCTION

The Wise Virgins is a *roman à clef*, and like most novels that make use of real characters and events in disguise, it gave offence to those who thought they recognised themselves in its pages. Of nobody was this more true than the author's mother, Mrs. Woolf, who was deeply affronted by the portrait of her in the guise of Mrs. Davis. And she clearly meant what she said when, having read the manuscript, she told Leonard that if the book was published, "I feel there will be a serious break between us". The book was indeed published, in October 1914, with a few minor changes of which some at least were at the suggestion of its publisher, Edward Arnold. But Leonard's mother was not placated.

It is not difficult to understand why Mrs. Woolf, an exemplary wife and both a devoted and practical mother, was hurt by the fact that Leonard chose to represent her in his novel as a fat elderly Jewess, snobbish, peevish, and forever complaining about 'the servants' in her "nasal, monotonously quiet voice". Moreover she is shown as being much given to tears, and to sentimentalizing over the activities of her family and friends. Nor is it difficult to see why Leonard, after the liberating experience of four years at Cambridge under the all-pervading influence of the rationalist philosopher G.E. Moore, and seven years in Ceylon, found the atmosphere at Colinette Road, Putney, stiflingly conventional and culturally sterile. No wonder that he declined to re-write his delineation of it in *The Wise Virgins*. But other events supervened. In August 1914 the First World War broke out, and as Leonard reports laconically in *Beginning Again*: "My second novel was published simultaneously with the outbreak of war. The war killed it dead and my total earnings from it were £20". Nothing more. Indeed it is significant that in the Index to *Beginning Again*, which Leonard himself compiled, there is no reference to it whatsoever. There might well have been another figure for his total earnings had he ever reprinted the book under The Hogarth Press imprint, or allowed anybody else to do so. But he resolutely declined to, and seems to have put it firmly and permanently behind him—perhaps out of consideration for his mother, who lived on until 1939. Whatever the reason, the book has never been reprinted until now.

I began by saying that *The Wise Virgins* was a *roman à clef*, but it would perhaps be more accurate to say that it is only partly one. For while it is undoubtedly true that some of the characters in it, and some of the scenes in which they appear, are portraits of real people set against recognisable backgrounds, I think it is equally true that the book has a great deal more to offer than these pseudo-likenesses of living characters. For that reason I would like to discuss first the three major themes around which the novel is written, and to postpone until later any discussion of the 'impersonations', however interesting and revealing they may have become in the light of subsequent events.

First, then, *The Wise Virgins* is a study of class distinctions. The distinctions are finely drawn, and are very subtly woven into the fabric of the narrative. In them Leonard analyses, with acute perception and some astringent—not to say caustic—humour, the social and cultural differences between the ambience, ethos and *mores* of an affluent upper-class family living in Kensington, and those of a conventional middle-class family living in Putney (Richstead). To do so, he has recourse to a number of characters and scenes which vividly exemplify the leisurely life-style of the former, and the humbler occupations and recreations of the latter. An example of the latter is the river picnic on which the Garlands and the Davises go, a succession of scenes whose evocative accuracy anybody familiar with the Thames on a hot summer afternoon, even today, will surely corroborate. Leonard, I think I am right in saying, nowhere gives us a precise date for the events he describes, but some of them are sufficiently close to actuality to make it reasonably certain that the action takes place in or around 1912-13. What is certain is that he began writing the novel in September 1912, and finished it some time between June 1913 and the end of that year. In reading it today, therefore, one has to bear in mind that it describes things as they were more than 60 years ago, before the First World War, when the great majority of people went to Church on Sunday as a matter of course, and long before female emancipation had become at all widespread.

The second theme which Leonard explores in *The Wise Virgins* is again a matter of distinction, but this time not of class or culture, but of religion—or the lack of it. Between, that is to say, the orthodox Christianity of the suburban Garlands on the one hand, with their good works, their regular church attendance, and one eye on the Vicar as a possible husband for an unmarried daughter; on another hand, the intellectual, free-thinking, agnostics in the shape of the Lawrence family and their friends; and on the third hand, the views of the Davises, the newcomers into the enclosed social world of Richstead, who are Jews. Not surprisingly, Leonard writes of what this conflict meant, to them and to him, with a good deal less detachment and much more passion than he wrote about their other differences. Here again, one must bear in mind the climate of opinion that obtained in 1912, a quarter of a century before Hitler came to power. And although it is true that this country had, from 1880 at least, opened its doors to immigrant Jews fleeing from oppression in Eastern Europe, it is also true that there was a great deal of latent anti-semitism about, especially in the middle and upper classes. So that it is not in the least out of character for Leonard to make May Garland say, after the Davis's first visit to her home: "I hate Jews". Or to write the scene between Harry Davis and Trevor Trevithick on Waterloo Bridge, in which Harry burst out at him:

"You talk and you talk and you talk—no blood in you! You never *do* anything."
"Why do you think it is so important to do things?"
"Why? Because I'm a Jew, I tell you—I'm a Jew!"

Harry is always complaining that the Lawrences and their friends, as well as the Garlands, never *do* anything, and of course it is perfectly true that young women of their class, in 1912, never did. They sat at home reading, writing, painting or sewing, patiently waiting for an eligible suitor to turn up. And when Harry Davis turns up in Camilla Lawrence's life, the repercussions set up by the fact that he is a Jew are considerable. Leonard describes them with extraordinary vividness in the scene between Harry and Camilla, when they go for a walk on the Downs and Harry explains to her what it means to be a Jew, and what Jews consider "worth while". In this connection one should not forget that, when Virginia finally decided to accept Leonard's proposal of marriage, she wrote to several friends saying "I am going to marry a penniless Jew".

The third and last, but by far the most important strand in the novel, is the love affair between Harry and Camilla—or, if you like, between Leonard Woolf and Virginia

Stephen. There can be no doubt about the character identification, and, because the novel was written very shortly after their marriage had taken place, its picture of their courtship (apart from its conclusion) is largely accurate. It is also very revealing about certain aspects of both their characters, and that of Virginia's sister Vanessa (Katharine Lawrence in the book) as well. Leonard's sister Bella, of whom he was very fond, saw in Harry Davis all Leonard's "less pleasant characteristics magnified to the nth". That may be; but I do not think Leonard saw himself as Harry Davis: rather that in Harry he created the image of a young man with Leonard's background, education and intellectual gifts, but without the wisdom and experience which Leonard had acquired through his years as a Civil Servant in Ceylon. Had it not been for that experience he might well have behaved as silently, sullenly and egotistically as Harry Davis does in the book. Many intelligent young men do behave so when they find themselves—as Harry did—in a family circle whose conventions they have rejected and whose beliefs they have outgrown.

The portraits of Katharine Lawrence and Camilla Lawrence are in a different category, for both of them are seen through the eyes of Leonard, who admired and loved them both. Vanessa's calm wisdom, her beautiful voice, and her practical good sense are marvellously conveyed, as are Virginia's beauty, her strangeness, her sexual frigidity, and her wonderful propensity for imaginative flights of fancy. A superb example of the latter is Leonard's description of her plan to live to old age among a flock of chickens.

There are one or two other, less important, portraits in the story. Mr. Davis père, Harry's father, is a shadowy figure who bears no resemblance to Leonard Woolf's father, a distinguished Q.C., who died at the early age of 48, leaving Leonard's mother with nine children to bring up and insufficient means on which to do so. Hence the move from Lexham Gardens to Putney—a significant step down the social ladder.

Camilla's father, Mr. Lawrence, is likewise no more than a mere sketch of the august and formidable Victorian man-of-letters who, virtually single-handed, created the *Dictionary of National Biography*. The sketch, nevertheless, is brilliantly vivid and convincing, despite the fact that Sir Leslie had died in 1904, eight years before the events in *The Wise Virgins* are presumed to have taken place. Indeed Mr Lawrence is really Sir Leslie seen through Virginia's eyes, as we can tell from her description of him in *Moments of Being*.

Lastly there is the portrait, or rather the caricature, of Clive Bell in the character of 'Arthur'. As an undergraduate at Trinity College, Cambridge, he was highly articulate, which is not the same thing as being garrulous or a chatterbox. But Leonard did not like him, and was frequently irritated by his ebullient talkativeness. And in many respects Clive conformed outwardly to the popular image of a well-to-do philistine undergraduate at the turn of the last century. But Cambridge opened his eyes to the delights of literature, especially poetry, and alone among the Cambridge friends of that period who ultimately constituted 'Old Bloomsbury' Clive had a passionate and informed interest in pictures. It was this, no doubt, which first attracted him to Vanessa Stephen, herself destined to become a distinguished painter, whom he married in 1907. So that when, in June 1911, Leonard came home on leave from Ceylon, it was to find Clive and Vanessa installed in 46 Gordon Square. We know, from Leonard's correspondence with Lytton Strachey in 1908-9, that the successful outcome of Clive's courtship of Vanessa would have been particularly distasteful to him. This,

I believe, sufficiently explains Leonard's unkind and very unfair representation of Clive in *The Wise Virgins*.

*   *   *

Although *The Wise Virgins* was published in October 1914, Virginia did not read it until January 1915, probably because Leonard thought it unwise to show her so personal an account of their courtship until she had recovered from her third attack of mental illness. Here is her reaction to the book, as recorded in her Diary for January 31st 1915:

> "After tea, as no one came (we've hardly seen anyone this week) I started reading *The Wise Virgins*, and read it straight on till bedtime, when I finished it. My opinion is that it's a remarkable book; very bad in parts; first rate in others. A writer's book, I think, because only a writer perhaps can see why the good parts are so very good, and why the bad parts aren't very bad."

That is a judgment with which many readers will possibly concur, although it seems to me to do rather less than justice to the book's merits as a whole. The novel certainly has its faults, though as Virginia says they are not very grave. There are *longueurs* in the middle (the Richstead garden-party is too long drawn out) and Gwen's overhearing of the conversation between Harry and Camilla in the shrubbery is an unconvincing contrivance. Some of the characters, too, lack credibility in certain respects: nobody could for a moment believe in Harry's painting, or for that matter in Camilla's. They are given these attributes simply in order to confuse the identities of the Stephen sisters and to enable Harry to become intimate with Camilla. Moreover, younger readers will no doubt find the dénouement surprising, even melodramatic;

but that is a reflection on the social conventions of the time, not on the author.

But these are relatively small blemishes when set beside the novel's merits: its wit, the suppleness and appositeness of the dialogue throughout: the skilful organisation of the plot, which builds up to its climax with growing tension; and above all the accuracy and perceptiveness with which the author describes a whole range of visual experiences so that they come vividly to life. Take, for example, the passage about the barges on the Thames which Harry sees in the darkness from the parapet of Waterloo Bridge, or the evocation of the devastatingly dreary Eastbourne hotel in which the final stages of the drama are played out. It takes a writer, as Virginia saw, and she used the term advisedly, to achieve such effects.

April 1979   I.M.P

THE WISE VIRGINS

BEGINS WITH WORDS IN A GARDEN

Man is not naturally a gregarious animal, though he has become so under the compulsion of circumstances and civilisation. You can see this in the history of his dwellings. In the beginning he and she lived in a cave, like leopards and other flesh-eating animals, savagely remote from their fellows; or they burrowed holes in the earth, or high up in trees made huts of branches and creepers. The caves and the holes and huts were still individual. Then they came together into villages, and there too each man made a hut for himself. So are houses still built in the country, in villages, and in the East even in towns; they are unlike one another, individual, the dwelling-places of individuals.

But in our towns we build houses in rows and in avenues, in roads and in streets; the walls have joined up, the blocks stretch out into a long uniformity of red brick and doors and windows. The builder builds streets, not houses, for classes and incomes he thinks, not for individuals. But the builder is wrong: the thin brick walls and the manners of civilisation divide the stockbrokers, the lawyers, the merchants, the rich and the poor into families, as effectually as the jungle and ferocity divided their savage forefathers. It was their naked and feeble bodies and their cunning brains that herded them into the blocks of great houses, into the avenues of snug villas, into the rows of mean streets; but behind the long lines of brick and window and gable and front door, and under the thin uniform of class or profession, each is still a monogamous and solitary animal, mysteriously himself in his thoughts and his feelings, jealous for the woman who has come to him, despite the clergyman and the gold ring, as she came to the cave, to be possessed by him and to possess him and to bear him children in the large brass bed.

Intellectual people who really do live in London, sometimes when they go for a walk in the suburbs do not see all this; the builder deceives them with his bricks and his gables and his stucco. They shudder at the rows of red mushrooms springing up in the old market-gardens and orchards, all with the same florid cheerfulness and prettiness of wood and plaster, and later of blind half-drawn and white curtain, and they exclaim: "Oh, these red-brick villas! All exactly the same, like the people who live in them!"

But they are wrong, just as the builder was wrong. It is only on the outside that these solicitors and "people who are something in the city" are the same, only in the thin crust which civilisation has formed over the fires of their primeval feelings. They wear the same straw hats and muslin dresses in summer, and in winter bowlers and dark dresses; they think the same things and in the same way, because the ways of this strange world in which they find themselves wandering are so difficult to understand, and they humbly and gratefully take what is given to them. That is why they go into the builder's stuccoed villas; for them the stucco and the red brick and the wooden gables and the delicate pink of the almond blossom, that brings spring for a brief week into the front garden of every third house, stand for comfort and cosiness. They have been told these things and therefore they believe them; in that, it is true, they are all the same. But in themselves, in the feelings that no one has taught them, under the painted plaster crust of straw hats and opinions, they burn each of them with a fiery individuality.

They are rather frightened of this individuality, which goes back so far to the creepers and huts and jungle; they cover it up as much as possible under their straw hats and coats and Christianity, but it comes out every now and then and here and there when they are not thinking of it. It comes out in their gardens. Those people who think of Nature with a big N, and talk of Pan and Mother Earth, will say that it is the smell of the earth that brings it out.

In Richstead, when the builder builds his rows of red villas, he makes, by building three brick walls seven feet high, behind each a parallelogram of bare earth, and calls it a garden. It is bare earth with sometimes an old apple-tree or pear-tree in it, saved from the devastated orchards. In the beginning every parallelogram is the same, as uniform as the villas to which they are attached. While the builder is running up his villas, the first sprouting of the weeds upon the earth like the first growth of beard upon a man's face, makes them sordid and unkempt and dreary. But when the houses are let, the parallelograms become the gardens of stockbrokers and merchants. The owners stand upon bare earth there, and some even dig in it. Every garden becomes different: grass lawns are made and flower-beds and pergolas and arches. In some the weeds are allowed to spread in strange luxuriance, in others there are ordered rose gardens. There are fashions in hats and jackets in Richstead, in promenade concerts and bridge drives; there are no fashions in gardens, for in each even the weeds are different.

One day in the suburb of Richstead it was June in the Garlands' garden, a hot June afternoon. Mrs. Garland was not strictly a virgin, but she was a widow with four virgin daughters, and a widow of so many years' standing that she might almost have been said to have reached a second virginity. And the garden had nothing masculine in it. No bare patches marked or marred the square of close-cropped grass, upon which stood two laburnum trees like graceful maidens who every year in spring let down the golden glory of their hair. Jasmine and a sterile peach broke the bare monotony of the three brick walls; tall hollyhocks and sunflowers, little clumps of pinks and pansies filled not too full the narrow flower-beds that ran between the walls and the yellow gravelled paths. But the pride of Mrs. Garland and of Ethel and May and Gwen was the show of white arum lilies and roses in the circles and half-moons, which after serious consideration they had decided to cut out of the grass "lawn". There the lilies stood like virgins and the roses bloomed; it was a real garden and the scent of its roses and lilies reached even to the dining-room, when the windows were open. They tended it very carefully, cutting off the brown and shrivelled blooms with a pair of scissors—which hung on a nail in the hall especially for that purpose—every morning before breakfast. The girls took it in turns to perform this duty. The garden was the envy of St. Catherine's Avenue; innumerable ladies had remarked that it was wonderful that such flowers could be grown so near London. It is true that Mrs. Garland's roses really did open with leaves intact like real roses, instead of remaining obstinately half-closed, with frayed magenta petals covered with hundreds of little green bugs lying lethargically one upon the other, as was the rule with roses in other gardens in St. Catherine's Avenue.

It was still hot in the garden, though it was half-past five. The buzz of bees among the roses and the heaviness of the still air made it feel like an August rather than a June day. Ethel and May and Gwen had had their tea under the solitary old plum-tree, that stood on the margin of the lawn and path. They had not spoken for some time. Gwen was lying back in the canvas deck chair, a novel in her lap. She was watching her two elder sisters in that vague way in which one often looks at and scarcely sees the things and persons, the house and furniture and relations with whom one has lived one's lifetime. There was Ethel sitting up so straight on the straight-backed garden seat, intent upon the fine white insertion which she was working at, and May bending forward, her legs wide apart, her feet firmly planted, elbows on knees, reading the other library novel.

There was a vague feeling of discontent in Gwen's mind, a feeling which lately had become more and more frequent to her. It was, she knew, wrong for her to have it, and so of course she would not for the world have told anyone about it. But it was there; she could not attend to her book. Suddenly the intentness of Ethel's pale blue eyes, then the sweet expression of her pursed lips, then the sturdiness of May's legs and the rolls of cheek pressed up by her hands, as she bent over the novel, annoyed Gwen a little. She yawned loudly and sprawled back in her chair. Neither of her sisters moved. She watched the swifts tearing in a straggling line round the roofs; their screams, as they appeared for a moment over her head and then disappeared between the houses, to appear again and disappear again in the same place time after time, irritated her. She stuck her legs out before her and yawned again still more loudly.

Ethel looked up from the insertion. "You're showing a good deal of leg, dear," she said in her mild voice.

"Not as much as May, at any rate."

May lifted her eyes from the book, and without moving examined Gwen. She then slowly removed one hand from her face, and felt for the bottom of her skirt with it. She was satisfied: the skirt was only an inch or two from the ground.

"I don't know what you mean," she said stolidly. "It simply isn't true, is it, Ethel?"

"Well, Gwen," said Ethel indistinctly, drawing a white thread slowly through her lips, and looking from May's substantial brown shoes to Gwen's offending leg, "I really don't see quite what you mean. I can only see May's feet, but I can see your leg almost—well, almost to the knee."

"Ha, ha! Gwen," said May, and returned to her book.

"O Lord!" said Gwen. "What does it matter? But one can always see May's legs."

May looked up again, frowning. "What *do* you mean now?"

"One always does seem to see your legs, May dear, however thick your skirt is. They're so substantial."

Ethel interposed gently: "Don't you think we've discussed legs enough? You don't seem to get on very fast with that book, Gwen. Isn't it good?"

"Just like Gwen!" grumbled May. "Anyone says anything to her and she turns on somebody else." But she tucked her feet in under her chair and pulled her skirt out over her knees.

"It's called 'Youth and the Prow.' It annoys me. It's so—so——"

"Oh, I read it," said Ethel. "I liked it, I remember; it's so clever, I thought. Why does it annoy you?"

Gwen frowned, sat up in her chair, and looked at May. "I say, May," she said, "I'm sorry I said that about your legs. It was untrue, and beastly of me. I'm sorry."

"All right," May mumbled without looking up from her book.

"Oh, Ethel, don't these novels annoy you sometimes? They *are* so clever. The people in them—they make me envious, like reading about people who are rich and have everything they want. Don't you often think you're just like the heroine?"

Ethel's thirty-seven years were written in her face, in the lines round her pale blue eyes and in the network of little veins that were too sharply red. An almost imperceptible blush came into her cheeks.

"I used to, Gwen, but I don't think I do now—very much."

"I do. I suppose everybody does. But then sometimes I

don't. I see how absurd it is. We're not a bit like the people in books—they're so superior. Look at Clare in this book."

"She lived in Richstead, didn't she?"

"Yes, that's just it. And she was twenty-one. I'm twenty-four."

"Well, dear?"

"Well, look at what she did and what happened to her. You can't imagine anything like that happening to Hilda Lynton, can you? Imagine Hilda going off with an artist for a week to Cornwall! Or speaking to him as Clare does to Stephen all about the sea and rocks and earth? Can you imagine even anyone telling Hilda she's like the sea, her 'cool purity touched into luminous warmth by the moon'?"

"I don't see quite what you mean."

"I expect Hilda would think she was rather like Clare, if she read this. And it's just as absurd for me. I don't believe things ever do happen like that in Richstead—not to people like us. It's absurd."

"But, Gwen, dear, it's a book. I don't think I want things to happen to me like that."

Gwen looked at Ethel; she saw something of the patient sweetness of her face. She smiled.

"But, Ethel, don't you ever wish that something had— would happen, I mean?"

"Well," said Ethel brightly, "it does. No. 21 is taken, and mother's calling there."

"She's been an awful long time too," said May, shutting up her book.

"I wonder what they're like," said Gwen. "Byron didn't look a gentleman, I thought."

"Who's that?" Ethel asked.

"The son with the turned-down collar. May and I saw him pass the house this morning; we call him Byron."

"I don't know why mother always will call on new people," said May. "Nobody else does now: after all,

Richstead's London. It's much better not to know one's next door neighbour. I don't expect they're gentlemen—they certainly don't dress like it."

"It might be more fun if they aren't," said Gwen.

"I thought the young man I saw looked rather nice," said Ethel. "Rather foreign looking and artistic. I don't know why you should say they aren't gentlemen. The father is a solicitor; it's absurd to say that solicitors aren't gentlemen."

"How d'you know the father is a solicitor?"

"Mrs. Lynton told mother—and here is mother."

Mrs. Garland came through the small iron gate that led into the garden from the drive and little half-moon of lawn which, with lilac trees and bushes and a stunted monkey-puzzle, formed the front garden. She was dressed in black, and had a black bonnet with dark violet flowers in it upon her head. One could imagine Ethel, having borne four children and outlived a husband for many years, looking exactly at fifty-nine what Mrs. Garland looked, as she slowly walked across the lawn. There was clearly far more of Mr. Garland in May, and still more in Gwen. Mrs. Garland looked what she was, a large, patient woman whom the years bringing a husband and family had passed over and had left a widow, with a round red face, very much what they found her as a sweet-tempered girl of eighteen. She had reached the age when one wears black clothes, and walking is something of a burden, and one's thoughts and conversation turn about what has happened rather than what will happen.

"Well, dears," she said, smiling slightly, as Ethel came quickly to meet her, and May and Gwen got up.

Gwen ran up to her, took her by the arm, and made her sit down. "Now, mother," she said, "out with it quickly—you know we're dying to hear what they're like."

Mrs. Garland smiled at Gwen. It was Ethel's smile, a smile

which was often on the lips of mother and elder daughter, very sweet, very patient, but a smile which very often seemed to the person to whom they were talking to be curiously unintelligent, curiously unconnected with the smiler's actual thoughts. When you first saw it it made you happy to think that it was you who had called it forth, that it was directed to you—and then came the disappointment at finding that you had nothing more to do with it than the chair on which you were sitting.

"I only saw Mrs. Davis and the daughter. They both seemed very nice—rather foreign, I think."

"I expect they're Jews," said May.

"Do you know," Mrs. Garland said in her low, serious voice, "I believe, May, you're right; I think they may be. They don't seem to go to church."

There was a silence. A feeling of disappointment came over Gwen. "But what are they *like*, mother?" she said. "Were you in the drawing-room?"

"Yes."

"What is it like?"

"It's very nice; they've got some very beautiful things in it, I think—china and vases and that kind of thing, and a piano and a table with books on it. I'm not sure that it isn't a good idea to have a table like that—it makes the room look less stiff. But it's much fuller than our room, more small tables with china and silver on them, but very few flowers."

"And they?"

"Well," Mrs. Garland went on quietly, "Mrs. Davis is quite a lady, I thought; she must have been a very good-looking woman, very well preserved. She doesn't know anyone in Richstead. The son is an artist—"

"Byron," May nodded to Gwen.

"And Mr. Davis a solicitor. Mrs. Davis talks a great deal. They must have been better off at one time; she talked of having kept a carriage. They lived in Bayswater."

"And the daughter—what's her name? How old is she?"

"She must be twenty-five—yes, twenty-four or twenty-five. Her name? Now, let me see, I heard her mother call her—what was it? Oh, yes, Hetty. She talked a good deal, too; rather clever, I should think, a nice bright girl. You'll like her, Gwen dear. Oh, and I asked them all to come in after dinner to-morrow. Ethel, dear, you must remember, we must get some little cakes and things to-morrow."

Ethel had been sitting with her head a little on one side, her pale blue eyes fixed on her mother's face with no intentness, with the look habitual to them, as if the words were entering into her mind through the ears and that was all. She understood them, her attention was fixed somewhere around them, but they did not really interest her. But the mention of something to do, to be done by her, focussed her mind at once; the eyes lost a little of their fluttering vagueness.

"Yes, mother," she said brightly; "I'll go down to the shops to-morrow morning."

May and Gwen were both wondering whether the young man would come the next evening. May said nothing; her large, cold eyes were looking steadily at the sky. She was thinking that it was rather a bore that these Jews should come and dump themselves down at Richstead and in her set, perhaps: they might make things uncomfortable. Then she thought of the young man, and wondered what he was like, and again whether he would come in after dinner next day, and if he did how she would impress him. She decided that she would wear her blue dress. Suddenly she heard Gwen say:

"Are they all coming, mother? Did Mrs. Davis say they'd all come?"

"She said she thought they'd be rather a large party, but I said they were all to come. She and Miss Davis and the son are coming, at any rate. She's not sure that Mr. Davis will get away in time. But I must go and take off my things. Don't forget about the cakes, Ethel."

The iron gate had clicked energetically, and Mrs. Garland's second daughter was already in the garden before her mother had finished the last sentence. No one would have guessed from seeing or even knowing Janet Garland that she was the sister of Ethel or May or Gwen. She was one of those female "sports" born into so many families in the 'eighties. If she had been born in Kensington or in the 'nineties she would have been a militant suffragette: as it was, she played golf perpetually, tried to drop her g's, and dressed in pleasant, rough grey tweeds. Hanging like Mohammed's coffin between the nineteenth and twentieth centuries, between the soft, subservient femininity of Victorian women and the new woman not yet fully born, she compromised with life by finding it only in the open air and on the golf links. Life in return had made her singularly pleasant to look at; the process of continually walking after and hitting a small white ball had hardened her muscles so that even under the rough jacket and rough skirt, which always looked as if it might at any moment change into trousers, one realised that there were human limbs; her face was startlingly and provocatively sexless; the feminine sex of the hair and delicate texture of the skin cancelled out the male sex of the shape and expression, which were those of a boy of eighteen.

Janet had a putter in one hand and a golf ball in the other. She stood in front of Mrs. Garland.

"Cakes? Who's comin' to tea—or is it an after-dinner show?"

"Mother's called on the Davises. They're coming in to-morrow evening," Ethel explained.

"Oh, that's the podgy girl you pointed out to me, May. Does she play golf, mother?"

"No, I asked, but she doesn't."

"Lord, I'm tired—beat Nelly Smith twice to-day." She began to practise putting on a part of the lawn specially kept by her for the purpose.

Mrs. Garland walked slowly into the house, followed by Ethel. May and Gwen did not move. Both felt a little excited, as if life were moving a little faster than it had before they had heard of the young man. May chewed the end of a piece of grass thoughtfully. Her mind moved slowly; she thought again of her blue dress, and what impression she would make. Gwen thought of the young man in the turned down collar. It was rather exciting his being an artist; she imagined him sitting next day in the drawing-room, talking to her. She would have to talk to him about pictures, and she didn't know anything really about them, she felt. She tried to remember the names of—what were they?—pre-Raphaelites or post-impressionists? She was not sure what exactly was the difference between them. She began imagining the conversation. Perhaps the best thing would be for her to tell him that she knew nothing about pictures, and ask him to explain things to her, and then he would be very kind and nice.

May got up to go into the house. There was a slight frown on her large, cat-like face.

"I suppose everyone thinks me clumsy," she said. She felt that if they did it was true, but that it was at the same time unfair of them if they did. She hoped too that Gwen would say they didn't.

"Oh, May, don't think of what I said. No one does really. I was a beast to say that. It isn't true."

"I expect it is," said May, feeling less depressed already. "I know I'm clumsy—but it isn't pleasant to have it thrown in one's face."

"You aren't clumsy, really you aren't!"

May stood hesitating for a moment; it almost gave her

pleasure to admit her clumsiness. It was a melancholy fact, and yet pleasant to feel that one was not personally to blame for it, and pleasant too to hear it denied by Gwen. She felt drawn to Gwen. She went and patted her on the shoulder and then she walked slowly into the house. Gwen watched her, thinking to herself that there could be no doubt that May was clumsy. It was very true what she had said: you always could imagine those thick, long legs under the skirt. Yet she was a nice old thing. She smiled: "Poor old May."

II

THE WORDS OF MRS. GARLAND AND
MRS. DAVIS

The next evening at a quarter to nine Mrs. Garland and Ethel were sitting in the drawing-room waiting for the arrival of their guests. Janet, May, and Gwen were still upstairs changing their dresses. Mrs. Garland was in a discreetly good black dress, to which black jet in places, by reflecting the incandescent gas, lent the only colour. She was trying to concentrate her attention on a book which she thought interested her, "The Royal Palaces and the Royal Family," but she was rather tired, her eyelids were heavy, and she had difficulty from time to time in repressing a yawn. Ethel was dressed in a "high" dress of soft dove-grey material with a high lace collar; she was sitting as usual very upright on her chair, and doing some embroidery. She had bought the little cakes and seen that Agnes, the maid, put them out on plates and a large silver tray, with a glass jug of lemonade and the three decanters around whose necks silver labels upon silver chains declared that they contained port and sherry and claret.

At five minutes to nine the front door bell rang. There was a shuffling of feet on the doorstep and later in the hall, and then the door was opened by Agnes, and Mrs. Davis with her son and daughter came in. Mrs. Garland put down her book, and walked forward with the smile on her face and her face pushed a little forward.

"My dear Mrs. Davis, this is good of you."

"This is my son, Harry. I'm so sorry, my husband isn't home yet—but I'm afraid we're a large party already. What a charming room, isn't it, Hetty? So cheerful and open, and such flowers. What a difference flowers do make to a room! And I do like a room not too full; really we've too much in ours, I think—there's scarcely room to turn round."

Everyone stood during this speech of Mrs. Davis. After it was over, Hetty and Harry shook hands with Mrs. Garland and Ethel. They settled down in the half-moon of chairs around the fireplace, in which stood, in order to hide the fireless hearth of summer, a curious screen made of brass and coloured glass.

"My dear Mrs. Davis," Mrs. Garland began again, "this is good of you," when the door opened rather suddenly and May in her blue dress, a little out of breath, moved slowly into the room. She shut the door, which shot open immediately to let in Janet and Gwen. Everyone got up again for the introductions. Hands were put out and drawn back awkwardly at wrong moments, in the efforts of six people to shake one another's hands at the same time in a confined space. Harry's hand just touched Gwen's as he tried to shake May's, and May's just touched Mrs. Davis's as she tried to shake Hetty's. Each felt the uncomfortable feeling of unexpectedly touching a stranger's bare skin. An awkward silence fell upon them as they sat down.

Mrs. Davis sat between Ethel and Mrs. Garland. At the other horn of the half-moon were Gwen and Hetty, and in the centre May and Harry and Janet.

"It's what I like about the suburbs," Mrs. Davis plunged at last, "the friendliness and all that. So different from London. Here we are friends already, though we've only been here a fortnight. Now in London—why, I never spoke to my next-door neighbour, though we lived next door to one another for twenty years."

Hetty laughed a little through her nose. "Except to complain of the pug dog, which barked at Harry. It frightened him so, poor dear, didn't it? that you had to be brought round with a little brandy."

Harry looked rather uncomfortable, but smiled mechanically.

"It wasn't a laughing matter really," Mrs. Davis protested, as if some slur had been cast on her son. "He was only nine, and a dear little boy—don't blush Harry, you *were* a dear little boy once. It might have frightened the child into a fit. People oughtn't to keep animals like that; it shouldn't be allowed. Altogether I don't see why people want to keep dogs; they're more bother than they're worth, bringing a lot of dirt into the house."

Hetty and Harry exchanged quick glances.

"I just read in this book," said Mrs. Garland, "about King Edward's dog—the one which followed his funeral, you remember."

"Wasn't it too pathetic?" said May.

"It was devoted to him. He commanded it to be brought to see him only a few hours before he died."

"Do you like dogs?" said Ethel to Harry.

"Oh yes, of course. They appeal to one's worst instincts."

There was a silence. "Worst instincts?" said Gwen.

"Yes; if they do anything you don't like you say they've done wrong, and then you beat them. You can only do that with a dog, you know. And the more you beat them the more they love you—which is so comforting. They say it's the same with a walnut-tree and a woman, but then," he added under his breath, so that only Ethel heard him, and she pretended to herself that she hadn't, "I don't know about that—the woman, I mean."

Mrs. Davis smiled in a way that showed that she did not quite like this. "Harry's so funny," she said to Mrs. Garland; "you mustn't think he believes all he says."

"He must have been a very wonderful man—King Edward, I mean," said Mrs. Garland, "so truly kingly. Have you seen this book?"

"No, I don't think I have."

"It's very interesting."

"Dear me, there's so much to read now. And there's so much to do with a large house and family, I seem to get no time at all for reading."

"You find that? I always say the same myself."

"Yes, there's nothing I enjoy so much as settling down with a nice good book—a good book, you know, one that gives you something to think about, and all that—but when do I get the time? There always seems something to do, what with the distances and people interrupting and letters to write. And there are the servants. You've got to be always at them. I don't know what we're coming to."

"Yes, I'm sure. I'm very lucky myself—knock on wood. My Agnes, now——"

"Ah, the girl who let us in? A nice looking girl. You've had her a long time, of course? You are lucky."

"Yes, I'm lucky; she's been with me now eight years. She's——"

"Yes, you're lucky. I know what it means myself. I had a housemaid fifteen years. I've never known a moment's peace since she—she left to be married two years ago. They don't know when they're well off; she's got twins now, and a husband who probably drinks—at least he looks as if he does. They live in two miserable rooms—yes, they find out the difference when it's too late. And the ingratitude! Fifteen years that girl was with me, in as comfortable a home as you could find, and she left me at a month's notice!"

"To bear twins to a husband who looks as if he drinks!" murmured Harry.

"And she was a good servant, mind you," went on Mrs. Davis. "You don't get them like that nowadays. Clean and respectful, never had to tell her a thing twice. Now, what with their education, useless education I call it, and piano-playing and pretensions . . . they have their day out, they see whom they like, and then they won't stay because you ring the bell for them while they're at dinner!"

"They won't stay," said Harry suddenly, "because they're not treated like human beings. They prefer working nine hours a day in a factory all the week, like free people, and having Sundays to themselves, to being chained to your roast beef on Sundays, as well as to your mutton on week-days."

Hetty laughed: "Harry thinks no one ought to be allowed to be a servant. It's one of his pet subjects."

"I don't think anything of the kind. If anyone likes to live in a cellar, tied to someone else's bell, well, let them. All I say is, you'll find less and less women will like it, if they're strong enough to work in a factory or pretty enough to—" He stopped.

"I don't see," said Mrs. Davis in her nasal, monotonously quiet voice, "that they've anything to complain of. We all have to do things we don't like. They have a comfortable home and no cares. The truth is, they come under false pretences: they can't even do their work. It shouldn't be allowed."

"Yes," said Mrs. Garland, "servants are becoming quite a problem. I'm sure I'm very lucky to have my Agnes and Charlotte."

"It's terrible, it really is, it's terrible. If it goes on much longer it simply won't be possible to get servants at all. I don't see what people will do. And it's the same in large establishments: there's my cousin, Mrs. Sylvester—she lives in Lancaster Gate; she keeps eight servants, one a man— she told me the other day she couldn't get a scullery maid for love or money.

"You don't say so." Mrs. Garland stifled a yawn.

Mrs. Davis was now started upon a subject about which she really felt. You could hear it in her voice, the voice which, quiet and precise, seemed to fit so ill with her appearance. There was no doubt she had been a handsome woman—in fact, robustly and boldly, she still was a handsome, large woman. The big curved nose, the curling, full lips, the great brown eyes would have made a fine old woman of her, if she had been squatting under a palm-tree with a white linen cloth thrown over her head and drawn round her heavy oval face. The monotonous sing-song of her voice would have sounded all right if she had sung the song of Miriam which tells how the Egyptian horse and his rider were overwhelmed by Jehovah in the sea; it came incongruously through the large nose in her quiet, precise, voluble and thin-sounding English.

However, that was the voice in which for the next quarter of an hour she poured out the lore of servants, their follies, stupidities, and vices; the unmentionable horrors of their bedrooms; their dirtiness, carelessness, ingratitude. She told the tale of Marys and Ellens and Kates; how one had broken a valuable old glass that "my poor brother" had brought from Venice, how one had been discovered "quite intoxicated" on the kitchen floor, and another—this in a whisper—had had to be bundled quickly out of the house for disgraceful behaviour, or rather the result of it. Mrs. Garland, tired and yawning though she was, gradually became absorbed in the subject. The two ladies now pulled their chairs together, bent their heads to one another, and spoke in lowered voices. An atmosphere of the scullery and the dirty-clothes basket gathered around them. And through it all to Harry, sitting moody and bored on the uncomfortable plush chair, floated only disconnected sentences and the long list of women's names, Mary and Ellen and Agnes and Ethel, that excited and irritated him by vague suggestions and the romance of all that they might mean. Familiar and endearing, they seemed to be used with cynical mockery of him in the sordid, greasy chronicles of his mother and

Mrs. Garland. Mary, Agnes, Ellen, Ethel! The names sang in his ears with snatches of poetry that came to him again and again. "Mary Beaton and Mary Seaton and Mary Carmichael and me." "Bertha Broadfoot, Beatrice, Alice, and Ermanyard, the lady of Maine, and that good Joan whom Englishmen at Rouen . . ." "Mary Beaton and Mary Seaton and Mary Carmichael and me."

But he had to go on talking to Ethel. She had hesitated at first, as he lolled back silent in the chair, just realising the sternness of his face and the gloom of the drooping corners of his mouth. But his silence was uncomfortable.

"And how do you like Richstead?" she turned to him.

Harry brought his eyes down from the large portrait of Mr. Garland in a frock coat, which had not entered into his reverie. For an uncomfortable moment he looked into Ethel's fluttering blue eyes.

"Oh, well—I like it very much, I think. I haven't seen very much of it yet."

There was a pause.

"Have you always lived here?" he went on.

"Oh yes. At least, as long as I can remember."

"Good Lord!"

For a moment she did not know quite how to take this. Then she decided that it was all right; he was eccentric, his mother had said that he was always so funny. She laughed.

"Why do you say that?"

"I'm sorry; I oughtn't to have, I suppose. But—well—I shouldn't like to live always in the same place."

"And have you moved about a great deal?"

He frowned. "I've moved from Bayswater to Richstead; it's taken twenty-four years."

She was more comfortable and smiling now.

"I expect it will take twenty-four more to move back from Richstead to Bayswater," he went on.

"But it's very uncomfortable, moving, isn't it? Didn't you find it so?"

"It's hell—I mean, it's simply awful. I don't think we'll ever be comfortable again."

"Then why do you want to be always moving?"

He was uneasy, he almost always was "in company." He felt that he must go on with the subject, that, if it flagged, it would be impossible to begin another. She wasn't interested, he felt that; she was half listening, as he was too, to the two mothers. Agnes, Ethel, Mary, Ellen! He felt sorry for her pale eyes, her stolid red cheeks, her pale yellow hair.

"Persia and Ecbatana," he said; "don't you want to see *them*?"

"I don't know that I do very much."

"You sail on a boat down the Caspian Sea to a place called Rescht, I think it is. And there the caravans start, and you ride down on camels through the plains of Persia, Mesopotamia, Arabia, the plains of Persia! O Lord! they're vast, those plains there, all pink and blue, rolling away to the huge hazy mountains, and great slow rivers and little white towns set among palm-trees. To ride through them swaying on a camel! Don't you want to do that? And see all those places, Ispahan, and Teheran, and Tabriz, down to Bushire on the Gulf, the Persian Gulf? It's a desolation of desolation there; nothing but blue water and sand on either side, and little white lighthouses sticking up which the British Navy has dotted down to mark shoals, and rocks and things. And you get a B.I. boat to India! Don't you want to do that?"

"It sounds very attractive, but I don't know that I do."

"Oh, Ethel!" the voice of Gwen broke in across Hetty and May's conversation; "how can you? It sounds too fascinating."

"If you want to talk to Ethel you'd better change

places with me," said May rather sharply, getting up.

Gwen sat down next to Harry. "It sounds too fascinating. Have you been there and done that?"

"Oh no. I read of it in the *Times,* that's all I do."

"Mr. Davis doesn't approve of Richstead, Gwen," said
Ethel.

"That's not quite fair. I don't disapprove of Richstead.
If I lived in Ispahan I should want to go and see Rich-
stead. I live in Richstead, and so I want to go and see
Ispahan."

"Oh, so do I," said Gwen.

"You mustn't put these ideas into her head," said Ethel
archly. "Besides, one must live somewhere."

"Why?"

"Oh, well, you couldn't be always moving about. It
would be so uncomfortable."

"I must say," said Gwen reflectively, "I'm always
precious glad to get home again after six weeks away in
the summer."

Harry felt the dull sense of depression creeping over him
again. "It's so bad," he said, "to be comfortable. That's
why you want to go on for ever in the same place."

"But I like being comfortable," said Ethel decisively.
"I don't think it's bad at all."

Harry remained silent; he couldn't think of anything
more to say. Gwen watched his rather heavy face. She
could not make him out; she was not sure whether she
liked him or hated him at first sight. He seemed to be
exceedingly ill-mannered, she thought. There was a look of
discontent, discomfort, almost of suffering in his face, as
he sat with crossed legs staring at the carpet.

"But why is it bad to be comfortable?" she said. "Are
you uncomfortable as a rule?"

It seemed to him that there was a note of eagerness,
perhaps of pity, in the voice. He looked at her for the first

time. "Fresh, pretty," flashed through his mind, "uneducated." But her evident interest warmed and flattered him a little.

"If you're going to be comfortable at twenty-four, what on earth are you going to be at forty? If you're comfortable you're middle-aged already."

"But you're comfortable, aren't you?"

'I? Good Lord, no!"

Ethel laughed: "You are funny," she said.

Harry relapsed into silence. A feeling of irritation came over Gwen. Were they all very stupid, except this self-satisfied, uneasy young man? There was something in him which answered to many of her own feelings, but there was something else—if she had thought clearly, which she did not, she would have called it a certain cynical hardness —which was rather repulsive to her. Did he despise them? Was he laughing at them behind the mask of his face? For the first time probably in her life there came to her the keen desire and the bitter hopelessness of ever knowing what another person is thinking about. Up and down behind that mask of coloured skin were flickering the little tongues of thought and feeling, just as they were doing behind her mask, and May's, and the loquacious Mrs. Davis's—but she was cut off utterly from his as he was from hers, as they all were, the one from the others.

She turned impulsively to Miss Davis, breaking into May's description of the tennis club dance.

"Miss Davis—I'm sorry, May—"

"Look here, we've decided on Christian names," said May; "we're certain to come to it sooner or later, so it's better to begin at once."

"Yes, it's much nicer. But, Miss Davis, Hetty—mine's Gwen, you know—does your brother ever mean what he says?"

Hetty laughed. "Oh, well, sometimes, I think. Don't

you, Harry? What's he been saying now?"

"He says he's always uncomfortable, and that it's bad to be comfortable."

"He certainly believes in the doctrine of discontent," said Hetty drily. "At least, to judge from his practice."

"But you don't believe that, do you?"

"I? I hate being uncomfortable. But then I don't think I often am, except when I put on clean stockings or cut my nails."

"Oh, that sort of uncomfyness!" said Gwen. "It's not as bad as the first time you get up after being ill in bed for a few days."

"And all your clothes stick to you and feel like cold oilskin paper."

Janet had been sitting in the background a little outside the circle, silent. Her silence was deep and protracted in any drawing-room, but it was scarcely ever uncomfortable. At this moment Harry, half turning, happened to catch her eye. He had been scarcely aware that she was sitting there. It was pleasant suddenly to see her bright face and the round cheeks brown from sun and air and wind.

"I shouldn't think you're often uncomfortable," he said.

He noticed that her eyes seemed extraordinarily steady as she looked at him.

"Do you play golf?" she said.

"I have."

"Well, d'you know the feeling that you haven't got hold of your club right? It lasts a whole day sometimes, that feelin'—that's uncomfortable."

She breathed hard and resumed her silence.

"Were you uncomfortable at your first dance?" May said to Hetty.

Hetty considered. "No, not very," she said seriously. "Of course I was nervous at first, I suppose, but it went off very soon. I wasn't comfortable—it seemed all a little ridiculous."

"Ridiculous?" said May.

"Ridiculous?" said Gwen. "Don't you love dancing?"

Harry smiled. "Hetty doesn't *love* anything," he said in a voice too muffled to attract any attention.

"Oh yes, I like it immensely. I like the music and the swing, and all that, as long as one doesn't look at one's partner, or the other people. But it always seems a little ridiculous, if one thinks about it or looks at it. Going round and round in somebody else's arms—whom you don't know."

"I never think when I'm at a dance," said Gwen. "It's too exciting."

"I don't think I do find it quite as exciting as all that."

Harry smiled again. Ethel noticed it, and turned to him.

"I suppose you don't do anything so frivolous as dancing," she said gently.

For a moment Harry thought she was sarcastic, but it was clear that she was never that. It was her quiet sense of humour.

"I don't dance, but I don't despise it. I find it a little too exciting. But I don't dance principally because I can't."

They were silent. May was describing the tennis club dance again, which she had enjoyed. Harry's face was impassive, almost cruel, as he looked at Ethel.

"You don't dance either," he said at last.

"I? I don't go to dances often, no."

"Why not?"

"Oh, well, I don't know. There are so many other things to do."

"You ought to dance more."

"You do say queer things," Ethel laughed rather nervously. "Why do you say that?"

"There are some people who ought to dance; it does them good."

"And you think I'm one of them?"

"Yes, you're one of them, certainly."

"But you don't know anything about me."

"I know everything about you—and I know you ought to dance."

Ethel sat very still; she was as near to disliking Harry as she could be to disliking anyone at first sight. There was a rather frightened look in her blue eyes. She tried to get away from the subject, but she could not think of anything else to say, at the moment, but automatically: "Why?"

"You wouldn't like it at all if I told you why."

"Oh yes, I would. I wouldn't mind at all."

"You would be shocked. One can never tell people the truth, you know—not when it comes to reasons—about themselves."

"Then don't you ever tell the truth?"

"Only up to a point; then I lie or run away. I'm going to run away now, at any rate."

They both awkwardly pretended to listen to the conversation going on near them.

The conversation ranged now rather widely in facts and platitudes. May and Hetty and Gwen found plenty in common upon such subjects. Their laughter rose now and again girlish and a little forced. Harry became very silent, only speaking to answer some question, and then almost completely monosyllabic. Sometimes his mother nodded at him mysteriously; he knew it was a sign to make him speak to Ethel or Janet. He ignored it, frowning a little. Ethel was almost uncomfortable; now and then she made little attempts to enter into the conversation of the other three and to draw Harry into it. The thought of her bed and the quiet of the little room up there and the hour, which must soon come to release her, when the people would go, was very pleasant and comforting to her. Mrs. Garland and Mrs. Davis had reached the Richstead shops and the price of mutton. But even Mrs. Davis's volubility was slackening and stifled yawns became more and more frequent.

They were all rather tired now, and after two silences that were universal, Mrs. Davis got up with: "I'm afraid it must be very late."

Mrs. Garland rose too with alacrity. "Oh no, it's quite early still, and you must take something before you go."

She rang the bell, and the food and drink were brought in and handed round on the silver tray. Conversation flickered up again under the warming influence of food. A general rearrangement of chairs and their occupants had taken place, and Gwen was unfortunate enough to find herself rather isolated sitting near Harry, who was dejectedly silent. She thought of how she had imagined the evening and her conversation with him. He did not look very kind or nice now, nor as if he would explain things. But she felt she must say something to him.

"It is true that you're an artist?"

He examined her face coldly, not meeting her eyes. The freshness and prettiness, the clear skin and the curve of the brown hair as it curled up, the kindness of the voice pleased him. It irritated him that there was probably nothing more. And yet unconsciously he would have liked to please her.

"I paint, or rather I'm trying to learn to paint."

"It must be fascinating. I'd rather be able to paint than anything."

"Well, why don't you?"

"I? Oh, I couldn't draw a line to save my life."

"You don't want to, to be a great artist. Anyone can paint—that's the great discovery of modern times. But what do you do?"

"I? Well, I—but what exactly do you mean?"

"Well, what do you do all day? How do you exist?"

"I don't do anything, I suppose. I'm very fond of

music, I play a good deal and have lessons."

Harry looked at her thoughtfully. "I expect you'll think me very rude," he said slowly.

"Oh no; why should I?"

"What I should like to know is," he went on in a lower voice, "how you live, what you do with yourself all day. I don't understand it. That's what's interesting."

"It's so difficult to say. One seems to do nothing, when one comes to think of it."

"Well, but what have you done to-day?"

"To-day? What *have* I done? Oh, I practised after breakfast, and I went down to the shops to get something for mother, and in the afternoon I read and people came to tea."

"You read? What did you read?"

"Oh, a novel, a silly novel."

"Do you only read novels? I say, it's very rude to cross-examine you like this."

"I don't mind. But what did *you* do to-day?"

"I? I went to Paton's, that's the art school, you know, and tried to paint, and got bored by a horrible model. So I didn't go back in the afternoon, and went and lay on the grass in the Green Park."

"All the afternoon?"

"Yes. I met rather an interesting man there, a loafer. He—"

At this moment Mrs. Davis got up. It was half-past eleven, and there was a note of finality this time in her: "Children, we really must go." Harry got up quickly. They moved by degrees into the hall, and on to the steps, and at last with many "Good-nights" into the street.

"Very nice people," said Mrs. Davis, as they walked away.

"Quite nice," said Hetty, yawning loudly, "rather dull, though."

Harry walked gloomily in the gutter.

"Really, Harry," said his mother, "I wish you would talk more when you go out. It's almost rude to people."

Harry made no reply, and they walked in silence to the house. They yawned together in the hall as Harry bolted and barred the door.

"I suppose we'd better go straight up," said Mrs. Davis wearily.

"It's twelve o'clock," grumbled Harry.

He put out the lights, and went up to his room, and fell dejectedly with a muttered curse into a chair by the open window.

His dejection seemed to weigh upon him like something physical. "What do I want?" he thought to himself. It was a thought that often recurred to him. "Agnes, Ellen, Ethel, Mary, and Ermanyard the lady of Maine." (To understand Harry Davis and his place in the universe and what he made of it—and this applies to nine hundred and ninety-nine out of every thousand noble and inarticulate human beings for whom bed and night so often bring the horrors of self-revelation—it would be necessary to have some account of the thoughts which now came to him. Convention and the keepers of the public conscience make this account impossible in the English language. The reader must fill up according to his or her ability eight to ten minutes introspection.) . . . She hadn't liked him. He twisted himself angrily in his chair, as he thought of the pretty, fresh face of the girl he had talked to. She hadn't liked him, none of them had. He hadn't got on with them; he never did with people. They were so dull, so stupid. But she had been interested in him, he had seemed strange to her. Even the one with the fluttering eyes had been interested in what he said. But they couldn't understand him. Did anyone? Was he to wander up and down the world always between rows of cold, dull eyes? The intolerable dullness of life! And yet the interest! He almost laughed at himself. "Egoism," he thought, "damned egoism! I never think of anyone except myself, or in relation to myself. But I *am* better than they are, for at any rate I know I'm an egoist." He looked out at the dark street; the silence was unpleasant. He shuddered a little. "The horror of the night is that we're alone with ourselves. No one to mop and mow before, to play the fool before. Only our miserable, naked selves—and we'd mop and mow and pretend before ourselves, if it were any good. And that's just what I'm doing." He jumped up, flung his clothes off and huddled into bed. "Damned fool! Damned fool!" he said aloud, as he settled himself to dream.

"They're Jews," said May, when the front door was shut and they had wandered back into the drawing-room.

"And what if they are?" said Gwen rather sharply.

"I hate Jews."

"*I* don't like Jews," said Janet, as if she was rather astonished to find that she did not like them.

"What Jews do you know? We don't know any."

"There was May Isaacs at school, horrid little beast; I suppose you'll say she wasn't a Jew? Besides, I know the Davises now."

"I don't see anything to hate in the Davises, May," said Mrs. Garland gently.

"I don't see anything much to like in them, at any rate," said May.

"Then why did you ask her to come on the river with us? I heard you," said Gwen.

"One must say something."

"Well, I'm going to bed."

"Gwen's fallen in love with Byron. I hope you'll make him wear different collars, Gwen dear."

Gwen did not answer. She kissed her mother and went up to bed. She undressed at once, but slowly. She was dejected and discontented. Was he nice, that dark young man? Had he liked her? Had he despised them? He had thought her stupid, dull. There was something unpleasant, cynical about him. And yet he thought in a way in which none of the people whom she knew thought. Was she really stupid, and was life dull? She would ask him straight, next time she saw him, why he despised them. She, at any rate, had spirit. And she too settled herself to dream.

III

THE WORDS OF ART AND INTELLECT

Mr. Davis sat opposite to Harry at the breakfast-table. Harry watched him over the edge of the newspaper, with the settled, silent, filial irritation of years, putting too large pieces of toast and sausage sideways into his mouth. They were alone at breakfast. There was no conversation; they ate steadily, reading the papers. Mr. Davis was a small, domestic man with a grey face, a large nose, and great grey eyes which the observant observer might have very easily mistaken for the eyes of a dreamer. As a matter of fact, Mr. Davis rarely dreamed even when he was asleep, and never when he was awake. At the moment, the prices of stocks and shares—he had the Jewish habit of manipulating his capital—were sinking into his supple brain through his eyes as quietly and unconsciously as the sausage through his mouth into his excellent stomach. In the brain they were dealt with in company with other facts, of which alone life was composed, golf and books and people and Home Rule, as automatically and effectively as the sausage was in the intestine. In the one the little pieces of masticated hot pig were analysed and combined again into proteins and hydro-phosphates and oxygen to be packed away to liver and heart and kidneys; in the other with equal impersonality the facts of life were analysed and packed away to their separate cells to be combined again into other facts in a ceaseless succession. To Harry it seemed as impossible to see that there was any "I" dealing with the facts in the brain as with the sausage in the stomach.

Marmalade and toast followed the sausage. At this stage

Mrs. Davis entered, and had to be kissed good-morning. She was sorry that Mr. Davis had not been at the Garlands'; they were very nice and neighbourly. He too was sorry. Then, with his eyes and his mind following the torturing cross-examination of the last murderer, he heard in full the story of the previous evening's visit. At nine, however, the last piece of toast was swallowed, he pushed back his chair, put his hands on his knees, and jumped to his feet. Standing upright, he gave himself a little shake; the real business of life and of the day had begun, and Tintos stood at seventy-eight.

"Are you coming with me, Harry?" he asked in the sharp quick voice of affairs.

The ten minutes' walk to the station was through spring and early summer. The sun danced on the leaves shining with last night's rain; the blackbirds and thrushes called to one another in the little squares of gardens; they hopped briskly on the lawns searching for the morning worm. Harry and Mr. Davis joined the thin stream of men setting towards the city. They came out of front doors and clicked gates sharply behind them, brisk and elated to leave the stuffy breakfast-tables and families for the fresh morning and the day of doing before them. Harry's spirits rose suddenly in the general air of expectation and hope about him. Not even the political argument with his father —it always occupied the ten minutes to the station—could damp it. He grew still happier in the train among the crackling newspapers and red shaved faces and the cheery, masculine jokes. He manoeuvred in order to sit facing a fresh, pink-faced girl preening herself in colours among the many males.

He left Mr. Davis at Tottenham Court Road, and pushed through the crowd up Oxford Street. He walked fast, still expectant and hopeful, though there could not have been said to be any conscious content of his hope and expectancy.

As he entered the studio he glanced instinctively towards an easel, and almost unconsciously there was a drop in his spirits when he saw that the owner was not there. The model also had not yet arrived. There were only two people in the long, light, dusty room. There was a little man with sandy straight hair, carefully parted in the centre, and a thin, nervous face, at work on a canvas. A tall, unshaven young man, whose curly black hair by its length and disorder would have proclaimed his pursuit and therefore his temperament anywhere, was standing in front of an easel and talking vehemently. He spoke in a surly voice, as if it were an offence or at least an impertinence for anyone to listen to him, thereby showing clearly to all artists, art critics, and others of the initiated that he was an admirer, if not a personal friend, of the most celebrated living painter.

"Morning, Grayson," said Harry to the little man.

"Oh, good-morning, Davis," said Grayson, looking up, and showing a pair of weak, rather melancholy eyes.

Sainthill, the other young man, paid no attention to Harry's entry. "Colour!" he said disdainfully, "colour's nothing at all. It doesn't matter what colour you put anywhere in a picture."

Grayson was putting the finishing touches to a study of the model of the previous three days. He painted with minute, meticulous care. His study was faithful enough to show that the model had been a fat Jewess under the nun's dress which covered her.

"I don't agree with you," he said in a soft voice. "I've been trying the prism tip the last few days. You look at what you're painting through a prism, you know. That gives you the true values."

"True values? True fiddlesticks. What d'you mean? There aren't any values."

"There are. The prism shows them plainly. Suppose

you're painting Davis, now. You look at him through the prism: well, he becomes outlined with a spectrum. You look at his nose—the outside colour there is, say, violet—then you paint it violet. You look at his chin—the outside colour there is, say, green—then you paint it green. I tried it the last three days in the afternoons, and got very good results. The only thing is, it rather hurts one's eyes; after looking through a prism for two or three hours you can hardly see anything; it makes your eyes water so."

"Where did you get that tip from?" asked Sainthill, clearly rather impressed.

"Carson told me; he's a great man on colour, almost an authority. The prism is a French tip; he told me Gauguin used it."

"I can imagine Gauguin," said Harry seriously, "sitting on the shore of the Tahitan sea under a cocoanut-tree, squinting through a prism and painting the Tahitans with violet noses. I expect he used a blue prism, so as not to hurt his eyes in the tropical sunshine."

"I don't see anything to sneer at," said Sainthill angrily. "I expect there's a good deal in it. It just proves what I was saying. Colour's nothing; it doesn't exist—not as we see it."

"I don't see how it proves that, quite," said Grayson.

"Why, you look at Davis through a prism. You see violet rays coming from his nose, green from his chin. Very good. I'll allow you've got down to the real thing—I'll even call them values, if you like. Paint his nose green, violet, I mean, and his chin green. But nobody *sees* his nose violet and his chin green."

Other students had by this time arrived, and one or two of them broke into the discussion. Sainthill was in the minority, and became even more gruff and domineering. Harry did not listen to the argument, but idled over his easel, canvas, and colours. A young woman came in, and

went to the easel at which he had looked on entering. He
was aware instantly of her presence there, though he did
not look at her—of how she crossed the room, her eyes not
meeting any of the eyes turned on her, curiously self-
conscious under their gaze, and yet aloof too and remote
and unheeding of those who surrounded her. He was irritated by his wanting to speak to her and by his hesitation
to do so. "Damned fool!" he kept on saying to himself,
"Damned fool!" and suddenly crossed the room.

"Good-morning, Miss Lawrence. Will you be able——"
He saw she did not remember; his spirits dropped suddenly
again. "To-day, you know—you said you'd sit to me, in
the afternoon."

"Oh yes, I forgot; of course. But it will be all right. I'll
come to your studio. Paston Street, isn't it?"

"Yes, 69. Will you come about three?"

"Yes."

She smiled thoughtfully. He interested her; she wanted
to find out what he was like. He was so different from the
other boyish students, so open in their poses and soft in
their minds and faces. He was so obviously hard and clever,
and there seemed under the crust to be something intricate
and perhaps violent. She wanted—it was purely curiosity—
to see, if possible, what it might be. And it must be added
that she got some personal pleasure from noticing his
interest and admiration.

She certainly did interest him, though he had very rarely
spoken to her. Ever since he had been a child he had found
the need of something romantic for the thoughts that were
never spoken and for the dreams that he was accustomed
to dream by day. That something had to be attached by no
matter how slender a thread to his actual life, because he
was not one—being the son of Mr. Davis—to be satisfied
with absolute impossibilities or unadulterated dreams. At
the moment she was romantic, mysterious to him. He liked

to recall the purity of her face and her voice: the remoteness of a virgin, he said to himself. When one knows the coarseness and tortuousness of one's own mind, the foulness and ignobleness of one's own thoughts, he used to think to himself, such purity of beauty is almost frightening. One longs to be intimate with it, but is there any point of contact? She seemed to be in another world from his, and that attracted him all the more. Sometimes in that sentimental quarter of an hour before sleep she seemed too to belong to two worlds, to bring, in what she said or might say, the fragments of songs and sights of a stranger and more beautiful world into the stupid tangle of Sainthills and Graysons and Garlands.

In the studio, waiting for her that afternoon, he was very nervous; elated and yet dreading the thought of having to talk. He tried in a desultory and ineffective way to put some order in the litter of dirty things in the dirty room. She was late, and he had plenty of time to imagine all the horrors of uncomfortable silences. The reality, when she did come, was of course far easier. In the bustle of arranging the chair on the dais, and the screen and her position, neither had time to realise that they were alone in the bare, dirty room. They were already naturally themselves and willing to be comfortable in silence when he started painting.

"People seem to interest you enormously," he said when fairly under way.

"They do, of course. But how did you know that?"

"Oh, I've noticed it at Paton's—among all those fools. They all interest you equally, I believe."

"Not equally, oh no. But I want to know about them all. In there, of course, they're like a lot of sparrows met on some leads, hopping about and chirping and ruffling up their little feathers before one another. But I should like to know them when they go off in the evening. Laura

Stenning now—I wonder what she is really like."

"The girl with the spotty face?—the result of too much tea and liver sausage; tea and liver sausage for two out of every three meals is not good for the complexion."

"I daresay she lives with her mother in a little house at Richmond or Hampstead. And they have high tea with poached eggs and a madeira cake when she gets home from Paton's. I expect the mother is a widow, crippled by rheumatism or measles or something like that. She's rather querulous, being poor, and sits at the window all day, when Laura's out, knitting Laura's underclothes and reading 'The Anatomy of Melancholy.' She has a passion for the 'Anatomy of Melancholy'—there are people like that, you know."

Her face was very still, and yet extraordinarily alive; to Harry a calm and depth of reflection and the fire of imagination appeared to show through her eyes. She roused a curious excitement of mind rather than of body in him. The dirty room seemed to be full of the keen warmth of spring which blew in over the chimney-pots from the pale blue sky through the open window.

"Go on," he said, "go on. God! I wish I could paint. What happens when she comes home?"

"Laura is very good to Mrs. Stenning, who lives upon the 'Anatomy of Melancholy' and the late Stenning's memory. He was a stock-broker or a veterinary surgeon. She bullies poor Laura and makes a grievance of Laura's art. I expect her art is her one revolt."

"Isn't that damned strange?"

"Why?"

"Oh, it's true, I know—but it always does seem so strange to me. These thin-blooded creatures! How they get passions for perfectly impossible things (Laura Stenning for art, good God!), and go soaring off on them, breaking ties and traditions—and full-blooded people next door go grinding away in their old ruts their whole lives!"

"But it's good, don't you think?"

"Good? You call it good? I don't know, I don't see what good is ever going to come out of Miss Stenning drawing models at Patons and painting woolly landscapes afterwards, until rheumatism cripples her hands."

"Oh, well, I do think it is a good thing that she's got out of that stuffy room away from that terrible old woman for five hours at least every day. She has broken loose from her fate, and at any rate that is something."

"Poor old Mrs. Stenning. I don't see why you make her out to be such a ghoul. I expect really she's a dear old lady and very advanced."

She laughed. "I believe she would appeal to you."

"Why do you say that?"

She looked at him with some intentness. "I believe," she said, "the darker side of humanity always would rather appeal to you."

Harry did not answer. He painted in silence, thinking of what she had said. She watched him as he frowned over his work. She had almost a sixth sense of sensitiveness, and through this the curious sense of coldness and hardness and concentration about him repulsed her. At one moment she felt that she never wanted to see him again; at another moment his intelligence and his obvious quickness to feel what she was feeling appealed to her. And there was something behind it, a little dark and gloomy, perhaps, but also unlike what she had known before. And after all, what one wants to get out of people, if one is still young, is just something which one hasn't got before.

"And what's going to happen to Laura?" he broke in on her thoughts.

"Laura? I expect they know very few people. She won't have many chances of marrying. I daresay there's a young man, about thirty now; he's the son of her father's confidential clerk. He's not quite of their station in life, but he has done very well for himself, a steady, faithful man, quite well off now. He still calls her Miss Laura, and twice a week he comes and sits with her and her mother after dinner. He plays the flute to them."

"The flute?"

"Yes, he plays Mendelssohn to them on the flute. He has been in love with Miss Laura ever since he was twenty-four."

"And she? Will she marry him?"

"No, I think not. He probably proposed three years ago, and she refused him. You see, she thinks he's just a little below her—and that means a good deal to her. Old Mr. Higgins was only a clerk! And then he's just like a faithful, dull old retriever dog, rather short in wind and breathing heavily through drooping red moustaches."

"She's a fool not to take him."

"I don't know, I don't know. At any rate it's too late now. He won't propose again. And if he did she would probably refuse him. She's thirty-one, I imagine."

"At thirty-six she would take him. But he won't propose then. By that time he will have married a big-bosomed strapping wench who will henpeck him finely. Laura's a fool."

"Is she? She's romantic a little, artistic. She wants something better than a faithful old retriever dog. There's something rather fine, rather noble in her. After all, she really does stand out for something, and, poor little wretch, she takes the risk."

He stopped painting, and stood, with his brush lifted, looking at her. "They appal me sometimes, those spinsters drifting on through life to be dried up into disappointed, soured middle-age. There they sit in a great circle round London, waiting, waiting, in the suburbs—the suburbs are full of them. It's horrible."

"I daresay they're tragic, but there *is* something fine, almost noble, in them. I like their point of view. It's alive, they're alive—so much more alive than those cow-like married women."

"But they miss something immense; not only children, I mean, and child-bearing. The—the romance of life. It gives me the horrors sometimes to think of it. *I* may miss it too; *you* may even—though I don't suppose you will. It all seems so purposeless, so futile, idiotic. That's what dries them up mentally, just as their breasts and bodies are dried up. And little hairs sprout under their chins."

His voice was dull and passionless. His dark view of life seemed to her to throw a gloom over the bright day. She fought in herself against that view. He had not said what those dried-up spinsters missed, what he was afraid for him and her missing. In his mind it had meant what the male wants, a certain fierceness of love, mental and bodily; something which romance and civilisation and all the generations which lie behind mankind have made, at least in our hopes and imaginations, a flame that shall join and weld together and isolate from the rest of the world. She knew vaguely, felt vaguely what he meant. But it was not in her, a woman and unmarried, to know the want. There was no gap yet in her life. She was too beautiful to have lacked or to lack admiration and the love of men, and too alive not to like and to be excited by it. And there her knowledge, her experience, and therefore her desires, ended. Among men, as among animals, it is the young male who is fierce and dangerous, and roars and bellows and makes all the noise.

She burst out: "Life's so wonderful."

"And so damnably disappointing."

"Don't. I won't believe it—it's untrue. There's not a minute of my life that I don't enjoy, and I *will* enjoy it. The possibilities of it! It's so interesting, exciting always.

Painting and people and even walking about the streets. Just to watch the faces passing you! Why, anything may happen, you may meet anyone. It's like a great adventure—isn't that romance? It's absurd to sit here painting in this stuffy room. Come out now, and I'll show it to you, and then we'll go back to tea and eat strawberries and cream."

They walked down Oxford Street into the park at Marble Arch, and then by the side of the trim and railinged grass and the orderly, most English, and well-mannered flower-beds to the little green chairs near Hyde Park Corner. There they sat and watched the people passing and repassing: the shining motor cars in which beautiful ladies lay back looking down contemptuously upon a world which could never hope to sit upon the cushioned seats beside them; old and middle-aged gentlemen walking slowly with silver-knobbed sticks under crooked arms, white spats over gleaming black boots, and the red of innumerable good meals in their smooth cheeks. These latter were more tolerant of the human beings around them than the scornful ladies, often even casting an appreciative glance over some young female form that would obviously never sit in a motor-car; and yet they sometimes took off their hats to a smile from some car, and were strolling to or had strolled from a bow-window looking on to the Green Park.

Harry and Miss Lawrence watched them and the watchers of them, the weary governess and the dapper clerk, the seedy old man with the disreputable nose and fumbling feet, and the little woman with battered black hat askew on her wisps of grey hair, madness in her eyes and white dancing shoes on her feet. They did not talk much; she was thoughtful, almost distraite, but to Harry there was a curious satisfaction in her mere presence. In the gentle afternoon sun it was, as she said, as if the spring had been caught and caged here, and the cage was so large that one almost forgot the bars.

He went back with her to tea to the house in Horton Street, where she lived with her father and sister. They found them and a young man, whom he had met there before, called Trevor Trevithick, sitting in immense arm-chairs eating strawberries and cream.

"I'm glad you didn't come earlier, Milla," said Acton Lawrence in a weary voice, putting his empty plate on the floor and stretching out his legs.

"Why?" asked Camilla.

"I might have felt that I couldn't have that second plate of strawberries. However, there are probably enough left for you two to have a plate each."

Harry and Camilla found two more immense arm-chairs and sat down in them. Mr. Lawrence took out his watch and looked at it intently for some time; then he yawned loudly.

"Three hours until dinner," he said. "This undoubtedly is the worst part of the day."

"It's not as bad as the afternoon," said Katharine Lawrence.

"It's worse, really. One does sometimes go out in the afternoon, and sometimes the afternoon really is too hot or too cold for going out. But after tea there's no excuse on a day like this for staying in, and there's nothing to do."

"One might read," said Trevithick.

"I read all the morning, and I read all the afternoon. It's not much change to begin again after tea—especially when one may have to read after dinner."

"And in bed," said Katharine.

"One might bathe," said Camilla. "I expect it's the best time for bathing."

"Bathe?" said Katharine. "How can one bathe in London?"

"Anywhere. There are all sorts of places, I'm sure. I expect one can bathe in the Serpentine, or on Hampstead Heath."

"Milla has the oddest idea of London," said Mr. Lawrence. "She really believes that there are bathing machines and a beach with nigger minstrels somewhere in it."

"I shouldn't be surprised. I've seen the most extraordinary things in London. I saw a fishing-boat and five brown bears being taken through the Euston Road last week. You never go out, so you never see what goes on in London."

"It's so ugly," said Katharine, "one can't go out."

"Probably Duffelsdorf is uglier," said Trevithick.

"Duffelsdorf? Why Duffelsdorf, Trevor? Where is it?"

"In Germany, I expect, isn't it?"

There was a pause while Trevor lit a pipe. He took a long time to do it, and then said nothing.

"Why do you say London is ugly?" Harry asked Katharine.

"Well, first of all you can't see it. It's always right on top of you, a great, grey, formless jumble."

"Do you know Hungerford Bridge?"

"Oh, of course there are a few places in London which are beautiful about once a year—"

"Usually at night, when you can't see them, or at sunrise, when Wordsworth's the only man to be out of bed to see them," put in Mr. Lawrence.

"But everything's so grey and dark and dirty, never any colour; and then the buildings are so ugly."

"Father and Katharine are a pair, good Lord!" said Camilla. "You ought to have been born in the middle ages. You are like two old schoolmen or scholiasts, or whatever they were called—Duns Scotus, I mean—sitting one on each side of life, judging, summing up, condemning. Look at them—Katharine as old as father and father as young as Katharine. They're eternal. They rule out all poetry, all imagination, everything but the most exquisite good taste. They'll go on sitting here long after we're dead, summing up and delivering judgment. I imagine them with horror one on each side of my coffin, pitilessly going through my faults and frailties—the most charming part of one—and condemning, condemning."

Harry looked at Mr. Lawrence, whose pale face was that of a very wise, very refined, very old baby on the top of a man's large, loose, fat body. It was impossible, from looking at his smooth face, to guess what age he might be between twenty and sixty; most people, including his children, solved the difficulty by treating him as a contemporary. Camilla's forecast seemed highly probable. He looked as if he had been sitting for ever, as if he would sit for ever talking, talking, talking in his immense arm-chair. Life would flow past him on each side of his arm-chair, for the noise and the sweat and the blood of it to be commented on now and again with caustic contempt. But his immobility partook of the permanent and his lassitude of the sempiternal.

"Camilla," he said, "is one of those unfortunate people who are so conscious of what she calls her faults and frailties that she can never keep away from them. She always brings the conversation round to them. I don't see what all that's got to do with London."

"Because you treat everything in the same way. You don't see the poetry in me, and you don't see the poetry in London. You're so formal. Because the buildings in Piccadilly don't have the outline of the best form—primitive or Norman or Romanesque, whatever happens for the moment to appeal to the really refined taste—you condemn them. You don't see them as a whole looming up into the grey mist out of the roar of life below. And the park with its trees and tulips and green chairs and bandstand. And the superb fadedness of Bloomsbury. And the red horror of West Kensington."

"Of course if the horrors of West Kensington are poetical——" began Katharine.

"What you want are little green windows on pink and yellow walls everywhere against a perpetual blue sky, and old churches, exquisite, noble, dead, and beautiful, slumbering on remote from life in unending sunshine."

"At any rate you can see Pisa and Florence," said Katharine. "You can even see Paris."

"But they're dead—even Paris is dead; you feel it as soon as you see their antediluvian omnibuses. And as for seeing it, why, you can see Shakespeare's England at Earls Court, but nobody wants to live in it. To go from London to Paris is like going from the twentieth century, which is alive, straight into the nineteenth, which is dead, and to Italy the fourteenth, which is deader, and to Spain the tenth, which is decomposing and stinks accordingly. I like seeing them, but I'd rather live in Peckham."

"That," said Mr. Lawrence judicially, "isn't the question."

"Why not?"

"Katharine said that London was ugly; you're now saying it's the only place to live in. I might be prepared to agree with both of you."

"I agree with you, father," said Katharine. "Milla can never be logical."

"The place you live in must be comfortable—that's the first thing. People must leave you alone; there must be proper arrangements for moving your mere body from one place to another place when you are foolish enough to wish to move; the food must be eatable; people must speak to you in a decent language. I expect, my dear Milla, London is the only place which is properly arranged in those ways. Anywhere in Germany, of course, is impossible —they are such intolerable people. In France, there's the food, it always upsets the digestion; and Italy's the same, only there it affects one rather differently. All foreign languages are intolerable."

"You might speak Latin," said Trevithick. "I've

found it useful in Sweden once or twice."

"And what did you speak in Duffelsdorf? Swedish?"

"No, but I did, I think, speak Latin in Duffelsdorf too—to a Spanish professor."

"What was a Spanish professor doing in Duffelsdorf?"

"I don't know. I think he said he was on his way to America."

"Where from? Sweden?"

"No, he lived in Saragossa."

Everyone laughed, but Trevithick remained quite serious.

"Now, Trevor," said Katharine, "we must get to the bottom of this. What was your professor doing in Duffelsdorf on his way from Saragossa to America?"

"There was a cousin of his at Leipsic."

"And what was the cousin of the Spanish professor who lived in Saragossa and met you in Duffelsdorf doing in Leipsic? Was he also on his way from Saragossa to America?"

"I don't think he said what his cousin was doing in Leipsic. Well, yes, I seem to remember he did. He was on his way from Vienna."

"Where to? Duffelsdorf?"

"No, they were to meet at Leipsic."

"But what was the professor doing?"

"Which? They were both professors."

"Good God! the professor who was on his way to America, I suppose."

"But they were both going to America," said Trevor, smiling. "They were going together, that's why they wanted to meet."

Katharine gave up in despair with: "Trevor, you're outrageous."

Trevor got up and knocked the ashes out of his pipe into the fireplace. He stood looking down at the four persons lying back like corpses in the large arm-chairs. He smiled at them half-tolerantly, half-apologetically. An air of immeasurable wisdom hung over him as he filled his pipe. No passion, no feeling even to which weak humanity is subject had ever moved or vibrated through the sallow, parchment-like skin of his face. No one spoke. A stranger, coming suddenly into the silence, might for the moment have mistaken Trevor, in his black clothes, for some wise and discreet and fatherly and old-fashioned solicitor, who had just broken the news of some terrible family catastrophe to the four persons lying back stunned and silenced in their chairs.

At last Camilla sat up, and looked at Trevor. "Come, Trevor, we've got to get to the bottom of this."

"Very well; it's quite simple really."

"There were two professors, both Spanish and cousins?"

"Yes, they were cousins, and probably both Spanish."

"One lived at Vienna, and the other at Saragossa? They were both professors of butterflies or lizards."

"You are very near, Camilla. They were zoologists."

"And they were going to America to collect lizards."

"They were going to investigate the habits of the American rodents."

"There, I told you so. That was pretty brilliant."

"Anyone could have done that," said Mr. Lawrence. "The question—and a dull enough question too—really is, why a man who wants to go from Saragossa to America goes via Duffelsdorf."

"I don't believe he did," said Katharine.

"I don't see why he shouldn't," said Camilla rather wearily.

Trevor got up and went over to Katharine. "I'll send you that book," he said in his soft voice. He looked up at the ceiling for a moment as if he saw perhaps a bird or a butterfly flutter gently across it; then almost imperceptibly he smiled round and down at the others, and very quietly and unhurriedly glided out of the room and shut the door softly behind him.

"Well, Trevor's gone," said Mr. Lawrence, yawning and stretching out his legs. "I thought he'd stay to dinner." He took his watch out again and examined it for some time. "Still an hour and a half till dinner," he muttered.

Harry got up and said he thought he must go too. He said good-bye awkwardly, and awkwardly in the silence got himself out of the room. As he walked quickly towards Rupert Square he caught up Trevor, and they went on together.

"I suppose," Harry said after a time, "they always go on like that."

"Who?"

"Those two, sitting in their arm-chairs."

"I suppose they do. I see them two or three times a week, and they usually are doing that. But don't you like it?"

"Like it? Don't they ever *do* anything?"

Trevor laughed softly. "Why should they? What if they —or at any rate she understands everything? Isn't that enough?"

They were in the Strand. Harry was in a state of unusual excitement and suppressed irritation. He wanted to talk to someone; he longed to talk, not openly, of what he only half acknowledged to himself that he was thinking and feeling, but in veiled language that the other might or might not half understand. Trevor with his pale face and soft voice, with his apparent obtuseness and his obvious penetration and understanding, was extraordinarily sympathetic, the ideal confidant whose silence, we can afterwards console ourselves, meant of course that really he didn't understand. Down the Strand Harry was silent, thinking of Camilla and that quiet, bright-coloured room and Trevor's question. Trevor felt that Harry wanted to talk, and though he was going away from where he lived, he walked on with him. On Waterloo Bridge they both stopped instinctively, and hung over the parapet of that little rectangle jutting out from the pavement, and occupied usually by suicides, lovers, or drunkards.

"I wonder if she feels anything," said Harry.

"It would be difficult to understand so much, wouldn't it, without feeling anything?"

"I wonder if she understands so much?"

"She is, I think, the only woman I know to whom you can say anything or everything."

"And what about"—he paused—"her sister?"

"Camilla? Well, there are some things which one probably could not say to her."

"What things?"

"About herself."

As they looked down at the water slipping away silently under the bridge and brilliant with the light from the clear spring sky and the innumerable lamps, suddenly and silently a dark mass slid out from under the archway, and then another and another, blotting out the bright water like enormous clouds in a bright sky. A funnel loomed up at them and the tug heaving swung round above the bridge to moor the string of empty barges. There was no sound and no sign of life; only the great black masses surged backwards and forwards, swaying and straining in the stream. There was something ominous and threatening, almost frightening in their sudden and noiseless appearance out of the darkness, in their stillness and blackness. And then, quite suddenly, as Harry and Trevor looked down on them, out of the darkness of one of them appeared a face: a man stood up from some hidden hole down there and looked at them. They saw his face quite clearly, very white, and the hand just raised to put the short clay pipe into his mouth, and the little bristling moustache. For a minute he stared up at them and they looked down at him—the whites of his eyes shone like those of a nigger in his blackened face—and then he spat into the water; and the face disappeared below again into the darkness.

Harry felt extraordinarily intimate with Trevor. "What couldn't you tell her about herself?" he asked.

"The truth. You couldn't always tell her the truth."

"Why? Because it would be unpleasant?"

"I don't think so—not necessarily unpleasant. She might think it was; she might not understand."

"I should have thought she understood even more—at any rate as much as Katharine."

"Of the truth? With her, I should think, it's imagination. Bare truth she might misunderstand; she is more female than Katharine. But Katharine's the only woman I've ever met who understands the bare truth."

"Truth?" burst out Harry. "Truth, good God! What d'you mean by that? I'd give all the understanding in the world for a little imagination. Truth! what is Truth? God! she was right about you schoolmen—your logic-chopping and your facts! What right have you to call them truth? Truer than what you get by imagination?"

Trevor smiled. Harry could just see by the light of the lamps his thin, pale face, smooth of all passions and desires, and lined only a little as if by pain—like the face of some sexless ascetic.

Harry turned on him. "You're a Christian," he said contemptuously, brutally.

"I hope not," Trevor smiled.

"I'm a Jew."

"Yes, I know. Well?"

"You can glide out of a room and I can't: I envy you that! But I despise you. I like that big baby sitting all day long in his arm-chair, but I despise him. I admire your women, your pale women with their white skins and fair hair, but I despise them."

"Do most Jews feel like that?"

"All of them—all of them. There's no life in you, no blood in you, no understanding. Your women are cold and leave one cold—no dark hair, no blood in them. Pale hair, pale souls, you know. You talk and you talk and you talk —no blood in you! You never *do* anything."

"Why do you think it's so important to do things?"

"Why? Because I'm a Jew, I tell you—I'm a Jew!"

Harry looked at Trevor a moment and then turned and walked away at a great pace over the bridge towards Waterloo station. Trevor watched him swinging along and thumping the pavement with his stick. He smiled as he too turned and slowly walked away in the opposite direction, humming a little tune.

IV

OPINIONS UPON A RIVER

Mrs. Davis was right up to a point in her philosophy of localities: friendliness or a certain type of friendliness is more common in the suburbs than in London. Mere acquaintanceship ripens more quickly and naturally into an intimacy in which the young call one another by their Christian names and the old and even middle-aged call one another "my boy" and "my dear." A suburb is not a village, but some traces of the village community feeling still work in the outskirts of London. If on three days in every week you travel in the same train with some one, and he or she gets out at the same station, and walks behild or before you up the same length of street to a house which is to all appearances exactly as your house is, a seed has been sown which may at any time ripen into friendship.

It is true that it does not always ripen into friendship. It may ripen, in an adverse sky, into a very bitter discord. And that too is the way of villages. Usually the seed is dropped casually by the male; after that for some time he remains a good deal in the background, as an encouragement and an incitement. The seed is borne in and ripened by or hatched out among the females, not without a considerable amount of clucking. Many a middle-aged suburban city gentleman might still be in the limbo reserved for unborn babies if his mother and his mother's mother had made up their minds—and they very nearly did make up their minds—not to call on his father's mother and his father's sister. His father and his mother's brother had said "Morning" to one another before the call for many mornings; they were not without their importance in the

minds of the ladies even then; but the call was undoubtedly
the moment when the friendship was conceived.

After the call the ripening process may develop very
rapidly. It did in the case of the Davises and Garlands. One
must shop, if not in the morning, then in the afternoon,
and therefore one meets by chance very often among the
shops. One joins forces there, "takes" mutton "off" the
same butcher and fish "off" the same fishmonger, buys
ribbons over the same counter, and cakes for the day-at-
home off the same plate. Hetty and Ethel and May and
Gwen met often enough in these occupations, and their
mothers did also. They walked back to St. Catharine's
Avenue together under their loads of paper bags; they
did not always part at the gates of their houses. The ordinary tea of everyday life, not the solemn tea of callers and
days-at-home with its intricate ceremonial, was often
taken together. In the garden Mrs. Davis would finish her
disquisition upon Whiteley's, or May her confidences to
Hetty about the vicar, begun among the fish, the cakes,
or the meat.

They came naturally to dropping in in the morning to
ask what the other was doing to-day. They planned and
carried out expeditions further afield, "to town" for the
more important shopping and the dressmaker, who, com-
paratively reasonable and yet court, lived on the threshold,
but not over it, of fashionable dressmakers; the threshold
stands somewhere near Victoria station. In these expeditions the male was not actually present, though he stood
always somewhere near in the background, the flavour of
him to be snuffed up every now and then in the conversation, in order to tune up life and the intimacy a little.
The Garlands were always glad to hear of Harry, and to tell
of Cecil Lynton or the vicar. Cecil Lynton was the best
tennis player at the club and danced divinely.

But the time came when the male would again be

required, a little closer than the taking off of hats and good-evenings, which Ethel and Janet and May and Gwen received from Mr. Davis and Harry on their way to and from the station. Only a woman can understand the curious shades of feeling and the hidden motives that lie behind the friendship between two women. Popularly it is assumed to be always platonic, but platonic friendship between a woman and a woman hardly ever exists, at any rate almost as rarely as between a man and a woman. Inter-feminine friendships are usually either of passion or convenience, and this is the reason why often they die so young; for on a rough calculation it takes about as short a time to get all the love as to get all the use you want out of anyone. Women, and especially young women, are continually suffering little bursts of passion for one another, which last for a day or two up to sometimes twelve months. This is the result of the atrophy of the power of spontaneously loving males, which the conventions of civilisation impose upon the women under thirty whom alone one is supposed to meet and talk to. Such passions are, fortunately or unfortunately for the human race and its continuance, of short duration; they die down soon enough into ashes or memories or habits.

It is probable that for the first week at any rate there was a little passion in May's friendship and feeling for Hetty. It would be rash to think that one could say what there was in Hetty's feeling for May. She herself, being intelligent, often wondered whether really she had ever felt anything except sensations, boredom, and interest. She was not intelligent enough to see that life for her was simply a business. One had to know people and to have friends, just as one had to know how to put on one's clothes and just as one had to have and read books. Some people were nicer, pleasanter, and more interesting than others, just as some clothes were nicer and more convenient,

and some books less boring than others. Again, one had to
know people and to have friends, partly because the business of life might entail marrying and getting a home, a
husband, and children. One also had to pass a certain
amount of time out of bed and not reading, and it is
customary not to pass the whole of this time in one's
own company.

In the background, as I have said, and not very far away,
stood Harry with the vicar, Cecil Lynton, and the more
nebulous figures of the known and unknown young men
who slept in Richstead and apparently spent about eighty
per cent of their days somewhere in the neighbourhood of
either the Mansion House or Temple Bar. Their presence,
if the intimacy was to continue, became necessary, not
only to keep the intimacy intimate, but because mothers
naturally prefer to think of their unmarried daughters in
the company of young men than in that of young women.
But there was a difficulty: neither Mr. Davis nor Harry nor
Hetty would join the tennis club. When Mr. Davis was not
engaged in his own business or in the mysterious rise and
fall of prices or the still more mysterious rise and fall of
parties and politicians, he played golf at Richmond. A
mixed double at tennis had no attractions for a man of
his tastes and years. It had still less for Harry, who saw no
reason why, if the best place to spend Monday, Tuesday,
Wednesday, Thursday, and Friday afternoons was an area
covered with houses in the centre of London, one should
spend Saturday afternoon in a boarded rectangular
meadow in Richstead.

A river party was the inevitable conclusion. It could not,
like Saturday afternoon tennis, become a habit; and so
Mr. Davis and Harry were definitely engaged for one
Saturday. May's vicar and Cecil Lynton were to make up
the four male oarsmen that the number of ladies made
necessary for the two boats. The provisioning of each boat—

there was to be a tea and a supper—was divided between the two families, with a tacit understanding that Mrs. Garland's tea would vie with Mrs. Davis's and Mrs. Davis's supper would vie with Mrs. Garland's. The choice of the place of embarkation was the cause of much discussion. Mr. Macausland, the vicar, favoured Shepperton, as being near and select. Richmond and Twickenham were too vulgar, though they were pressed for by Harry because it is easier to enjoy oneself if there are others around you who are vulgar enough to show that they are enjoying themselves. The real river, it was agreed, only begins at Maidenhead, but the mothers feared the distance and that nightmare of getting home to a suburb late at night. However, no one knows better than the elderly mother or widow in Richstead, with unmarried and fortunately still nubile daughters, that it is a law of nature that parents must sacrifice themselves for their children. The last train from Maidenhead and other river "resorts" on any Saturday night in May or June displays in the draggled, weary forms of these elderly matrons—who have spent nine hours under the unaccustomed sun (and not seldom rain) of the open heavens, upon a bare board scarcely tempered by a thin cushion, in the narrow space afforded by a fifteen-foot open boat, destitute of all necessary modern conveniences, and in periodic and often reasonable fear of being capsized—as noble an example of maternal unselfishness as the breast of any pelican bleeding to make a nest for its fledglings. So Mrs. Garland and Mrs. Davis, obeying without many complaints the law of nature, yielded with smothered sighs to Maidenhead.

They all met at the Garlands'. There was a disappointment, for Cecil Lynton could not come, being kept by business. But Mr. Macausland, the vicar, was there. "He will get on so well with the Davises, especially with Harry Davis," Mrs. Garland had said to Gwen; "he's so intellectual and broad-minded and artistic." He was a clergyman, too, which in some suburbs is still an asset. He was a hard-featured, red-faced man of thirty-six, whose wide-open eyes showed you quite clearly that he knew what a sinner you were and how the knowledge pained him. He had taken a bad third-class degree at Cambridge after three years at Selwyn, and his artistic and intellectual claims rested upon his lectures on Browning and a three weeks' personally conducted tour in Italy.

After the introductions, in which Mr. Macausland exhibited the courtesy for which he was celebrated among the ladies of his parish, the hampers and baskets were collected in the hall, distributed among the males, and the party started. A clear blue sky, and the earth still fresh with young green from the spring, and a fine hot day, and soft white dresses and white shoes and stockings and gay hats, and even the black parson ending in white trousers—they started in high spirits and high good humour with everything and everyone, that not even the drag of a heavy hamper on the arm all the way to the station could damp even in Harry.

Harry found himself walking next to Mr. Macausland. The vicar was still thinking regretfully of Shepperton.

"It's Maidenhead, isn't it?" he said to Harry.

"Yes, we're for Maidenhead."

"I can't help thinking it's a mistake—a little mistake. Shepperton is so much quieter, more suitable for ladies in every respect. And the river there is very lovely; not perhaps so obviously lovely as at Maidenhead, but to the cultivated eye— You are an artist, I believe—you would appreciate that quiet beauty. Langly, the novelist, you know—he wrote that charming book, 'A Day of Roses'—a dear friend of mine from Cambridge days—I've often heard him say that row of poplars, as you come round the bend at Shepperton, always reminds him of Ravenna. It is. I can speak from experience; it is just like the country round Ravenna. In every way preferable to Maidenhead."

A certain sensual droop of Mr. Macausland's lower lip as the conversation proceeded, and the way his eye wandered over the substantial charms of May's figure, showed Harry that the vicar was enjoying himself in his character of mere man as well as in that of moralist.

"I never think Maidenhead quite suitable for ladies," he lowered his voice confidentially. "I've seen sights there, things going on, you know, in boats—in the evening, of course, but still daylight—openly, quite openly, that make it very awkward if you have ladies in the party. It isn't as if you can go another way on the river; if it's at all crowded you may be forced right on to them."

"Oh, well," said Harry maliciously, "one must enjoy oneself when one's young."

"I don't think I'm a prude," said Mr. Macausland stiffly, "I trust I'm not; I trust I'm open-minded. But there's a class of person which goes on the river at Maidenhead and makes itself—I'm not overstating it—a public nuisance to decent people. You don't get that class of person at Shepperton. I'm all for people enjoying themselves. I'm not a gloomy man myself, and I don't take the gloomy view of my office and duties that some Anglican priests take, or are supposed to take. I'm all for people enjoying themselves. I'm going to enjoy myself to-day"—he waved his hand to the white flounces ahead of him—"with youth and beauty. *Dulce est desipere*—you know the old tag."

"Poor old Horace! I expect he'd have called what you see at Maidenhead *in loco*. He probably belonged to the class of person you object to.

> *To sport with Amaryllis in the shade,*
> *Or with the tangles of Neæra's hair,*

as he says somewhere else."

"Milton, Milton, I think, surely—the famous ode to Lycidas. But that by the way. This is a most interesting question. I'm all for liberty. I'm a Liberal, both by tradition and inclination. But nobody should have liberty to make himself a nuisance to others. It's disgraceful and shouldn't be allowed. There must be some by-law preventing it; and if there isn't, there should be at once. People should be compelled—educated is the better word— to enjoy themselves decently. We've done it with the lower classes to a great extent. Look at their bank-holidays: what a difference even in your time there must be! They don't think it necessary any longer to get drunk in order to enjoy themselves."

Harry was very serious now. "I don't know Maidenhead well," he said; "in fact, I've only once been there. What class of people are they and what do they do?"

"Do? You can imagine what they do. Young men about town and, I should say, the less desirable sort of actress, with a sprinkling of shop-assistants and clerks. Do? I've seen them lying in one another's arms, literally, in the bottom of punts. It's most unpleasant with laidies in the party."

"Oh, Mr. Macausland," May broke in, for by this time they had reached the station and had all collected near the booking-office, "what is this important question you and Mr. Davis are discussing? Your voices sounded so serious."

Mr. Macausland was one of those men who have one manner for men and another for women. Like a chameleon, he seemed to reflect automatically the colour or tone of his sexual environment. His manner changed instantly from one of serious, rather matter-of-fact good-fellowship, but always dignified, to one of elaborate courtesy, suaveness, and playfulness.

"Ah, Miss May, we were having a very interesting discussion about—well, principles. But that is the worst of us men—that sort of thing is too serious and too deep for a fine day like this. We men, you know, as soon as we get together, become too serious. We want the ladies to bring lightness and grace into our conversation—as into our lives."

Mr. Davis, who stood near and whose one method of conversation consisted in the statement of facts and arguments, looked at May and Mr. Macausland rather as if they were a pair of strange animals. He noted May's robust and clumsy charms, and listened with astonishment to Mr. Macausland's little speech. "The man's a fool," he thought, "of course he's a parson." And yet there was a very distinct twinge of envy in his contempt for the parson: he himself would never have thought of making a little speech like that, nor have had the self-confidence to say it, even if he had thought of it. He looked at the parson for a minute longer, and then, with the tickets which he had taken for the whole party in his hand, he moved away, mentally shrugging his shoulders, to the platform. The others followed, and eventually all packed themselves with the hampers into the train.

Conversation was spasmodic and awkward in the train which took them to Maidenhead, and there was a general lowering of spirits, despite a pun or two from the vicar. But the long platform of Maidenhead station and the walk down to the river, among the other white dresses, white stockings, and white shoes, and white flannel trousers and clean young men in straw hats and blazers, raised them again. At the river rose the inevitable problem and discussion how to divide the party among the two boats. May was to take the oar that should have been Cecil's, and hoped silently to scull behind the vicar; but, as usually happens in these cases, after a rambling discussion, the division is suddenly made by one of the party who is blind to all the delicacies of personal affinities, and many a one is depressed to see that just the one person they did rather hope to find in their boat is sitting in the other.

"We can't stand here talking all day," said Mr. Davis suddenly, and made the division. Harry and Mr. Macausland were to scull the two mothers and Gwen; he and May would take charge of Hetty, Janet, and Ethel.

It was, there can be no doubt, about as bad an arrangement as could have been devised, and everyone felt it to be so except Mr. Davis. The two boats were to proceed up the river as near to one another as possible, so that conversation might be general. But it is not really possible to talk across two scull lengths, and the attempt to do so caused continual irritation to the scullers and alarm to the passengers by the sudden clashing and interlocking of sculls owing to the erratic steering of Hetty and Mrs. Garland. After this had happened two or three times, and Mrs. Davis in one boat and Ethel in the other had got well splashed in the process of disentangling the sculls, it was decided to proceed at wider intervals.

The conversation in May's boat was not altogether a success. Mr. Davis, when he took off his coat to row, disclosed braces, a most depressing sight to suburban young ladies on a river party. To May and her two sisters he was an old man, but being a new phenomenon ought to be entertained by them. Their attempts at conversation disclosed the fact pretty soon that he was not a lady's man. With him silence took the place of small talk; he was a utilitarian, and even an afternoon on the river, with four ladies, could be put to some more practical use than talking: you could get as much exercise out of it as possible by sculling. This he proceeded to do, carefully inquiring from time to time of May whether he was sculling too fast for her. Though she saw the small round bald patch on the top of Mr. Macausland's head drop away further and further behind them, and though two blisters very soon formed on her hands, she assured him that she liked the exercise. Hetty, who could always be relied upon to keep up a bright conversation even in the most chilly social atmosphere, discussed books and theatres with Ethel and Janet, and drew in her father as much as that was possible. But nobody except Mr. Davis noticed that the time was passing pleasantly.

In the other boat they were already beginning to enjoy themselves. Mr. Macausland, it is true, would have liked to have been with May, but, being a man, he was less affected by these little social disappointments. He was out for a holiday, he had to entertain two elderly ladies and a young pretty one, he could score off the conceited young fellow behind him, and the actresses and young-men-about-town in the boats passing them had not yet begun to misconduct themselves. And after all, the river on a hot day of early summer is very pleasant.

"Well, aren't you glad you did come here instead of stuffy old Richmond and Twickenham, mother?" said Gwen.

"It's certainly very charming, dear, very charming—but comparisons are odious. There is something about Richmond——"

"Our young friend behind me," said Mr. Macausland, "can tell us that Ruskin—wasn't it, or was it Turner?—used to say that the view from Richmond Hill was the finest and most English view in England."

"Delightful, delightful!" murmured Mrs. Davis, nodding her head and looking round her at everything and nothing in particular with eyes that obviously saw very little. "There's something about water, just being on it, I mean, which is quite peculiar. It has a charm of its own. That little bit now—one couldn't want anything more beautiful than that, could one?"

"Yes, that's very true," said Mr. Macausland; "water does give a view something quite peculiar. A lake now—

there is nothing more beautiful than a lake."

"Lovely, lovely!" murmured Mrs. Davis.

"Most lakes—all, I expect—are repulsive," ejaculated Harry.

"Ah," said Mr. Macausland tolerantly, "there spoke the younger generation. And why are most or all lakes repulsive?"

"They are all the same—intolerably dull. They were especially made for self-satisfied people to admire: that's why they look so self-satisfied themselves, laying themselves out to be picturesque."

"Have you ever seen the Italian lakes, may I ask?"

"No, but I know what they're like. They're all just the same. They were created for picture post-cards."

"Ah, if you saw them you might modify your opinion. In my humble opinion—and I've had the advantage, you may call it disadvantage, of seeing them—I have seen few more beautiful sights in nature than Desenzano, the Sirmio of Catullus, you remember, on Como."

Mrs. Garland was delighted. The vicar and young Davis obviously suited one another; the conversation was quite intellectual. "Such an interesting man," she whispered to Mrs. Davis confidentially. "So well-read and travelled; it's quite a treat to hear him. Your Harry, too, such a clever young man."

Mrs. Davis sighed as inaudibly as possible. She did not altogether approve of Harry's methods of conversation, saying these strange things so dictatorially. Where was the sense in it? Everyone knows that lakes are very beautiful. Why, she knew herself that Harry had hever really seen a lake; she must tell him afterwards that it is bad manners to lay down the law like that about lakes, that they aren't beautiful. How disappointing, how exasperating one's own children can be to one! But she nodded her head to Mrs. Garland, and smiled with her mouth, while her eyes roaming over the trees reflected in their look her irritation with Harry.

"I should just love to see Italy," Gwen had meanwhile remarked.

"Ah, but which Italy, Miss Gwen? There are two, you know, and so different. Where are you going to start?"

"I want to see both—everything," said Gwen, afraid of displaying her ignorance of the fact that there are two Italies.

"Then Rome is the place for you; that's where they meet. There you have the glorious monuments of the mighty Roman Empire side by side with the still more glorious works—and how different!—of the Christian renaissance."

"I went to Rome on my honeymoon; that's many years ago now," said Mrs. Davis. "I suppose it's changed a good deal since then. But what a marvellous town—St. Peter's, I remember, and that other place, the Colossus, isn't it?"

"Colosseum?" suggested the vicar.

"Yes, that's it, I suppose."

"I don't expect that's changed very much since you were there, mother," said Harry.

"You can never tell nowadays. Everything changes." Mrs. Davis spoke plaintively, as if all changes were a personal and malicious insult to her. "Everything changes. What with penny-steamboats, I'm told, on the Grand Canal at Venice—and all that."

The conversation was here interrupted by the boat arriving at the entrance to a lock. All attention on the men's part was now needed for getting the boat safely through, and on the ladies' part for staring at the occupants of all the other boats surrounding them. The passage was accomplished in safety, and waiting for them on the other side they found May's boat.

"I say, you have taken a time," she remarked, looking at the vicar.

"Isn't it too heavenly?" asked Hetty generally.

Everyone seemed to feel suddenly that they really were enjoying themselves enormously.

"Half-past four," said Mr. Davis. "We ought to find a place for tea."

The thought of tea added to the general buoyancy.

"The cup that cheers," said the vicar, smiling. "Hurrah! we'd better pull for those willows, and tie up there. Then those who like can have tea up on the bank."

They tied up in the shade of the willows. Mrs. Garland and Mrs. Davis preferred to remain in the boat, and Ethel joined them; the others sat or lay upon the grass above the boats. After tea, when the men lit their pipes and stretched themselves on the grass, and the peace of the hot afternoon, and the river slipping away below them with only the faint sound of water lapping against the two boats, stole over them, they mellowed to one another in disjointed conversation and small jokes. Only the two elder ladies sitting there below the bank began occasionally to realise that the seats were of wood under the cushions, and to weigh the nuisance of getting out of a boat against the discomfort of pins-and-needles in the feet. But fifty years of river parties and picnics had taught these two ladies the patient wisdom which is so pathetic a characteristic of civilised elderly ladies. When for more than eighteen thousand two hundred and fifty days you have never been comfortably at rest except in bed or with the foot at right angles to the leg, the leg at right angles to the thigh, the thigh at right angles to the trunk, it is natural that your body can ill accommodate itself to the bare earth even with grass upon it. Mrs. Garland and Mrs. Davis, therefore, patient and wise, preferred to face another five hours in their usual position on the hard seat and in the narrow confines of the boat than to sit upon the earth, which never seems to support one in any direction except from below, and there with excessive pressure. There they sat, shifting the position first of one leg and then of the other from time to time, talking bravely, happy that the "young people" were enjoying themselves, yawning occasionally and looking forward to supper and the end of the day.

On the bank the conversation after tea tended to become particular instead of general. May, who was a pillar of the church and parish work, steered herself into a discussion of it with the vicar. Such was their skill that they contrived successfully to flirt over the children's crèche, which was the centre of May's activities. The others at first formed a group, chatting easily and without effort. Harry lay on the grass, a little back from the circle, where he could see the others without being seen by them. He stretched himself out in lazy happiness, giving himself up to the feeling of physical well-being which came of the gentle heat, the good tea, and the peacefulness of flowing water and the shade of willows after the exercise of sculling. At first he noticed only the little eyes of blue sky that looked down on him from between the leaves, and the slender arms of the willow-wands that seemed to reach down to caress the flowing water with their pointed leaves. Then—just in front of him sat Gwen. Once again her freshness and prettiness appealed to him. He knew that he was sentimental—he was fully conscious of that—but it gave him pleasure to watch and note the pink cheek, the wonderful colour and texture of the hair, the innocence of the mouth and the white dress.

It would be pleasant to be like that—to have what is called a simple outlook. Complexity—that's the curse of human existence. Life must be so simple to a creature like that, so free of desires and difficulties. And wasn't it really just as good? And she would bring no difficulty into the life of anyone else; things would be marked out for her, just the ultimate events, the great landmarks of life, birth, marriage, child-bearing, death. Yes, one might live simply and happily with anyone like that. One? Yes, one, it's always one, never I. How different other people, the complex, the sophisticated, the people who think and understand, like—like Camilla, for instance, or Katharine even. There would never be any simplicity, any easiness for Camilla. One didn't think somehow of her pink cheek or innocent mouth. He seemed to see her face clearly above Gwen's against the dark trees across the river. He compared them: Camilla's, in beauty alone, was incomparably more beautiful. But there was something else in it which made the other look like a child or a wax figure in a hairdresser's shop—the sensitiveness of the forehead and mouth, the light and sadness and aloofness of the eyes, the sensuous lips.

"You are a Tory, father, through and through," he heard Hetty say to Mr. Davis.

"How many women take any interest in Home Rule or Tariff Reform? You want the vote and you don't know anything about the questions you would have to vote on."

"Does your son think the same as you do?" Gwen asked.

"Harry's asleep," said Hetty.

"No, I'm not," said Harry, sitting up suddenly, "but I'm not going to discuss woman's suffrage on a day like this. I'm pro-suffrage. If they want the suffrage, I'd give it 'em."

"But there's no proof they do want it," said Mr. Davis.

"All the more reason for giving it to them. If they don't want it, they ought to. I'm for giving everybody everything. You can't get out of the argument; it's what's called in leading articles cogent. Hullo! 'Riparian Ownership'—I never saw that; we're trespassing. Let's go and explore," he turned to Gwen.

Gwen got up. "Isn't anyone else coming?" she asked, but they were too comfortable to move. She followed Harry, who was strolling up the bank. They were in a wood, the trees close enough together to hide them very soon from the others. Both at first felt a little awkward and shy. "We'll strike inland," Harry said, "and see what there is to be seen." There was nothing to be seen at the moment except the tall, straight trunks of trees; almost immediately all sounds were cut off from them, of the river and voices and the oars in the rowlocks of passing boats, and the little bursts of laughter from other parties scattered up and down the banks. In the still atmosphere of the small wood the heat was rather oppressive.

"Now for it," thought Gwen. "I shall ask him point blank."

She looked at Harry slouching along by her side with his hands in his pockets, apparently absorbed in thought. The truth was that he did not quite know what to say. His mind was distracted between a feeling that he must talk to this girl, and continual vague recurrence to his previous thoughts about her and Camilla.

"Isn't Mr. Macausland interesting?" said Gwen.

"Very," said Harry, with too obvious irony.

"Why don't you like him?"

"I don't particularly dislike him. I don't like parsons."

Already the feeling of being hurt, irritated, disappointed by this sneering young man came back to Gwen. "Why not?" she said coldly.

"I don't like their trade. With people in other trades, if they will only talk shop, it's ever so much more interesting than anything else they've got to say. Now parsons won't talk shop; they're afraid to, I suppose. There's Macausland: he won't talk to me about the Athanasian Creed or the Virgin Birth, and yet he will never allow me to forget he's a parson."

"Is there anyone you don't despise?" she asked slowly.

Harry stopped and looked at her, startled. His first feeling was one of irritation with himself. She was so pretty; a hot afternoon, the river, and this pleasant, peaceful wood! Anyone else would enjoy himself like a young man—be natural, happy, flirt. Here was he fretting, arguing, hurting.

"I?" he stammered. "I don't think I despise people. I'm too extraordinarily humble for that."

"You're sneering at me now."

"Why do you say that? I'm not, honestly I'm not. I don't despise people. Any amount—I like very much."

"The other evening, the first time you came in, I made up my mind to ask you straight why you despised us."

Harry became interested at once, his self-composure returned. "Let's sit down," he said. "Now why do you say that? It's quite untrue. I hadn't any thought like that."

"I know it's true. You're much cleverer than I—we are, of course. But is that everything? It's so difficult to explain; but is it merely that that makes you so contemptuous?"

"I say, don't say that, Gwen; it isn't true. I never meant to be like that. But—by God! I'll tell you the truth. You do amaze me."

"Well, but why?"

"What are you at? That's what I want to know. Ethel, now—you don't mind my talking like this? You're sure?"

"No, I don't think so."

"Well, Ethel—she's a fair puzzle. What's she at? What does she think or feel? Is she satisfied with life, to go on like that year after year until she dies? She seems somehow to be cut off from all reality. I don't despise her, but, Lord! I do pity her. Don't you?"

As he spoke in his short, sharp way, Gwen's excitement increased. She remembered her vague discontents, her irritation with her sisters, her astonishment at their placid content with their existence. Yes, she pitied Ethel, but what, after all, lay before her, Gwen herself, but what had once lain before and had now come to Ethel? Poor old

Ethel! How often she had thought of her as poor old Ethel. One can pity with some complacency the old maid marked with disappointment and emptiness and no hope of the romance and adventure of life; one can listen with complacency to another's pity of her. But to hear and to feel the same pity of oneself! "Poor old Gwen! Poor old Gwen!" It might come to that; there was no reason why it should not. She fought against a vision of the future, her own future, in refusing to agree with Harry.

"Pity her? I don't know. Why should one? She's quite happy, quite contented—more so than most people. She wouldn't like to be pitied."

He divined some of her thoughts. He himself felt the pity of it, and unconsciously his manner softened, became kinder, almost affectionate.

"Do you believe that? In your heart you don't, you know. And if you did believe it you would pity her all the more. She wouldn't tell, of course; nobody will ever know. She has spun herself round in a cocoon and hung herself up in her little corner of life in St. Catharine's Avenue. She'd rather die than let anyone peep inside the cocoon. (That's a woman!) But she didn't spin it until she'd given up all hope of life. I don't call that contentment, happiness."

"I suppose you mean that the only thing in life, for a woman, is to get married?"

"Good Lord! no, I'd rather be Ethel than May."

"May? Why, she's not married."

"No, but she will be, and pretty soon too. I bet she'll marry the vicar."

She wanted to gain time, to readjust her ideas. "And what about Hetty? Do you include her?"

Harry thought for a moment. "One doesn't pity people like Hetty—very much. She's more armed, armoured against life. She meets it more on equal terms. If she gets knocks, well, I expect she can give a knock herself, if she's put to it. Hetty's as hard as nails. She knows what things are, and she knows just exactly what she wants—and she will probably get it in the end. No, one doesn't pity Hetty, unless one's going to pity her for God having made her what she is; and if one started doing that there would be no end to it."

"And Janet?"

"Janet? she's a dear." Gwen smiled. "One doesn't pity Janet, she's a *lusus naturæ,* she's happy. She's ancient Greece, Hermaphrodite, the soul of a young man of twenty in a woman of thirty. And yet even her golf links are only a cocoon."

They were silent. She tried to think of what he had said. Her mind was confused by this intimacy of conversation with a man. She tried to think of Ethel's life, the life of all of them in Richstead. Were they all cornered up in a back water, shut off for ever from the real things of life? It looked like it in "poor old" Ethel's case—she would go on, until she died, buying little cakes for tea at the shops, doing little things for other people, reading one library novel every fortnight, doing needlework. She had no friends, no husband, no children, no—no life. It was the case of novels over again—people in books, life in books were so different. Only with books one could always say, as Ethel had said: "Ah, they're only books." But this young man seemed to say that life, in Richstead even, could be so different, that there were great things to be done and felt outside St. Catherine's Avenue. She believed it; but what were they, these real things? It was all so vague, so difficult.

"I don't understand," she burst out, "I don't understand. You say Ethel's cut off from reality. What *do* you mean by that?"

"There are some important things in life, more important that just eating, sleeping, drinking, and dying.

Don't you agree?"

"Well, but what are they?"

"To produce, create—that's the best—pictures, music, books—"

"But everyone can't do that. Ethel couldn't, surely."

"Children, I was going to say. It's the one thing that I regret in not being a woman, that I can't bear children. And the doing and feeling of things, and people. It's difficult to explain without talking like a prig, but then so's everything worth anything. You can go out and meet life and live it like a live being, instead of letting it just come up to you and rock you gently along until it trickles out at the end, with you in it, into nothing at all."

Gwen's interest increased with her excitement. He seemed to be opening a new world to her. The conversation that evening with Ethel in the garden came back to her mind: they were talking now more like people talked in books. At any rate she had never talked with anyone like this. He was no longer hard and contemptuous; he was gentle to her. In some strange way she felt like a child being instructed by an affectionate elder.

She wanted to move about. She got up and they walked on slowly between the trees.

"I believe," she began haltingly, "I have felt that. I've been discontented. It seems all so meaningless sometimes. But there's no one to talk to. You must think me an awful fool."

"My good child, of course I don't. You're about two years old—that's all the matter with you."

She laughed. "And you?"

"I'm about seventy-two. I've never been two. I wish the devil I had, but Jews are born old, you know; they know good and evil from their birth, they take it in with their mother's milk, their original mother having eaten those apples—and they usually choose to follow the evil from the start. But I'll make a very good father confessor, philosopher, instructor, and guide to you. You must know things, if you want to live—unless you care to remain two years old all your life."

"I don't think I do. But how *can* one know things in Richstead?"

"You can read, that's always a beginning. Read Dostoievsky."

He looked at her. She was very serious; she reminded him of a child puzzling over a difficult sum. Suddenly it all seemed to him extraordinarily ridiculous, the whole conversation, and the idea of this pink-faced girl reading Dostoievsky in order to learn how to live. He tried to prevent himself laughing, and started a fit of the giggles. She did not know what he was laughing at, but the giggling was infectious and they were soon both laughing helplessly.

"What made you laugh? Me?" she said at last.

"No, no; I wasn't laughing at you—only the general absurdity of things."

"Who is Dostoi—whatever the name is?"

"A writer, Russian. I'll give you a book of his. Don't be frightened; it's a novel."

They had stopped to laugh, and had now turned back towards the boat. They had become intimate enough not to notice now that they were walking in silence; they were busy with their own thoughts. They were walking now along the river bank, and suddenly just below them Harry saw a boat. In the boat lay a young man and a girl, behind a pink sunshade, their heads on a pink cushion. Harry and Gwen were on the wrong side of the sunshade, which was arranged to shield the occupants of the boat from the curious eyes in passing boats. The young man had his arm round the girl's neck, and her arm was round his. He was kissing her on the lips.

"That's one of the things worth doing," said Harry as they passed the boat.

For a moment Gwen felt that the remark was unpleasant, in bad taste. She blushed slightly. Then she began to laugh again, and turned to reply.

"Hullo!" said Harry.

In front of them, and walking very slowly back to the boat, were May and Mr. Macausland. It was clear, as Gwen and Harry came up, that it was an uncomfortable moment for the vicar. "Er—Miss Ma—er—what—er—I was going to say——"

May turned her head and saw the other two. "Hullo," she said, frowning, "where have you two been?"

"Exploring," said Harry, smiling and looking straight into her rather sulky face. "We found all sorts of wonderful places in the woods, and under the bank of the river beneath willows strange sights we found. I say, Gwen, what did we find?"

Gwen laughed happily, but did not answer.

"I don't know what you mean," May grumbled.

The narrowness of the path brought Harry near the vicar for a moment long enough for the latter to murmur: "I told you so. Disgusting, sir, positively disgusting. Not fit—place—ladies."

"Have you been exploring too?" Harry asked him.

"Miss May and I have been for a stroll," said the vicar severely.

In the boats supper was already being prepared, and they joined in the unpacking and laying out of sandwiches and cold chicken and cakes. Time was short and the meal rather hurried, for it takes a long time to get from Maidenhead to Richstead, and they were soon in the boats again on the homeward journey. The long day in the open air had begun to tell upon them all. For those who sat still, sculled by the others, a comfortable feeling of lassitude crept over them, loosening those bands which seem to brace the mind and body to the tightness which society and its conventions demand of us. They sank into themselves physically and mentally on their seats, sagging comfortably out wherever collars or boots or stays or the equally rigid and confining limits of their own minds and characters allowed them. Conversation ebbed and sank quietly. The stillness of the summer evening and the pale green sky settled down on them. Their souls were soothed —just as they are soothed in that half-minute, which seems an eternity, before we sink into sleep—by the dim vision of rippled water and waving trees, shadowy houses and shadowed lawns, gliding by, gliding by, gliding by.

The boats shot on in rhythmical glides over the pale green path that the black trees and their still blacker shadows upon the water left reflected in the river. Nothing could be heard but the regular creak of the oar against the rowlock, the ripple that seemed to whisper against the bows, a little splash now and then as the blades dipped, and sometimes away out of the darkness, melancholy almost and visionary, the sound of voices and laughter. Gwen at any rate allowed herself to glide along into a contentment, a happiness that was new to her. Her walk with Harry had excited her more than she herself realised. In the unpacking and packing up, a new and special link of intimacy between them had made her meet his eye among the others with a smile. All rivers at night are melancholy, sentimental, sad, like emblems of the mystery and unreality of human things. Under their spell we seem to see things larger than our own small selves. This languorous sadness only softened Gwen's excitement into a quiet happiness, and as she saw Harry's face, moving rhythmically backwards and forwards over the oar, softened by the pale light, but set and firm, sad and reflective, she still felt the link of the intimacy between them.

Harry himself was in a trance. There was a vague up-lifting of spirits as he gave himself to the rhythm of the oars and boat. Forward, backward, forward, backward his body swung, the silver-green water glided by him and dripped from the blade; forward, backward, forward, backward, the great black shadows glided by. He heard laughter across the water die away; the whistle of a train far away across fields and trees; then deep enveloping silence. Forward, backward, forward, backward; why not row Camilla like this? He sank deeper into dreams that he was rowing Camilla like this—

Mrs. Davis and Mrs. Garland had grown very intimate during the day. They had at one moment arrived at the point of discussing Mr. Macausland and May. "He certainly is very attentive to her, but—" Mrs. Garland admitted in her quiet, ladylike manner. And Mrs. Davis had glanced at Hetty sitting up there on the bank—such an attractive girl, more attractive than May Garland, more attractive than practically any girl she knew; and yet—she had refused young Bernstein, and since then no suitable young man seemed to be seriously attracted by her. It really was disappointing; she must ask young Bernstein to dinner again.

But as the hours passed the physical discomfort of stiff limbs changed to the more tolerable, diffused, and deadened sense of utter fatigue. The gliding of the boat homewards finally lulled them both into drowsiness. Mrs. Davis was the last to yield to the humane feeling that it was no longer necessary to talk. She was awakened by the thud of the bows against the landing stage, and by a little stream of cold water which trickled down her neck from the vicar's oar as he unshipped it. She bore it with a set smile, just as she and Mrs. Garland bore with uncomplaining cheerfulness the aches and pains in back and legs as soon as they began to walk up to the station.

The party straggled along with the baskets and hampers,

yawning. A happy day seemed to be ending happily for Gwen when Harry came and walked with her. They fell behind the others.

"I expect," he said gently, "I talked an awful lot of rot there. Don't think about it."

"I have thought about it; I shall too. It wasn't rot at all."

"Well, at any rate, you won't any more think I despise you? You aren't hurt, offended?"

"Offended? Oh no. I've enjoyed myself immensely. And you'll lend me that book?"

They laughed. "Dostoievsky? Oh yes."

When they said good-night at the gate in St. Catherine's Avenue he said again: "I'll send you round that book to-morrow," and she felt again that she had enjoyed herself immensely.

"What book?" May said, when they were in the hall.

"Oh, some novel."

"I don't like Harry Davis," May grumbled, as she went up to bed.

V

OPINIONS AND EMOTIONS IN A
COUNTRY HOUSE

Harry did not forget to send Dostoievsky's "Idiot" to Gwen, and he laughed to himself not unkindly as he handed it to the Garlands' maid. He was putting strong wine into the mouth of a babe with a vengeance. He hoped it would not completely upset her digestion, yet he had not much compunction if it should make her feel a little uncomfortable, because, after all, that was what in his opinion these virgins of Richstead really needed—something to show them that life was not all Richstead, virginity and vicars, needlework and teas. And when he had said: "For Miss Gwen, please," he did not give very much more thought to her or "The Idiot."

He was giving a good deal more thought to Camilla Lawrence. He met her almost daily at the studio; he took as long as he possibly could to paint her portrait; he was continually at the house where, sitting with his two daughters, Mr. Lawrence seemed to be perpetually exercising his cynical eyes and tongue. He became one of the Lawrence circle, of which the outward and visible sign was the use of Christian names. He would have denied, and probably rightly, that he was in love with Camilla; other people would have, and did, as rightly affirm that he was at any rate falling in love with her. Harry did not know whether or not he was in love; if he had read Stendhal's "De L'Amour" he might have at once crossed the border and have decided that he was. With this subtle, violent, and complicated emotion it is perhaps impossible to fix precisely the moment that separates not loving from loving;

but one cannot be very far from that moment when one lingers with pleasure over the thought that possibly one is in love with some particular one.

Harry, even when he was in it, always retained the first impression which the Lawrence circle gave him: interminable talk and silences in very comfortable chairs. These epicures in the art of emotions and the emotions of art had emancipated themselves from the convention that there are some things that men and women cannot talk about, and they had done this so successfully that a stranger might at first have been led to conclude from their practice that those are the only things that men and women of intelligence can talk about. Such a conclusion would have been hasty. It was perhaps their weakness, at any rate intellectually, that they never did those things— but then they never did anything. In the mornings Camilla painted, and Katharine retired to a room called the study, in which, it was understood, she was writing a book. It was quite obvious to those who knew them that Katharine should have been in the studio and Camilla in the study. Mr. Lawrence was—or rather imagined that he was—daily in the only place in which he could suitably have been, the British Museum. Actually on the five days out of the seven which made up their "working" week he spent the hours between ten and eleven of the morning deciding that he could study Byzantine art as well in his arm-chair as in a museum, and between eleven and one he did so.

The centre of the circle was Horton Street, but from time to time that centre shifted to a little house among downs, fields, and trees in Kent. To sit in the arm-chairs in Kent was the final sign that you were in the innermost circle. This sign came to Harry about a week after the river party at Maidenhead.

"I've asked Harry to come down with us on Friday," said Camilla to Katharine on the Thursday. "I suppose you don't mind."

It was one o'clock, and Camilla had come into the study. The floor was littered with innumerable sheets of white paper; in the centre Katharine was sitting in an arm-chair with a pen in her hand and a sheet of white paper on a book upon her knees. She bit the end of the pen, wrinkled her forehead, and looked up dubiously at Camilla.

"You'll have to decide, you know," she said judicially, "whether you are or are not going to marry Harry."

Camilla walked over to the window and leaned upon the windowsill, looking down into the quiet street. The world of actual things which she looked at—the trees heavy now with their summer leaves, the dingy iron palings, the heat beating up from the strip of polished asphalt road, the draggled old woman tottering along on the opposite pavement, seemed for the moment so much more real to her than herself and Harry and marriage. Katharine's remark sounded absurd; she could not seriously think of it. Other people married, but one did not marry—not people one knew—oneself.

"He hasn't asked me to marry him," she said.

"I didn't say he had. But he will. I give him two or three weeks, possibly less, if he sees much of you down there."

Camilla came and sat on the arm of Katharine's chair. Her eyes wandered to the window, her hands smoothed Katharine's hair.

"Do you think I ought to marry anyone, dearest?" she asked.

"I don't think anyone ought to marry you," Katharine laughed.

"Why?"

"Well, he would have to be very much in love with you, and—"

"There's no reason in nature, is there, why he shouldn't be that?"

"No, that's just it, just what I'm telling you, if you'll

only listen. He would be; you would always want him to be; you'd insist on it, and so he probably would be. You're attractive enough, of course—to some people."

"Well, what more could you want? I seem to be made for marriage. Attractive: love therefore enduring until death do us part. *Mens sana in corpore sano*; so that all the marriage service can be read without blushes. And a mind on wings! Katharine, I'm simply made for marriage."

"It's never any good talking to you, Camilla; you never listen to a word one says. I never said you ought not to marry: I said no one ought to marry you. You can't marry a man without his marrying you."

"Pooh, you old raven, sitting there croaking your never-more at me. All that applies probably to every woman who has married since Eve, or who hasn't. You admit that I'm simply the ideal woman for marriage, so why go on croaking your nevermore at me?"

"I imagine a husband might not always be content merely to be in love with you. It isn't a normal male idea of the ideal wife."

"Ah—yes, I see; you mean I couldn't be in love with anyone? Wouldn't that show I'm a normal woman? But do you honestly think I'm as cold as all that, Katharine dearest? You know I love you far more than you love me."

"That's hardly the point we were talking about, is it?"

"But I'm not cold, am I? I couldn't be so very attractive if I were. I'm very affectionate, you know that, don't you? I like silk and kisses and soft things and strokings. I was told the other day that I was like hills with virgin snow on them; but that's nonsense, isn't it?"

"It does sound like it, certainly. But that wasn't what I said."

"But you haven't been in love; no one has ever seen you luxuriating, you old raven. Yet you don't think yourself an icefield."

"I shall marry, however, and I shall be in love with my husband," said Katharine with impassive conviction, and it was quite clear that she would be. Camilla looked at her. Her face was already like that of a mother's; her own would always retain something of the virgin's.

"Women don't fall in love till afterwards," she said thoughtfully, "and after all, I am a woman."

"A very queer one," said Katharine, getting up and scattering more paper over the floor. "However, you'll have to decide whether you're going to marry Harry."

She stood there in the middle of the room and in the middle of the sea of paper, looking down at it and thinking of Camilla, who sat absorbed in thought on the arm of the chair. Katharine never worried about anything, but she came as near as possible to doing so about Camilla. In the East she would have sat with other women around the great tom-tom, tapping out the monotonous note every now and then and saying that fate is fate—only she would never have cried out and beaten the breast with them when misfortunes came. Having been born a European, she did not talk of fate; she merely saw life steadily without delusions or enthusiasms. One had only to look at the two sisters, each thinking now and silent, to see the difference of character, and, one might guess, of destiny. Katharine's great dark eyes, almost motionless and, when they moved, moving slowly over the surface of things, seemed always a little wide open in order to watch the procession of life and her own thoughts. When you saw her for the first time you thought her darker, deeper, and more beautiful than she really was. Yet she was dark and deep and beautiful enough, those who had seen her oftenest would have told you. By her side Camilla seemed stranger and fairer than she really was. Even when she was sitting now motionless and silent thinking, her eyes seemed to have to dart quickly to keep pace with her thoughts. Middle-aged and elderly ladies, on first meeting her, because of her very fair hair and her smile, called her most erroneously a sweet young woman; young women and many young men found her fascinating but frightening; old men felt like a father to her without noticing that they had fallen in love with her. Harry was right, you did not think of innocence in Camilla's face; you thought perhaps of purity, coldness even, of hills and snow, of something underneath, below the surface, that might at any moment break out destructive of you—of her?

Between Katharine and Camilla there was that curiously strong love which often binds sister to sister and sometimes brother to brother. It outlives years and happiness and separation, violent quarrels, mutual knowledge, and knowledge of faults, vices, meannesses. It may be doubted whether it does not rest upon the first and the last feeling to flicker through the embryonic and the dying body of everyone, love of one's self; for in our brothers and sisters we always see some of the seeds of our father and mother, which we love so much in ourselves. Is not that why, however much we may dislike our own family, we always feel in our hearts that it is an impertinence for anyone else to dislike it? But to return to sisterly love; if it begins in and rests on selfishness, it manifests itself often with great beauty in supreme unselfishness. It at any rate made Katharine fear for Camilla in a world which she seemed to be—if that is possible—but half born into.

"You don't like Harry?" Camilla asked.

"Yes, I do. I should like him better if he didn't take himself so seriously. He fusses about life with a big L. He is one of those young men who have discovered themselves—and make as much fuss about it as a hen who has discovered for the first time that she has laid an egg. But I like him."

"Suppose he does ask me to marry him, do you think I should?"

"I don't know, Camilla, I simply don't know. You are such an impossible person. You weren't made for marriage, you weren't made for a husband and children and middle-aged domesticity. Yet you ought not to remain unmarried; you can't, you positively can't be imagined as a respectable spinster at forty."

"Oh, Katharine dearest, what am I to do? You don't want me to die young, do you?"

"No, not in some ways; though I'm not sure it wouldn't be the best thing: you would leave a better memory behind you, probably. We'd say: 'What a passionate lover! what a devoted wife! what a noble mother she *might* have been!' We mightn't, you see, be able to say all that after you've been married to Harry for two years. It's odd, I can imagine even father in love, but not you—whether because you'd never be content with only one man, especially a husband, in love with you, or whether because you'd never be content with your—your side of it—you'd be wanting to go on to something beyond, I mean. Love's stationary, I expect. And then Harry—there may be something in Harry underneath—*he* wouldn't be content with that. When he's properly in love, as he will be probably by next Tuesday, I expect he's just as violent as you are when you're not. No, I think it would be a failure—and then——"

"Good Lord! you are unkind to me. I really believe you don't understand, Katharine, what one wants, the difficulty. I shan't marry Harry; you needn't be afraid. But if you went on very long like that you'd soon drive me into marrying him or anyone else. I like his not being content; it would be the only way to be happily married, to be kept alive, to go on always finding things, new things, beautiful things, instead of lying down at twenty-six like some shiny, satiny, white old cow—chewing and chewing the same old cud, the rich, deep grass."

Camilla stopped talking, but continued the subject in

her thoughts. She was quite certain she was not in love
with Harry, and somehow or other she did not see how she
ever would be. She liked his sensibility, his vigour, and his
violence; she liked his hardness, and it repelled her; the
sombreness of his mind and his yellow face repelled her.
If nothing else were asked of her, she might, she felt, love
him as a friend; but to live in one house and close to him,
which after all one must envisage in marriage . . . And then
too he left her cold, as cold as Arthur Woodhouse left her.
It would be amusing to see those two together this
week-end.

"Well, I'm going to lunch," said Katharine. "But you'll
have to decide whether you're going to marry Harry."

Camilla seized her by the arms and rushed her out of
the room.

On Friday evening there were six arm-chairs filled in
Kent. Harry was in one, Katharine, Camilla, and Mr.
Lawrence were in others. Arthur Woodhouse tossed his fat,
round little body and his little, round, fat mind from side
to side in another. Officially he was a disciple of the few
papers on Byzantine art published by Mr. Lawrence in
obscure but learned periodicals; unofficially he now considered that Mr. Lawrence had gone off on a wrong tack
in Byzantine art, and had proposed to and been rejected
by Camilla. If one had opened his heart and applied to it a
magic thermometer to register the heat of passions and
feelings, one could have deduced from the temperature
chart that he might just as well at times have proposed to
Katharine. His mind and his body and his laugh and his
feelings were all equally restless. Feminine charms moved
him more easily and at random than he himself realised.
Nor was he fully aware of the effect of those charms upon
his mind and his other feelings; he was one of those men
so small mentally and morally that anything which took
place in his little mind or little soul naturally seemed to

him to be one of the great convulsions of nature. So he was very happy, when alone between the sheets, to recognise how susceptible he was and how virile, and still happier to believe that other people, including women, recognised it. It only remains to add that Arthur was a barrister who practised only as a literary critic, and earned a living by being neither one nor the other.

The fifth chair was occupied by "Lion" Wilton. Wilton was always known as "Lion." The name did not suit his appearance, and how exactly it originated was not remembered; he looked more like a gazelle than a lion. In the 'eighties he would have looked like Lord Byron, and young ladies would have fallen in love with him at first sight. Hockey and women's suffrage had, however, spoilt his market, which was still fairly large among married and older women who have not entirely lost their love of submission and of being ill-treated by the male. They liked his ill-treatment all the more because of his beauty and his woman's face, his large, melancholy eyes and his fair, soft skin and long hair. Perhaps they also liked the cruelty of his mouth.

Conversation had not flowed easily at dinner. When two or three were gathered together Wilton was always gloomy and silent and sulky. Harry was uncomfortable, and therefore silent and constrained, with an almost unconscious feeling of hostility to Arthur Woodhouse. Arthur himself had not bubbled with his usual spontaneity. The constraint followed them into the next room after dinner, and settled round the open windows. Only Mr. Lawrence was completely at his ease, smoking his cigarette and watching the silent figures around him with a tolerant smile.

Camilla roused herself. "I think I shall keep hens," she said.

"In London?" asked Mr. Lawrence.

"No, here. I shall keep a poultry farm."

"You would have to live here then; you can't trust hens to themselves—they would sit on their eggs."

Arthur's laugh sounded. "You'd have the whole place swarming with chickens in six months. They would become a pest, like rabbits in Australia; they'd begin to overrun the country."

"It will make the house intolerable," said Katharine. "They make disgusting noises, and you'll never be able to keep them in their place; and they have insects and—"

"Chicken lice," said Harry.

"Horrors like staggers and gapes."

"I'm tired of London, all those people. I shall live here," said Camilla. "They are wonderfully beautiful in troops on green fields, each with a noble cock, all in their different colours, yellow, and blue, and glossy black and snowy white. I'll have them marshalled in their glossy troops in the field in front of the house, and I shall sit all day long upon the terrace, watching them and the pattern they weave on the field as they strut about. Every evening I shall go out with a long, peeled, thin stick and drive them home into their huge henhouse."

"O Lord!" said Mr. Lawrence. "I suppose you're going to become one with the earth, as they call it."

"Or the hens," laughed Arthur. "I suppose it's the same thing."

"They are noble birds," said Camilla, "noble and stately. I shall grow like them. A great peace will descend upon me among my chickens; my dreams will be of great wings and of sinking gently into fields of white and blue and golden feathers. All sorts of visions will come to me as I sit on the terrace with the peeled white wand in my hand. I shall grow very old there. I shall be a great and noble figure, and people will come from America just to see me."

"I always thought," said Wilton, "that the Holy Ghost descended in the form of a dove."

"It will go up in the form of chickens. When I'm very old, one day I shall be sitting there, and suddenly I shall hear the beating of innumerable wings, and I shall see the chickens rise up in a cloud from the field to heaven; and I shall know that that is the end. And in the evening, when the old woman comes up to cook my dinner, she will find me sitting dead in my chair watching an empty field."

"You would soon get tired of the chickens, Milla," said Katharine; "they wouldn't appreciate your flights. You must have an audience."

Camilla's flights were famous in the circle, but it is doubtful whether the last one had been fully appreciated by any of the audience except Harry and Lion, and Lion's enjoyment had been spoilt by the envious feeling that he could never talk like that. The flights intoxicated Harry, for "l'harmonie la plus douce est le son de la voix de celle que l'on aime," and in the timbre of a woman's voice, when it is beautiful, there seem to be mysteriously harmonised all the desires and enchantments both of the spirit and the body. He, at any rate, seemed to hear a deep and rare note in Camilla's voice as she sat there very still and fair and smiling, abandoning herself to something outside herself, to another world from which ideas welled up and formed themselves upon her lips into the beautiful sounds of words. To those who loved or desired her, or were upon the point of loving or desiring her, like Harry and Arthur, this abandonment to something outside herself, something which seemed to belong not to the ordinary constituents of humanity and femininity, caused fear and a curious catch at the heart. To those who had to live with her it often caused irritation. She had eluded them, slipped from their grasp and from their power to inflict human feelings of pleasure and pain; she was so intolerably far from them! Who in this world can ever quite forgive a near relation for not being like himself, for touching anything in which he cannot share, for being in any way not in his power?

"Camilla's quite right," said Arthur. "She has found Christ, the great fundamental truth that we're too damned sophisticated."

"Back to the earth, one with the earth," chanted Mr. Lawrence. "I see you are all going to become market-gardeners and Christians."

"Camilla is right. I'm not going to be frightened by being called a Christian. We're too sophisticated to feel anything; that's why we're so damnably discontented."

Mr. Lawrence stretched his legs straight out in front of him and turned in his toes. "I'm not discontented," he said in a rather superior tone.

"I'm at any rate contented with the amount of content-ment which falls to me," said Katharine.

"You two! You've passed that stage, and are now in the stage of crystallisation. Camilla's certainly discontented, so am I. There's no need to ask Lion, you have only got to look at him. Are you discontented?" he turned rather stiffly to Harry.

"Always," said Harry decidedly.

Arthur got up from his chair and stood in front of the empty fireplace, waving his pipe in his hand to emphasise his words, as he held his audience.

"There you are; we go on talking and gossiping and criticising only because we never feel the important things, the simple things, the real things. If we could be Christians we might feel them; but we can never be that now. If we dug in the earth we might—all agricultural labourers are like that; you can see it in the way they work, and in their eyes and movements." His little pale blue eyes wandered restlessly round the circle. A deep, uncomfortable silence fell upon them as they listened to his cultivated and cul-tured Oxford voice. He looked at Camilla more than the others, seeking her approval and finding no sign in her passive face lying back against the cushion. A little uncertain, he hesitated, but began again, impelled by his restless little mind and his desire to talk and his passion for "intellectual excitement." "All great feelings are simple ones; look at Homer and Marie Claire. Every child is an artist, and every civilised, cultured man, whether he be Leonardo da Vinci or George Meredith, is a philistine. We went off on a wrong tack at the renaissance. Shakespeare hypnotised us and we've never got back. Wordsworth tried and Tolstoi, and Ezra Pound and Mrs. Susanna Smith are trying now. But we'll never really succeed until we get out of the towns."

"Video meliora proboque, deteriora sequor," murmured Mr. Lawrence.

Harry had not often seen Arthur Woodhouse in the circle. He knew that he had proposed to Camilla, and this knowledge had predisposed him to hostility. Listening now to the loud, assertive voice, which in some subtle way seemed to appeal to you to make allowances for it, he felt the sympathy which makes up part of the feeling of contempt creeping into his irritation. Most people are generous enough to feel some pity for the dog with some touch of the cur and mongrel in it, which finds itself in the pure-bred and often snobbish society of a dog-show. The circle liked Arthur "in many ways," and towards the ways they did not like they displayed the good but unpleasant manners of silence. When this happened the sensitive spectator or listener began to feel that subtle sense of discomfort which comes to him when he hears a public speaker making a bit of a fool of himself. What made it worse—or perhaps, the moral philosopher would say, better—was that in Arthur's case one felt that he himself felt it, that it exasperated him and goaded him on to further asserting himself.

"It's so easy to sneer—anyone can do that. If you mean

me by that, I do get the simple emotions. I believe Camilla and I are the only ones among us who do. I don't know about Davis, he is so silent that one can't be sure that he feels any."

Harry's face became more impassive than usual, if that were possible, at what he felt was a gratuitous attack. He felt hot with irritation, and as usual in such cases seemed to those around him colder and more reserved than ever. He looked at Arthur, but did not speak.

"I assume that silence means consent," said Arthur, with a laugh obviously intended to be genial.

"I don't understand what you mean by your simple emotions."

There was suddenly in the room that curious feeling of larger emotions, passions, having entered under the ordinary words of conversation. Katharine stopped her sewing, and, smiling her slow smile, lay back in her chair as if to watch what was going to happen next. Camilla also watched Harry and Arthur; she had what she wanted, here they were together. The feeling that she was between them could not but excite her. She compared them: Harry so cold and with that air of concentration and wariness that animals possess when they are seeking their own food or trying to avoid becoming the food of others; Arthur with all his pleasantnesses and follies and pettinesses bubbling out of him. Harry clearly would never give himself away, as Arthur was doing even now. Was there not something ungenerous in not being able to give oneself away? They seemed matched unequally, and instinctively her sympathy went out to the weaker. Harry himself felt something of what she was feeling: it made him shrink all the more into himself; he felt physically the weight of self.

"There are some quite simple feelings ordinary human beings have; they get them from simple things, like digging in the earth, trees, human bodies. You never get them in towns, except perhaps the last. There are always a lot of complications, associated ideas. Don't you agree?"

"Even if I did, I don't see there's any reason to suppose the one better than the other."

"Have you ever been in love?"

Harry hesitated; he wanted time to consider what his answer should be.

"You seem doubtful," said Arthur.

"I'm doubtful whether you would call being in love what I call being in love."

Arthur failed altogether to keep out of his voice the bitterness and irritation which he was feeling. "Well, then, have you ever been in what you call love?"

Harry waited this time deliberately. "No, I haven't," he said, "but *I* could."

"You mean, *I* couldn't?"

"I expect you're capable of imagining you're feeling anything; most people are. That's all you mean, isn't it?"

"At any rate, I imagine I have. I can't prove it to you, but I have. You can take my word for it or not—one can't prove those sort of things. You admit you haven't. You don't mind my saying so, but it's a characteristic of your race—they've intellect and not emotion; they don't feel things." Arthur laughed.

Harry did not answer. He thought to himself that he did not answer because if he did he would show that he was suffering and had lost his temper. This was only partially true; one reason why he did not answer was that no answer for the moment occurred to him.

"And that," Arthur went on, "is additional proof of my point. You were all right when you lived in Palestine before the dispersal. You were farmers and agriculturists; you produced Job and Ecclesiastes. Since then you've been wandering from city to city, and you've produced Mendelssohn and Barney Barnato. You never find a

Jew on the land. Don't you agree?"

"You seem to me," said Harry slowly, "to have a very odd idea of what are feelings. Don't you limit them rather? Contempt, for instance? Isn't that a feeling just as much as your lust? And it's one that even Jews feel; I know that from experience."

Before Arthur could answer, Katharine got up. "If you are going to argue," she said, "I'm going to bed. I never can follow arguments, they always seem so illogical."

"They are when there's any reason *for* them," said Wilton, smiling for the first time that evening.

The argument had certainly depressed Camilla. There had seemed to her something ignoble in it, and something ignoble in each of the arguers. She said good-night, and followed Katharine out of the room.

The atmosphere of the room seemed to change instantly. One could feel that the next remark, whatever it was, would be short and sharp and matter-of-fact.

"By God! it's hot, isn't it?" said Arthur to Harry.

"Damnably," Harry answered.

"Let's go outside."

Arthur went out through the open window, and Harry joined him. They stood together and looked at the downs, which seemed infinitely far away in the moonlight. Each felt very friendly towards the other. In the lighted room Mr. Lawrence and Wilton sat in silence; from an open window above them came the faint sound of women's voices. To each it seemed that only he and not the other heard and was listening to these voices.

"It will be a fine day to-morrow again," said Arthur.

"Yes."

"I hope you didn't mind what I said in there?"

"Not a bit. In some ways I agree with you—up to a point."

They were silent again. They were listening. In the room

above their heads someone came to the window and stood there looking out. They heard that—Katharine or Camilla, they did not know who. They could hear the voice of the other talking from within the room, but they could not catch the words. The voice stopped, and then in the stillness above them they heard Camilla say:

"But one wants so much."

She moved away from the window again into the room. A feeling of intense self-pity came upon Harry and Arthur, and with it a feeling in each of pity for the other. Physically they felt so small, as one does at night under an immense luminous sky, and before the white plain of water-meadows stretching away to the haze where the moonlight lay upon the downs.

"Let's walk, let's get up on to the down," said Arthur in a husky voice.

Harry nodded. They climbed up the steep slope in silence. At the top Arthur flung himself down on the grass. Harry stood for a moment by his side looking down upon the great plain of sleepy meadow and curving ploughland that rests peacefully in the lap of the downs. The moonlight lay so gently on it, covering it with a thin white veil, and the river lay like a great silver snake coiling on its breast. Not a sound came to them up there on the bare hillside.

Harry sat down. He felt suddenly worn out and very tired.

"God!" said Arthur, "I can't stand this."

Harry looked at him; he seemed to be in a state of very painful excitement.

"You're lucky if you've never been in love. Camilla—you know—I expect they've told you . . . I can't stand it any longer. I shall go away—I must. I can't sleep sometimes for days."

He looked as if at any moment he might burst into tears; his face was working like a child's who is preparing to open its mouth and howl. He was no longer a man, civilised and restrained; the hour and the place and something inside him were pushing him over the brink. Harry nearly laughed, but his voice was level and kind when he said:

"But she likes you, anyone can see that, so isn't there hope?"

The last bar to the flood of confidences fell. Arthur had tried to repress them. They said that this fellow Davis was himself in love with Camilla. It was quite obvious that he wasn't in love with anyone, probably he couldn't be; cold-blooded that way; one only had to look at him to see that. And so the desire to hear in one's own voice the story of one's creditable sorrows triumphed.

"Oh, I don't know, I don't know. That's what makes it so unbearable—the suspense. I sometimes think I'll go off, break with it all completely. I have too; I've gone off into the country for weeks, to ride hard, walk hard, forget, but it's no use. I come cringing back, whistled to heel again like some damned little puppy-dog. I wonder if any woman understands what it is to a man. They don't realise that we've got bodies. That's what makes it so intolerable: unless they are loose and vile they have no passions. What's noble in us is vile in them."

He turned over, and lay flat, burying his face in the grass. Harry felt as if he himself were turning into stone. He just managed to say:

"You think her absolutely cold?"

"She's a woman and a virgin: isn't that enough? Didn't you hear her say: 'One wants so much.' Wants? They don't know, they simply don't know what desire is. What they want is to be desired—that's all. And when they get that from some poor devil with a straight back and a clean face, they think they are in love with him, and he marries, to be disappointed. Only Camilla isn't like that—God! I almost wish she were sometimes. She has a mind, an imagination; they intoxicate me. But that isn't the point. She is one of the few women to see clearly. She wants to be desired like all of them, more than most of them; but she sees that that isn't enough. She wants so much. What she really wants, only she doesn't know it, is to be a man; and—damn, damn, damn—she never will be."

Arthur pressed his face into the grass again, and waved his feet in the air backwards and forwards over his buttocks. Harry could think of nothing to say. At last Arthur sat up. His eyes looked as if he had been crying.

"I suppose I've been boring you, when you wanted to go to bed," he said.

"Oh no," said Harry awkwardly. "It's always interesting to—what I mean is, I wish one could give—be of some use."

"It's a comfort to find anyone who understands, who is sympathetic. Strange that I should have told you all that; I'm not given to make confidences. Sympathy—it makes one say more than one ought or means to, probably."

Harry smiled. He wondered vaguely whether he or Arthur or both were mad. The time for intimacy or for any further word between them passed suddenly. They walked in silence to the house. Mr. Lawrence and Wilton had gone to bed. As they entered the empty room Arthur looked at Harry as if he were going to say something more, but he stopped himself, and said instead: "Well, I'm going to bed. Good-night." He sat for some time half undressed on the side of his bed, thinking: he was already regretting his confidences.

VI

KATHARINE'S OPINION OF HER SISTER

The note of the whole party next morning was rather depressed. There was no general coming together after the scattered breakfast. Katharine and Camilla seemed to be drawn to one another—Camilla to Katharine for protection, and Katharine to Camilla by some unconscious anxiety. They walked together up and down a path in the garden, talking little and at intervals in low voices. Mr. Lawrence had wheeled a large arm-chair into the sunshine, and now sat in it, calm, cool, and imperturbable, under a white umbrella, reading a folio. Some distance away from him in the shadow of the house sat Arthur in a canvas deck-chair, moodily pretending to read a little book of poems by Mrs. Susanna Smith, guardedly watching the two sisters and wanting to join them. Wilton appeared, dragging another deck-chair, and settled down beside him. It irritated Arthur, and what irritated him still more was to notice the pink and white freshness of Lion's face. Lion had no book; he lay back in his chair, quite silent. After a while they saw Harry walk across the garden in front of the house, go through the gate in the fence, and lie down in the field.

"I didn't know they had taken up that fellow," said Wilton.

"Which fellow?" said Arthur irritably.

"That Jew fellow. Who picked him up? Camilla, I suppose."

"I don't see anything very wrong with him."

"I don't see anything very right with him."

"He can paint," said Arthur, knowing that that was the surest way of irritating Wilton.

"Who says so? Camilla? I wouldn't give anything more for her judgment of painting than I would for her judgment of people."

"It wasn't Camilla. It was Lawrence. He's said to be astonishingly good. Lucas Wentworth raves about him, says he's the only English artist with any idea of significant form."

"Lawrence! Good Lord! Look at him now! And that ass Lucas Wentworth! He went about raving of me for six weeks, told everyone I had real feeling and significant form, far and away the best of the young painters. Now he hasn't a word bad enough for me. It will be the same with Davis in six weeks' time, and poor old Lucas will be raving about some house painter or scene painter. The place where he ought to be raving is a lunatic asylum."

"At any rate that has nothing to do with Davis being able to paint."

"There has never been a good Jew artist, and there never will be."

"Why not?"

"They're too like Davis—too cold and clammy and hard. They're just like crabs or lobsters. They give me the creeps."

"I rather like Davis; he seems to me rather particularly sympathetic."

"Does he?" said Lion, and they relapsed into silence. Harry lay in the long grass of the meadow, a book open in front of him. He was not reading it. The sun beating down from a cloudless sky produced in him that feeling of semi-consciousness that great heat brings. And the heat intensified the dull sense of discomfort which weighed upon him. At the same time he was nervously excited; he could not read, he could not think connectedly.

The smell of hot grass and the droning of many bees over the meadow made him feel very drowsy. Every now and then the little catch which keeps us above unconsciousness seemed to slip down and allow him to glide softly and deliciously into sleep. And then at once the excitement and vague depression pricked him; he was in this hard, real life. He flung himself over in the grass into a different position. He felt the eyes of those above him in the garden; two, four, six, eight little loopholes of critical hostility. There they were behind his back, watching him; they thought him silent, uncouth, ill-mannered. He looked at his watch: eleven Saturday morning—eleven Sunday morning—twenty-four hours; Monday morning, forty-eight hours. Forty-eight hours to spend here, of which, say, sixteen in bed. That left thirty-two hours with these people, thirty-two hours' torture; and then to be alone, natural, free! Even Richstead and his father seemed beautiful; his father walking to catch the train every morning for a lifetime, his father's acute, unseeing eyes reading the share list, his father beginning the political discussion with: "Well, my boy, have you read Bonar Law's latest? The party's going to the dogs."

Well, he would be in bed by twelve to-night. Thirteen hours before that! And he would dream there, dream deliberately before he settled to sleep, dream of what he wanted to have and what he wanted to be. Why shouldn't he do that now and slip away into another world from these hard and bitter things? He tried. He thought of himself standing up on some raised platform above a crowd, a hostile crowd threatening him. Stones were thrown, there was blood on his face, but he stood there shielding—someone, from the stones. His arm fell limply to his side, but he stood up straight still.

He flung himself over on his back. It wouldn't do, in the full sunlight and with the gentle breeze on his face. The eyes above him intruded into his dreams, and there was no place for them there; he must wait for the darkness, and solitude, and sentimentality of the sheets. He could just see Camilla reading now under the beech-tree in the garden; she seemed infinitely remote from him. She was so cool and cold and untroubled; she was a stranger. They were all strangers to him; there wasn't a soul up there of all the four to whom he could talk of what he was feeling or of what he wanted. They would not understand, they would be bored, they would laugh at him. The only bonds between human beings seemed to be dislike and scorn and jeering and envy; otherwise, completely isolated, they staggered and strayed through life. With a twitch of irritation he turned over on to his stomach and buried his face in the grass.

"Well, Harry, I see you're following Arthur's advice, and adopting the first principle of Christianity and Sunday."

He looked up. Katharine stood beside him under a large white umbrella.

"What's that? It isn't Sunday either, you know."

"To make yourself uncomfortable. For me the first day out of London is always Sunday." She sat down by his side.

It soothed him even to look at her. She was so calm and beautiful and wise, like some figure of spacious Justice sitting on the world and judging it, judging it to be good. The large, observing dark eyes, after encouragingly passing over the hills and plains, had rested upon him.

"Do you really believe this is the best of all possible worlds?" he asked.

"I believe one should make the best possible out of it."

"And you do, I think; you look as if you do."

She had come out into the field with a purpose: she wanted to talk to Harry about Camilla. But now that she was faced by him it seemed very difficult. His young face had the heavy and set mould in which age casts things; its sallow surface was a smooth, immovable screen which was unaffected by what was passing in his mind on the other side of it. Only the eyes and the voice in unguarded moments had shown her that things were passing there, things that made her kindly to him.

"I don't think *you* make the best of it, Harry; when an umbrella or a tree makes life for a few minutes heavenly in this country, you go and make yourself thoroughly uncomfortable in the sun."

"I like the heat; you haven't heard me complain."

"No, you wouldn't complain. But you want to go away into a corner and quietly ruminate on the eternal discomfort of the universe. I expect you will save it up to go to bed with."

Harry smiled, thinking of what half an hour ago he had saved up to go to bed with.

"What do you save up to go to bed with?" he asked.

"Old conversation usually. I think of all the brilliant things I might have said in them, and didn't. In the end I generally come to believe that I did say them, and then I fall asleep quite happy."

Harry scarcely listened to what she was saying. Her presence soothed him. The softness of her as a woman attracted him physically, the soft lines of her woman's body, the softness of her lips and skin and hair, the softness of the curves and folds of her dress, which seemed like a symbol of all that is physically desired in woman. She was quick to feel his inattentiveness. She liked men and to be with them and to talk to them better than women—she was rather proud of confessing to this always and with frankness. The reason for this was not that she was a man's woman or a flirt. "I prefer men," she used to explain, "because they are so much more reasonable." Probably she did believe this, but it was not true. Like nearly all women, more indeed than most women, she regarded men as a peculiar and unreasonable breed of children. In her heart she never treated them as rational beings.

They were children swayed by strange and violent desires; they had to be managed, to have perpetual allowances made for them. It is amazing that women do not always wink when they meet one another, like Roman augers; indeed, two moderately clever women, talking tete-à-tete about men or a man, very soon do wink.

Harry had to be managed. He was wanting all kinds of things, things which she did not understand, but which of course, like all men, he was wanting. He was in love with Camilla, though he probably did not know it. He was unhappy as a child is unhappy, crying for some impossible moon. One cannot sit by and not try to soothe the unhappiness of a child.

"I suppose you think that very weak?" she said.

"What?"

"Why, to pretend one is what one never can be, until in the end one believes that one is."

"Weak? Yes, I suppose it is, but everyone does that, of course."

"I don't think Camilla does."

Camilla's name came with a curious shock to Harry. For the first time he realised how much he had thought about her in the last weeks. It seemed to him that he *had* been in love with her. Was he now in love with Katharine? Through the physical attraction which he was at the moment feeling for Katharine Camilla's name had come with the shock of a blow. By an act of will he stiffened his body and his mind.

"What does Camilla do?"

Katharine noticed the change of voice and tone, consciously steadied by Harry.

"I sometimes think there is no dividing line in Milla, between her dreams, I mean, and her realities. She doesn't pretend. When we were children, you know, she never said: 'Let's pretend.' We had a game, I remember, called explorers: we turned the nursery table upside down, tied a cloth across the legs, and sailed in it across the nursery floor to New Spain and wonderful western islands which father read to us about of an evening out of Hakluyt. I used to say: 'Let's pretend we're explorers,' but Milla never did. I'm almost ashamed to think how old we were when we last played explorers, but the floor was still really the Atlantic to Camilla and the table a galleon. And she's just the same now, I'm sure; she never says to herself: 'Let's pretend.' She never thinks of the brilliant things she might have said, but of the brilliant things she did say."

"And did she?" Harry laughed. "You seem to hint that she didn't."

"God knows. Sometimes of course she did, and sometimes she didn't. It's of no importance to her; that's her danger."

Harry looked across the meadlow to the garden and Camilla under the trees. She seemed immeasurably far from him, herself like a dream. For the moment the idea of being in love with her was absurd. So white and delicate and fair, she was not a woman, but a fine lady in a dream or a play infinitely remote from him. And Katharine was very near; here was flesh and blood, moving him now as it flushed the fair skin red and the full lips. He could imagine kissing and being kissed; he could imagine marriage and a calm life of marriage, and that face across the breakfast-table and a copper urn. But he couldn't imagine kissing Camilla: fine ladies and Dresden china don't kiss one or pour out one's morning tea behind a copper urn.

Then he came back again to her last remark, which had lain latent in his thoughts: "That's her danger."

"Her danger?" he asked. "How is it dangerous to her?"

"Perhaps it's not so dangerous to her as it is to other people."

She smiled both at the boldness of her remark and at her own thoughts. She did not feel or see what he was feeling for her. The intervals between his and her remarks she put down to his caution and reserve. Here was a young man in love who would never give himself away—never, until he had arrived at the determination to do so. She liked confidences, especially from men. She would have liked some sign, even though he was in love with her sister, of his being moved by her presence. She felt their intimacy, so close together on the grass under the eyes of those in the garden; but so little from his side seemed to be coming from their closeness. At any rate he had her sympathy. She thought she saw suffering in his eyes, and she determined that he should recognise her sympathy.

"You meant dangerous to her, you know," he began again. "In what way?"

She smiled to think that he was avoiding what was dangerous to him. "Well," she said, "I do think it's danger-ous not to face facts. Not that Milla doesn't face them, exactly. She isn't a coward or sentimental, but she simply doesn't know the difference between facts and—and, well, I suppose, her own dreams. I sometimes think she's never completely awake—and somnambulism is notoriously dangerous. Suppose somebody woke her up one day much too suddenly."

He understood now what people meant when they talked of Katharine Lawrence's depth. She was enfolding him in her large and tolerant sagacity, soothing him with her unastonished wisdom. And Camilla herself became to him still more unreal, still more of a dream.

"Perhaps it's impossible to wake her up," he said.

"Perhaps. But the person who does or tries to—the danger to him!"

"And hasn't anyone?"

"Oh, well, people have fallen in love with Camilla; but

you can't take that very seriously—because she doesn't, you know. You've heard of poor Arthur; he's fallen in love with her several times. There has never been any danger there, because even in her wildest moments she has never dreamed of being in love with him."

He looked at her in silence, right into her eyes, quite steadily in a way in which one does not look directly at a person once in ten years. She met his eyes steadily too and smiling.

"You are kind," he said. "And amazingly beautiful."

Her eyes dropped at once, and she even blushed a little. It came as a surprise to her for the moment—and she was not easily surprised. It was a little ridiculous, and a little unpleasant to her, and yet she was pleased too, excited, flattered. Just at first she thought that possibly she might have been mistaken, that he was not in the least in love with Camilla; and then she came down again to a calm, sensible view of it. One had to expect these things from men, to women unintelligible and unexpected. And the unexpectedness was just the charm to her as a woman.

As she did not speak he thought she was offended. He burst out almost angrily:

"I suppose I ought not to have said that. Good God! I was just thinking before you came out here how beastly people are to one another. I tell you I hated you all, because—because I thought you hated me. Well, not hated perhaps—despised, disregarded: don't you know what that feeling is? No, I suppose you don't; women don't—not if they are beautiful. One can't talk to people, can't say what one wants—feels. It's just as if they were mere blocks of stone set up around one, like so many tombstones. And then it all seemed simply silly what I had been thinking, when you came and talked as you did. I thought I knew what you meant: I thought you understood, were kind. And now I've spoilt it all, I suppose."

She laughed. "You are rather silly, Harry. You haven't spoilt anything. It's so much better for people to say out straight what they mean. I feel I can talk to you far more easily now than I could have a quarter of an hour ago."

They both felt that, and yet neither of them spoke; it was clear to them that the conversation had come to an end, for the time being at least. It was as if a fireproof curtain had been lowered between the acts, a plain, undecorated, unlettered curtain, over the bright colours and meanings of their conversation and relationship.

They sat for a few minutes silent, and then Katharine got up. Harry walked with her to the house. Their approach brought all the others from their chairs on to the lawn.

"You've been quarrelling, I believe," said Mr. Lawrence.

"Harry certainly was rating you soundly at one point," said Camilla.

"With absolutely no effect on Katharine, of course," began Arthur.

"No, none whatever—I watched her sitting impassive there like a monolith, while Harry, like a Hebrew prophet, scourged her for her detestable vanities and vices."

"This is an awful place," said Katharine. "Two people can't have a little private conversation without being spied on by all the others."

"If you want to have a private conversation," said Mr. Lawrence, "you shouldn't go and sit and shout at one another in the middle of a field surrounded by four people who want to read their books in peace. However, you have given us something to talk about at lunch. Thank God, it's time for another meal."

He walked away very slowly into the house, went into the dining-room and sat down at the table. The others scattered to their rooms, and when they came down five minutes later found him still sitting patiently eating bread, waiting for his luncheon.

VII

CAMILLA NEGLECTS TO MAKE UP HER MIND

Harry had no opportunity on the Saturday or the Sunday of continuing what seemed to him his unfinished conversation with Katharine. And he never found himself, as unconsciously he desired to find himself, alone with Camilla. They tended to keep together compact as a party, at meals, on the lawn in garden-chairs and with books, and in the afternoons on walks. They mellowed to one another—a sign of which was the general increasing pleasure in the ever-increasing causticness of Mr. Lawrence's comments upon life, people, institutions, and even inanimate things. They listened tolerantly to Arthur's voice rising and falling in the pure air over theories of art and literature. They sank back into silence and their comfortable chairs, lulled by the open sky of hot summer days, by the smell of hot earth and rank grass and heavy trees, by the drowsy call of wood-pigeons and the cawing of rooks. They found pleasure merely in sitting upon the grass through the long evenings with unread books upon their knees.

Harry's forebodings were disappointed; the lazy hours slipped away pleasantly for him too. He was rather silent, rather outside the circle of easy conversation, but not as silent as Lion. On the Monday morning he was sitting alone on the lawn when Camilla came out of the house. She walked over to him and an empty chair, but he went to meet her.

"Let's go up on to the hills," he said.

He had felt a sudden desire to talk to her alone, but now that he was walking by her side he did not know how to begin, or indeed exactly what he wanted to say. Before his conversation with Katharine, the idea that he might be or become in love with Camilla had been continually with him and had given him pleasure. Somehow or other that conversation had suddenly brought him to a full stop and shown him where he was going. As he had looked at Katharine, and realised the beauty of her face and body, the stability of her character, he had almost cried out within himself absurdly: "If I am to be in love, why the devil am I not in love with her?" The reality of his whole feelings began to seem doubtful to him, and the reality of Camilla. What could she possibly have to do with him? There persisted in his mind that image of her as a fine lady, infinitely remote, something not to be touched, in silk and satin and lace and fine linen, and with lady's-maids around her.

Now that she was actually walking by his side the plea-sure in her mere presence returned to him. It is a fine thing for the spirits to climb a grassy hill on a fresh morning with a breeze on one's face and to the song above one's head of half a dozen larks. Perhaps too he felt it was a fine thing to be there up above the earth with a beautiful young woman; for few young men in such circumstances can escape a flattering reflection of this sort. It is certain that Harry did feel that Camilla's presence there alone with him was in some curious way a proof of his value in the world, showed him to be a finer and more of a man than all the other Toms and Dicks and Harrys, and Arthurs and Lions down below without her on the earth. It is just as certain, and might rather have dashed his spirits, if he had thought of it, that Camilla felt no such reflection of her value in his presence.

"Have you enjoyed yourself here?" Camilla asked him.

"Yes. Why? Didn't you think I had?"

"I don't know. It's so difficult to tell with you. Now with most people, Arthur and Lion too, you can always tell from their faces. You never give yourself away, I suppose."

"Let myself go, do you mean?"

"Both, I expect."

"I wonder if that's true. I don't think it is really. I expect I can let myself go much more than you or any of those down there, but I only do it when there's something worth letting oneself go for."

"Worth? Worth while? Yes, perhaps that's it—that's what makes you different from them."

"That's because I'm a Jew. Oh yes, you see what I mean, of course. We wait hunched up, always ready and alert, for the moment to spring on what is worth while, then we let ourselves go. You don't like it? I see you don't; it makes you shrink from me—us, I mean. It isn't pleasant; it's hard, unbeautiful. There isn't sensibility, they call it, in us. We want to *get*, to feel our hands upon, what's worth while. Is it worth while? Is it worth *getting*? That's the first and only question to buzz in our brains."

Camilla was silent. She believed what Harry was saying. It made her sad. She distinctly did not want him to be like that. And then she ought to be making up her mind. She did not want to have to think of such things, to have to make up her mind about anything. She wanted to enjoy the gayness of sun and wind and the song of larks. She sat down, resting her elbows on her knees and her face on her hands. Harry stood looking at her. It gave him rather a bitter amusement to think that she had chosen the very spot where on Friday night Arthur had become confidential to him. Was he going to take her confidences now? She scarcely seemed to be aware that he was standing by her side, watching her. Her whole attitude was one of sadness, coldness, and reflection. The power and charm of her presence over him had never been so strong. It made him angry with her and with himself.

"We're born that way; I suppose we were born that way twenty thousand years ago in Asia. Personally I'm proud of it. I like it. (The only thing that a Jew is sentimental about is Judaism, you know.) I don't like softness. I'm different from Arthur and Wilton, and—good Lord!—I'm different from you, and always will be. One can't be born again; once and for all one has one's father and mother in one, in every cell of one's body, so they say. I am a good Jew; I obey the fifth commandment, and honour my father and my mother—at any rate in myself. We aren't as pleasant or as beautiful as you are. We're hard and grasping, we're out after definite things, different things, which we think worth while. We don't drift, we watch and wait, wait and watch. Down here I've enjoyed myself, enjoyed myself immensely, but even here not like you others. I feel it. It's pure and fresh here, somehow, this air and sky, the trees and grass and the long, lazy days. The country—it's like the highest art, it purges the passions. One is more like what one was as a boy. But there it ends with me. I just feel it æsthetically. I can never give way to it, and settle back in my chair to chatter with a pure heart and childlike mind, like Arthur. I'm still looking out to get hold of things which—which are worth while."

"And what is worth while?" said Camilla very slowly and wearily.

Harry hesitated. He had been speaking almost angrily, with a desire to hurt her, to expose himself and to justify himself. What was worth while? There was one thing which at the back of his mind he had all through half believed that he meant as worth while. But he only half believed it, and he shrank from, did not dare the putting of it into words.

"Money," he said, "money, of course. That's the first article of our creed—money, and out of money, power. That's elementary. Then knowledge, intelligence, taste.

We're always pouncing on them because they give power, power to *do* things, influence people. That's what really we want, to feel ourselves working on people, in any way, it doesn't matter. It's a sort of artistic feeling, a desire to create. To feel people moving under your hands or your brain, just as you want them to move! Admiration, appreciation, those are the outward signs. They make you swell with pride and happiness. You feel you're doing something, creating things, not being tossed and drifted through life with a few million other helpless imbeciles. Then of course we get an acquired pleasure in the mere operation of doing things, of always feeling onself keyed up and absolutely alive. You don't like us? You don't like my picture of us? But you must admit that our point of view implies imagination?"

Camilla remained silent.

"You don't know what life is," he went on. "You live in a world of your own; it consists mostly of clouds. By God! I wish I could take you to Richstead and show you that. That's how nine hundred and ninety-nine people live out of every thousand in this, my world, like caterpillars. The males crawl out to their offices in the morning, and crawl back to their houses in the evenings. The females crawl about their own and other people's houses all day. They are crawling after food and eggs—food to keep themselves alive, and eggs to keep the race of caterpillars alive. They don't know what they're after; they haven't got the imagination for it. But we have, even in the worst sink we know we're crawling and after what. The lowest pawnbroker in the Whitechapel Road has enough imagination to get himself an ideal; he knows what he's after, what is worth while."

Harry stopped and looked at Camilla, waiting for her to say something. All the time that he had been speaking, Katharine's words were in her mind: "You'll have to make

up your mind." Still she did not want to have to make up
her mind; everything was too difficult. She felt that she
had met here something that was strange to her. It was as
if she were being jarred and jolted out of a pleasant, peaceful country of smooth roads and country lanes and dreamy
fields into a desert of jagged rocks and stones. She wanted
to say something to bring herself back into the old
pleasant dreamy lanes and fields, but she could not. She
watched the great stretch of land and the winding river and
the smoke hanging over the sleepy village at her feet.

She was surprised to hear Harry laugh. "Well, I've enjoyed myself immensely," he said, "but I'm going away."

"Why? What do you mean? Surely you are coming up
with us this afternoon?"

"No, I think I'll go by the next train. I'm going to run
away for good."

"From us?"

"Yes, from you."

"Why?"

"Why? Damnation! one never knows quite why one
runs away—because one's afraid, I suppose. If you make
me put it in words you'll make me give the wrong impression, or say more than I mean. I'm in a reasonable
panic, that's all."

"I don't understand what you mean. What has happened?
It's something to have made a new friend. We thought we
had in you; we were congratulating ourselves on it."

Harry thought for some time before he answered.
Camilla felt strangely impersonal, and yet interested, even
excited, as to what was coming next.

"I expect that's it," he said in a voice in which there
was now no trace of heat or anger. "You want me to
change my groove. You would hate to change yours; you
want to go on as you've always gone on. I mean all of you.
Well, so do I. It doesn't do, it is not worth it—not when

you see what's going to happen, and that you'll never get what you want, if you want it. You don't like me."

It came as a shock to Camilla. She was not sure exactly what he meant. She felt so impersonal herself that she could not believe that he meant it very personally. Katharine would say that now was the very moment for her to make up her mind. But it seemed all too far off for her to consider it in that light; also, she had that queer desire which comes to people in crises to remain passive, to watch what will happen, to take no part oneself in the altering of things.

"You know that isn't true," she said. "This is simply silly, Harry. We all like you."

"Not as I am. You may like me as you are, and of course I could become so—but I won't, I never will, you know."

"That's absurd. We like you as you are."

Her voice was affectionate, almost pleading now. Harry sat down by her side. His anger left him suddenly; he looked back nervously over what he had said to see whether he had not been making a fool of himself, and he was inclined to think that he had. Camilla suddenly touched him gently on the arm and laughed.

"You are silly, Harry. Tell me about the people of Richstead, and then we'll go back to lunch."

Harry looked at her and laughed too. After that it was extraordinary how suddenly everything had become very vivid and gay. First he noticed the point of light which danced in her eyes as she laughed, and then the red and gold of her skin, and the bow of the lips that smiled at him. For the first time he felt the breeze on his face, and saw the great shadows chasing the sunlight over the green fields, the purple downs, and the white villages that lay before him. He did not mind any more that he had made a fool of himself: he was happy.

They spent the morning walking together over the hills. Harry forgot that he might be in love with Camilla, and Camilla forgot that she ought to make up her mind. They became intimate and happy together for a few hours like the lower animals or unintelligent people—which meant that, forgetful of the past and unsuspicious of the future, they took each moment that came as one isolated point of living and feeling, and enjoyed it.

VIII

CAMILLA'S OPINION AND GWEN'S EMOTION

Harry had persuaded Camilla to come and see for herself
how the people of Richstead lived. The opportunity was
a garden-party, a garden-party to which anyone could
obtain admission by the payment of sixpence. The young
and old ladies of Richstead were not behind the young and
old ladies of other suburbs in the many-sided and flattering
pursuit of "doing good." This pursuit, which, in our complicated surburban civilisation with its minute division of
labour, is the special province of the female and the clergy,
gains a peculiar bite and flavour when it enters into and
combines with the pleasures and distractions of the pur-
suers. The spirit of "doing good" manifests itself in its
most pure and mysterious form in the outward and bodily
signs of Bodies, Societies, and Guilds, which often, alas,
spring up and flourish under one vicar only to fade,
languish, and die away under his successor. The particular
body which flourished under Mr. Macausland was "The
Poor Dear Things," and the garden-party was "in aid of
The Poor Dear Things."

Only a person who has lived among the four great castes
of India can fully appreciate how much stronger the caste
system is in Richstead; and the caste system alone explains
the existence of The Poor Dear Things. Mr. Macausland's
congregation belonged almost exclusively to the lawyer
and merchant castes of the middle-class; that is to say, to
the lower and middle-class. Now obviously you cannot try
to do good to your own castes or to castes higher than
your own without insulting them; and the really low
castes, which form the great lower classes, are so curiously

constituted that they are inclined to resent any attempt of the wives and daughters of the lower and middle middle-class to enter their homes and do good to them.

Luckily Providence has provided The Poor Dear Things. There is a region between the lower middle-class and the lower classes, occupied by unfortunate people who are no longer ladies and gentlemen, but have not yet become merely men and women. Here live the fallen gentlewomen (fallen, of course, in exactly the opposite sense from that in which the term is applied to those unfortunates who are fallen women), and those of whom Mr. Macausland was fond of remarking: "He is quite a gentleman, quite a gentleman, reelly." Governesses and tutors, the daughters of clergymen and army officers in reduced circumstances, are the chief recruits to those drab-clothed, shabby ranks; and when chronic indigestion or an affection of the sight or merely the infirmities of sterile old age leave them, as life recedes, tossed up and stranded in some sordid street, alone in one bare room or a burden upon a brother who is already burdened with a salary of three pounds a week, a house with five rooms and a wife with five children, then they become for Mr. Macausland and the ladies of his congregation Poor Dear Things.

The Guild of Poor Dear Things supplies necessaries such as shawls, bibles, and soup, and dainties such as jam and potted meat to the Poor Dear Things scattered through the parish. Sometimes, but on rare occasions, and with the consent of two members of the committee, it supplies a luxury, money. The zealous members of the Guild make it their duty to search out those "cases" to which the name by which the Guild is known can be appropriately applied. All this requires funds, and funds are legitimately acquired by bazaars, garden-parties, and theatricals.

It was a garden-party with this object at which Camilla was to be shown how the people of Richstead lived. As it was in the cause of charity, Mr. Macausland had made no objection to an entertainment (entrance sixpence and one shilling) being included in the programme. Things move so fast in Richstead that he allowed the entertainment to be and to be called Living Pictures, although a few years before the mere name could not have been mentioned in his drawing-room, because at that time one learned from the papers that Living Pictures were an excuse in music halls for women to expose too much of their bodies to the eyes of the audience. However, that scandal had passed away with so many others about things and persons nearer Richstead than the amount of clothing which a woman should wear in Leicester Square; and there was now no suggestion that May would not be fully clothed in a representation of the famous picture St. Bartholomew's Eve, when the wind blew over the screen a little too early on the lawn of Mrs. Luke Thompson's fine old garden (kindly lent for the occasion), and discovered May trying to contort her limbs under a nun's dress made of alpaca into the necessary posture of supplication.

In the drawing-room at St. Catherine's Avenue Camilla had been introduced to Mrs. Davis and Hetty. Mrs. Davis had looked forward to the meeting with the natural curiosity of an anxious mother, ever since Harry had said casually: "I've asked Miss Lawrence—she paints at Paton's —to come to the garden-party on Saturday." She was too wise to say anything to Harry, but her mind immediately flew to a vision of an untidy daughter-in-law in a crushed strawberry linen dress who painted.

"I wonder who these Lawrences are," she said later to Hetty. "Does Harry see much of them, do you think?"

"A good deal, I should think," said Hetty. "He seems great friends with the father." She laughed through her nose. "He stayed with them, you know, in the country."

Mrs. Davis nodded her head at Hetty, and a peevish,

worried look—the perpetually recurring tragedy of the bird watching its fledgling fly away with pleasure from the nest —came into her eyes.

"I don't know what's come over Harry lately; he tells one nothing. One doesn't know what he does or whom he knows. It isn't like as if he was one's own son any more. He goes out of the house in the morning, and how do I know where he is until the evening when he comes back to go to bed? It isn't treating one like a mother; one might be a stranger or a servant to him. Who are these Lawrences? I've never heard of them before."

Mrs. Davis was prepared to be quite stiff to Miss Lawrence. With this object she made herself even smarter than she otherwise, on such an occasion for being smarter than other ladies of the neighbourhood, would have considered it necessary to appear; for it is so much easier to be stiff to anyone in one's best clothes. She was very obviously in her best clothes, for she had succeeded in making herself look as if she had never had them on before and probably never would have them on again. To Camilla she appeared to be two white kid gloves and a very large, dark old woman in the middle of an immense number of rich and important clothes, with two pathetically big eyes, two strong, thick lips, two deep furrows in all that time had won from powder and puffs out of a sallow face under an enormous lop-sided festoon of purple ostrich feathers.

Camilla impressed Mrs. Davis favourably. She was a very sweet young girl, and so clearly a lady and lady-like. Even her hair was inartistically tidy. Though she wore her clothes as if they belonged to her, and though of course anyone could see that they were not smart, not really smart, yet—well, one doesn't know quite how to describe it—one could see she was a lady, very elegant, elegant and graceful, those were the words. She was silent at first as she walked with Hetty down St. Catherine's Avenue behind

Harry and Camilla. There was a little failing in the satisfaction that she had hoped to derive from so many circumstances, such as that she was wearing her smartest clothes
and a hat that quite a young woman, of thirty-five even,
might have worn, that she looked well in them and quite a
young woman, that she was not an old woman, that her
daughter Hetty was looking very well and smart. Mrs.
Davis was not given to introspection; she did not curiously
look into her own mind to find a reason for the vague
feeling that there was something in this Miss Lawrence
that had suddenly made Hetty seem to be sounding a false
note. She looked at Hetty; the full, dark eye, sensual and
hard and cunning and beautiful, the hard, closed lips so
ready to spring open with a smartly jocose remark, the
already luxuriant curve of her bosom, and finally the frills
and flounces that had come from the Victoria station
dressmaker, and the hat top-heavy with a bower of arti-
ficial flowers that had come from Oxford Street. And then
she turned her eyes inquiringly to Camilla's back.

"I don't know that I like these dresses of Madame
Duclose," she said irritably; "you must get her to look at
yours again. It's too full there in the front of the bodice;
it gives you too much of a bust. I wonder where Miss
Lawrence gets her clothes."

"It doesn't matter much where she gets them."

"Why?"

"That sort of girl looks well in anything."

"Really, you needn't be so sharp, Hetty; I wasn't
making any comparison with you. Besides, that's nonsense: clothes make all the difference in the world once
you're a lady. Of course if you aren't one it doesn't matter
what you wear. There's Mrs.—what's her name? we met her
at the Lyntons, didn't we? You ought to have bowed to
her, Hetty; and Harry not taking off his hat! Such rudeness! She's overdressed and rather loud, of course, but she

seemed quite a nice woman, and comes of quite a good family, Mrs. Garland tells me. It's such a mistake in a small neighbourhood like this to expect to be able to pick and choose, and not make oneself agreeable. Besides, the rudeness! I don't like Miss Lawrence's dress as much as yours; it's not as good, rather prim, don't you think? But it's in very good taste; it must have been made by someone good. I do like that style. It doesn't suit everyone, of course, but is very graceful and elegant, something refined and quiet about it."

Hetty smiled. "I know exactly what you mean, mamma dear. I am a lady and Miss Lawrence is a lady, but Miss Lawrence is rather more of a lady than I am."

"I never meant anything of the kind, Hetty. It's so easy to twist one's words; one can never say a word without someone taking offence. Didn't I tell you myself that she is rather prim?"

"I'm not a bit offended. Miss Lawrence is a Christian lady and I am a Jewish lady."

This sort of discussion was apt in the Davis family to terminate in what Mr. Davis called a family row, which in turn only found its termination in the interruption of strangers or the necessity of going to bed. In this instance the arrival at Mrs. Luke Thompson's gate, where Harry and Camilla waited for them, brought the necessary smiles to the faces of Mrs. Davis and Hetty.

The garden-party was in full swing. The garden was old and large and surrounded by high walls covered with ivy, in whose venerable branches, blackened now by years of London fogs and London smoke, great tufts of dirty grey webs showed where countless generations of spiders had spun and spun again their dwellings. Within lay a very large oblong lawn and an extensive shubbery intersected by several short and winding paths. Mrs. Luke Thompson, who was by nature inclined to a practical sentimentality, which had been encouraged by her spending six months of her girlhood in Germany and most of the rest of her life in a childless widowhood, had a passion for rustic seats and pergolas. In moments of more than usual depression she regarded the pergolas that spanned the paths of the shrubbery as emblems of her disappointed life, for instead of the romance of strolling through arches of fragrant roses, she had to be content with dodging occasionally a long, straggling thorny twig or noting the pathetic attempts of a blighted bud to open into a frayed rose, as she walked down a sort of cage of wire netting. The rustic seats—so long as you remembered that any sudden movement on their rough surfaces might do damage to frocks and trousers—were more satisfactory, and she inserted them in several places in the shrubbery and sprinkled them liberally around the lawn.

Upon this lawn, or rather that part of it which had not been screened off for the living pictures, there were now forty or fifty people scattered about in groups, engaged in the rather unpleasant occupation with which these sorts of parties begin, of trying to look at other people without catching their eye, in order to see whom one wants to recognise and talk to and whom one wants accidentally to avoid. At present the larger groups appeared to be forming according to sex and age. On the path in front of the house some chairs and small tables by their promise of tea had attracted the older ladies; and there they looked like a party of rooks, in the black clothes of widows and the dark clothes of age, nodding their heads at one another and hopping about among the chairs. They were certainly enjoying themselves more than the white and many-coloured party of young women who clustered together down on the lawn, talking in high-pitched voices or in whispers, and glancing occasionally at a group of nine or ten young men, whose gay gestures, loud voices, and bursts of laughter showed that they knew that they were observed.

The Davises did not know, in the technical sense of suburbs, many people in Richstead; or rather, those people would have put it that not many people in Richstead knew the Davises. Under ordinary circumstances the fact that the Garlands had become quite friendly with the new family would have brought them a very wide acquaintance, for Mrs. Garland was very much respected and knew all the best people in Richstead. But even Mrs. Garland could not be entirely a passport to a family no member of which had been ever seen either in the church or on the tennis-court. Everyone is open-minded nowadays, and liberal-minded too, but there is a very natural feeling that people should, like decent Christians, sometimes have a racket in their hands on week-days and a prayer-book on Sundays.

Mrs. Davis and Hetty, leading the way rather rapidly on to the lawn, as if they expected to see immediately many friends waiting to talk to them, were suddenly aware of no friendly faces about them, and stopped abruptly. They formed an awkward little group of four in which conversation had to be manufactured, with Mrs. Davis very distraite and continually glancing round to see whether there were not somewhere somebody to whom she could introduce Miss Lawrence.

"I am afraid you will find this very dull, Miss Lawrence," she said to Camilla. "We don't belong by rights to Rich-stead, you see. We've only just come here from town, and most of my friends live in town. Seriously—isn't that Mrs. Lestrange, Hetty? There—the tall woman who has just come, with the pink roses in her hat?"

"No, mamma; that's the woman who lives next door to the Lyntons. We don't know her."

"How stupid of me—I'm afraid I bowed; very stupid of me. But I've no memory for faces. I've got a wonderful memory for names, but none for faces. It's very awkward sometimes, because as soon as I think of a name I believe that it belongs to the next person I see. Well, what was I saying?''

There was a pause.

"You were saying," said Camilla gently, "that most of your friends live in town."

"Oh yes. You know it's so different here; it's like a village, and then again it isn't. There's no friendliness, no real friendliness. Seriously I was.in two minds whether I should come here to-day at all—and then one doesn't want to seem stand-offish, you know what I mean. In a small neighbourhood, and all that, one feels one must at least put in an appearance."

Mrs. Davis paused for breath and took another survey of the lawn. Suddenly her eyes lost their feverish, worried expression; a look of pleasure and relief came into her face.

"Oh, there's Mrs. Garland and Gwen—I must introduce you, Miss Lawrence. Such nice people, and great friends of mine. Oh, and there's Mr. Macausland too."

She began to hurry Camilla across the lawn. Harry and Hetty followed slowly. Each knew what the other was feeling, but their faces remained like blank walls, except that they showed their good-breeding by a trace of superciliousness in the way they passed people as if they did not exist. But Mrs. Davis was unfortunate that afternoon; she could not reach Mrs. Garland without a contretemps. A very large woman, obviously "out of it," was standing almost immediately in their path. She was alone, and swayed perceptibly on legs from which Nature was asking too much as the only support for all that was above them. As soon as she saw Mrs. Davis she put herself into motion with an effort and bore down on her. Two small, faded blue eyes in an enormous, fat white face reminded one immediately of a gigantic baby and a small pig; above nodded a black ostrich feather curling forward and set upright upon a small black bonnet; below, over immense protuberances that seemed inhumanly numerous, billowed black silk.

"And 'ow are you, Mrs. Davis, 'ow are you?" she said, without a flicker of expression in the little blue eyes or expanse of white face. 'And is this another daughter? 'Ow are you, Miss Davis, 'ow are you—pleased to meet you."

"This is a young friend of mine, Mrs. Brown, Miss Lawrence," said Mrs. Davis nervously and stiffly.

"Beg pardon, no offence, I'm sure. 'Ow are you, Miss Lawrence? Pleased to meet you, I'm sure." A large, fat hand opened near the folds of black silk, and Camilla put hers into it for a moment. The little eyes were fixed upon her and examined her minutely and intently; the lips just opened to allow the words to come through them, otherwise not a fold of fat in the white face moved.

"And 'ere is your daughter, Mrs. Davis. 'Ow are you, Miss Davis? And this is your brother, I can see that. 'Ow are you, Mr. Davis? No mistake this time; you're very like your ma."

Mrs. Davis and Hetty were both flushed; they caught each other's eyes and nodded.

"We are just—" began Mrs. Davis.

But Mrs. Brown was not to be moved like that; she swayed in front of Mrs. Davis, and the lips opened again, the eyes still fixed upon Camilla.

"Nice 'ouse this, nice 'ouse and garden. All just so, and very nicely kept, I'm sure. Do you live in the neighbourhood?"

For the moment Camilla did not understand that the question was addressed to her; then as the eyes continued fixed upon her face, she said suddenly: "No."

"Wimbledon?"

"No; I live in Bloomsbury, Horton Street."

"Bloomsbury? Really now! One can't live in Bloomsbury."

"Why not?" Camilla laughed.

"It's too low; you won't be able to stand it. It stands too low. Always a mist there in the early mornings, so I'm told."

"But I've lived there for years."

Mrs. Brown made no reply. She continued to stare at Camilla, and nodded her head very slightly backwards and forwards, as though she was telling herself that she had known from the first that Camilla was a very strange phenomenon; but as her face remained still as expressionless as a mask of dampish clay, it was impossible to be at all sure of what was passing in her mind.

"When I married my poor husband we lived first at Balham," she told Camilla. "It's a nice place, Balham, stands high, you know. Sometimes I think to myself, well, I'll go back there. But then my boy, he likes Richstead. 'Ow do you like Richstead, now you're settled in like?"

For the moment Camilla thought that the question was addressed to her, and she began: "I—I—," but Mrs. Davis came to the rescue.

"We like it very well, thanks," she said stiffly.

"In many ways a nice neighbourhood," said Mrs. Brown to Camilla; "it stands fairly high. But not friendly, not neighbourly. There are those who give themselves airs"—her eyes flickered, as if she were going to look round the garden and denounce them by name; but if this had been her intention she thought better of it. "My boy, now—you'd like my boy, a 'igh-spirited young fellow—he takes it 'ardly sometimes. 'Don't you fret yourself, Alf,' I say to him; 'you're young. What's here to-day's gone to-morrow. We can't all live in Grosvenor Square, and some there are who wouldn't, not if they could. We're 'appy where we are, and we won't be 'appier where we aren't welcome.'

I'm old, you see, Miss Lawrence, and he's young. But proud looks never broke no bones."

The fat cheeks of Mrs. Brown suddenly were moved as if by some subterranean earthquake, a trembling passed over them, then several large creases appeared, her teeth showed for one second, the eyes flickered, and Camilla realised that she had smiled. Camilla smiled back at her.

"I see you are a philosopher, Mrs. Brown."

"I don't know about that; but I'm sixty-four."

"And happy! You must be a philosopher."

"'Appy!" Mrs. Brown continued to look at Camilla for a minute or two in silence. It seemed to Camilla as if, swaying slightly from side to side like some old and gigantic elephant, she was looking back into her innumerable years of unfathomable wisdom and experience. For the moment Mrs. Brown, planted down in the centre of Mrs. Luke Thompson's lawn, under her nodding ostrich plume, with her swelling old body still swathed in all the paraphernalia of silks and petticoats and stays that creaked gently as she breathed, was to Camilla the embodiment and emblem of women's lives. Her silence as she paused to look back over the past was impressive. She was about to deliver judgment on life on behalf of all the women who had lived and died since Eve.

"'Appy! My dear, I've buried a husband and four out of five children. You're young, or you wouldn't talk to me of 'appiness. And you won't, not when you're an old woman like me. But I don't complain, so I suppose, if you like, you may say I'm 'appy enough."

Mrs. Davis had been fidgeting nervously all through this conversation, nodding at Hetty and shifting her feet and hands backwards and forwards, but not quite seeing how to break away from, or rather through, Mrs. Brown. Now, however, she could endure it no longer; she made a dart forward and took Mrs. Brown's hand.

"Good-bye, Mrs. Brown," she said hurriedly. "Perhaps we may meet later, but now I'm just taking Miss Lawrence to introduce her to Mrs. Garland."

"Well, I mustn't keep you," said Mrs. Brown with a sigh. "Good-bye, my dear." She nodded the ostrich plume confidentially to Camilla.

"One has to know all sorts in a place like this," Mrs. Davis whispered to Camilla as she hurried her away. "They call on you, and all that—you know what I mean. Her husband, I'm told, was very much her superior. A solicitor, quite a good practice, and a very refined and cultivated man. She was his house-keeper, or even his cook, they say. Of course, some people won't know her, but she means well, poor thing. And as I say——"

At this moment they reached the Garlands and Mr. Macausland. Camilla was introduced to Mrs. Garland and to Ethel, Janet, and Gwen, and to the vicar. They formed too large a circle for general conversation, so that after the introductions Camilla found herself rather isolated with Ethel, and on the other side of the group Gwen and Harry were in the same situation.

Gwen had read Dostoievsky's "Idiot" and several other books which Harry had sent her, but there had been few opportunities for talking alone to Harry since the day of the river party. She was not at all sure that the books had thrown any light for her upon the problems that he had presented her with, and there were many things which she would have liked to talk to him about. She had begun unconsciously to regard him as a sort of oracle upon life. She looked forward to chances of meeting him, and was invariably disappointed by meeting him where it was impossible to put to him the problems which he had helped to call into existence. Her feeling of discontent and her irritation with the aimlessness of her life in Richstead had grown more distinct and frequent, but neither Dostoievsky

nor Mr. Bernard Shaw nor Meredith nor Mr. Conrad, who
formed the mental tonic which the young man prescribed,
seemed to provide any cure for that uncomfortable state
of mind. This state of mind, common to the young of all
ages since Ecclesiastes, has at the present time no name;
the old-fashioned young men and women of the 'nineties
would certainly have diagnosed it in Gwen as weltschmerz.
It was, however, another kind of schmerz from which
Gwen was suffering at the present moment. She looked
at Camilla.

"Is that Miss Lawrence?" she asked Harry.

"Yes; how do you know that?"

"Oh, Hetty told May that she was coming with you to-
day." There was a pause. "She's very beautiful," Gwen
went on.

"Do you think so?"

"Yes, I suppose she's very clever too. She looks as if
she were."

Harry glanced across at Camilla, who was absorbed in
Ethel's account of The Poor Dear Things. He smiled. "It
depends on what you mean by clever."

"Oh, you know what I mean," Gwen said impatiently.
"All your family are clever, and we aren't. We are just
ordinary, stupid people. You talk to Miss Lawrence, I'm
sure, in quite a different way from what you talk to—to—
well, Ethel. I can't even understand 'The Egoist.' "

"And Miss Lawrence can't understand the binomial
theorem, and I can't understand you or Mrs. Brown,
though I love you both very dearly."

"You're sneering and laughing at me now," said Gwen.

Harry was astonished to see that there were almost tears
in her eyes. "What nonsense, Gwen," he said. "You think
much too much about cleverness and stupidity. 'Be good,
sweet maid, and let who will be clever.' Nobody could
call you stupid. If you're going to take 'The Egoist' as a

test—good Lord! nobody ever has understood it. A lot of gibberish. Nobody can understand it, because Meredith didn't understand it himself—he never took the trouble to think clearly. And as for Miss Lawrence, I don't suppose she has ever read it."

"I wonder if you mean that. I want to ask you about things so much, but—but it's so difficult here, and then you seem so sneering sometimes."

"I don't mean to be; but, look here, we can't talk in this place. You're going to Eastbourne, aren't you, for the summer, when mother and Hetty go? I shall be coming down then and we'll settle the universe there. Let's go and hear what Ethel is telling Miss Lawrence now."

They edged round the circle. Gwen felt half inclined to feel relieved.

"And are you on the committee, Miss Garland?" Camilla was saying to Ethel.

There was almost pride in Ethel's gentle voice as she said: "Yes, I've been on the committee some years now—six, I think, to be correct. It used to worry me rather at first, because you see we are responsible for the funds; and then, as Mr. Macausland says, we ought to be responsible for the policy of our branch. One must not pauperise people—you know that's the new theory. And then there are so many different forms to fill up, and I'm not very good at that sort of thing. And we all take it in turns to be secretary for six months each. I'm afraid I was a very bad secretary. Mrs. Maitland, that tall lady over there, used to get quite angry with me because I always forgot to use red ink in the right places; but one gets accustomed to those sort of things."

"I suppose you do an enormous amount of good. It makes me feel ashamed and rather small. Do you know, I've never done any good, I've never even been on a committee. And your sisters do this sort of thing too,

I suppose?" She turned to Gwen to bring her into the conversation.

Gwen smiled nervously. "No, I don't do anything."

"Gwen hasn't taken any work up yet," Ethel hastened to explain. "She has only just given up going to classes, and then there is her music."

"And sometimes they enjoy themselves in Richstead," Harry put in. "They play tennis, and dance, and go on the river."

"And May has taken up the crèche now," Ethel went on.

"The crèche?—I'm afraid I'm rather ignorant—what's that?"

"It's another committee. Mr. Macausland, our vicar, started it. The women, you know, of those classes, the quite poor, in fact lower classes, go out to work, and of course they have children, quite little babies sometimes. And they are so queer, you know, they won't stay and look after them. They go out and work almost at once, you know, when the babies are quite little babies, who couldn't be sent to a school. So Mr. Macausland has started a place where they can leave their babies when they go to work. There's a committee for that, and May is on it."

People had gradually been drifting in twos and threes towards the screens. At this moment Mr. Macausland, debonair with a large pink carnation buttonhole, bustled up to them.

"Ah, ladies, I'm sorry to interrupt you, but if you want to see the tableaux, or at any rate get chairs, you'll only just be in time."

He shepherded them courteously to the rows of chairs, and then, with a gay smile and a wave of his hand to his many friends, slipped behind the screens, and made for the shrubbery. He was met by girlish giggles and little screams behind the bushes. "Oh, oh, Mr. Macausland," May's voice was distinguishable, "you can't come here.

I'm getting ready. And oh, Mr. Macausland, could you ask Ethel to come and help pin me up properly?"

"All right, Miss May, all right. I won't take a step forward, and I fly to your sister." He waved a graceful hand towards the bushes, keeping his eyes fixed in the opposite direction.

Mr. Macausland was pleasurably excited. He was a moral man, being a clergyman, and also being a man who sincerely believed that morality was good; that was why he insisted in his talks to young men upon the Christian duty of keeping the body pure. Nay, more; if the unthinkable necessity had arisen, he could now, a lusty man of thirty-seven, full fed, full blooded with the juices of many mutton chops and much roast beef in his veins, have stood up in front of that screen and laid his hand upon his heart in the presence of the purest of the pure matrons and virgins of his congregation and truthfully declared that by practising what he preached he was as pure even as they. And not many men, even though they are clergymen, could do the same on a hot summer day. So much for the body—a subject which, however interesting and important, is considered to be as much out of place in a book, which the author naturally hopes will be patronised only by ladies and gentlemen, as at a garden-party also only patronised by ladies and gentlemen.

But the novelist who is concerned with the little tragedies and comedies that go on inside the brain of the paragon of animals, man, cannot leave the case of Mr. Macausland without a few more words. Many Christian moralists and teachers insist that purity of thought, though not of course as important as purity of body, is nevertheless desirable. In this direction all the vicar's ideals and honest resolutions were of little avail. Sometimes he found it difficult to get to sleep as soon as he laid his head upon the pillow, and on these occasions he would acknowledge to himself at 2 a.m.—that horrible and private hour at which we are so ready to believe worse than the worst of ourselves—that on the rare occasions when the Devil had the impudence to tempt him he chose that peculiar form of temptation.

Now Mr. Macausland had for some time been considering from a personal point of view the question of marriage. It is almost as great an anomaly for a priest of the Anglican Church to be unmarried at the age of thirty-seven as for a priest of the Holy Roman Church to be married. It is also, generations of matrons have agreed, most undesirable. Still, if a priest must marry, there does not seem to be any adequate reason why he should not marry someone whom he wants to marry. On the other hand there are many women—one sees them not only on the stage or in variety entertainments—whom any man would like to marry, and yet it would be obviously unsuitable for a clergyman to take one of them to wife. Mr. Macausland's problem had been to find the mean between suitability and inclination. For some time he had been nearing the conclusion that he had found the mean in Miss May. When he approached the bushes of the shrubbery he had not reached a definite conclusion. It must be admitted that he saw through the leaves a firm white arm ending in some white garment. As he walked away to fetch Ethel he suddenly decided to ask Miss May to walk back to her house with him after the party.

Ethel fluttered away to pin up May, and in due time the entertainment began. It did not rouse the enthusiasm of the audience, though Mr. Macausland clapped his hands loudly and indiscriminately, and many old ladies remarked audibly that one or other of the pictures represented happened to be their favourite pictures. After the last one, which was "The Doctor," the old ladies were not the least eager among the audience to make for the tea buffet.

The Davises and Garlands had tea together. Conversation

flowed suitably over the surface of things, beginning with
May and the living pictures, and going on to inanimate
pictures, theatres, books, and Richstead. To Gwen it became almost unbearable. She had caught a look passing
between Harry and Camilla after some gentle remark of
Ethel's, and instantly for her the spring had died out of
the day. It was Camilla she hated, and she envied her for
all the graces, beauty, cleverness, and culture with which
she endowed her. Here was a living Laetitia or Clara
Middleton—she made no distinction of persons in that
world in which all the women were both clever and beautiful, and all the men both clever and handsome. Miss Lawrence could talk as an equal to Mr. Whitford or Sir
Willoughby. She herself was a contemptible cypher,
laughed at just as Poor Ethel was being laughed at now.
She wanted to be alone, so as soon as she had drunk the
tepid tea she got up, saying that she would go and find May.

The first person she met on the lawn was May, rather
flushed and obviously excited.

"Come here, Gwen," she said, taking her by the arm
and leading her off towards the shrubbery. "I want to say
something to you."

They found a rustic seat half hidden among the rhododendrons. May's legs were planted firmly wide apart, a
smile of satisfaction was on her face.

"Did I look all right?" she said.

Gwen nodded.

"My word, that Smith girl!" she went on. "Did you
ever? I never saw such a guy. She spoilt the whole show,
I think. Mr. Macausland was very kind about it, of course,
but I could see what he thought."

Gwen waited for what was coming. "Now, look here,
Gwen," May continued, "I want you to do something for
me. See that mother and Ethel don't wait for me or make
a fuss. I shan't come back when you do."

"Why? What are you going to do?"

"There you are, it's always the same. One can't do a thing without everyone prying into it, and fussing over one. Well, I suppose I may as well tell you, but don't go and tell the others. Mr. Macausland has asked me whether he may accompany me home."

Gwen looked at May. She was still flushed; she was clearly pleased and excited.

"Are you going to marry Mr. Macausland?"

"He hasn't asked me yet," May laughed.

"Will you, if he does to-night?"

"Oh, I don't know," May spoke patronisingly. "I'm going to get some tea now. Are you coming?"

"No, I think I'll stay here."

"Well, be a dear for once, and don't forget."

Gwen was quite certain that Mr. Macausland would propose to May and that she would accept him that night. So May was in love with him. Somehow or other it all seemed very disappointing and depressing. She tried to think of the vicar as a lover: the thought was displeasing to her; he did not fit into the world of romance in which alone lovers exist. He would kiss her. She felt uncomfortable physically as she did sometimes when Mr. Macausland was near her. Suddenly the scene in the boat came back to her when she was walking with Harry by the river and they saw the young man kissing the girl. That was one of the things worth doing, Harry had said. It disgusted her to think of the vicar doing that to May.

She was startled to hear Harry's voice close behind her. "Let's sit down here."

"Well, what do you think of us?" he said after a pause.

Then Camilla's voice: "My God! Harry, I should go mad very soon if I lived in Richstead. Poor wretches! Poor wretches!"

"Whom are you talking about? Do you include Mrs. Brown?"

"No, not Mrs. Brown, I think. She is too immense, too noble, too tragic for pity. There is always some contempt in pity. One pities poor old Oedipus, but one doesn't pity Job. No; I would kneel to Mrs. Brown; but the girls, the poor pale-eyed girls of Richstead, I pity them. After all, the mothers have their children, and the men their work; but imagine those poor Miss Garlands waiting, waiting for those abominable young men in straw hats and that disgusting clergyman to come up and ask them to marry them."

Gwen jumped up, her one idea to get away from those terrible voices and words. There were tears in her eyes. Camilla and Harry were on the other path, separated from her only by a single row of rhododendrons. If she moved they might see her; they would know that she had heard from the tears on her flaming cheeks. She sat down again, bitterly determined to listen to the verdict and sentence to the end.

"Do you know, Camilla, I think most of them are thoroughly happy," she heard Harry say. "That's the worst of it."

"I don't believe it, I can't believe so badly of humanity. They are bored to death. They simply don't know what to do with themselves. They are lost and they know it. You can see it in those fluttering blue eyes of Miss Garland. Heavens! how bored those eyes are with life. They are just like the pathetic, stupid eyes of one of those little squat toy-dogs belonging to some old maid; you know the kind, it sits on a chair and looks at you; it's been dandled and over-fed and nursed through life, and has never been allowed to run about or bark or smell at other dogs; it does not know what on earth it all means or what on earth it wants, and so it sits up round a committee table for Poor Dear Things, and begs. Good God! why don't they break out?"

Harry laughed, and at the sound Gwen crouched down almost against the arm of the seat. "Now you're going to abuse men," she heard him say; "I know you are, Camilla. One can always hear it in a woman's voice a sentence ahead at least, when she's going to slang men."

"Well, it does make me almost hate men. The injustice of it. It is their fault. And look at them, those imbecile, cackling young men and that gross clergyman. They've got the range of the world. They've been to Eton and Oxford and Cambridge."

"No, no, not Eton. Don't make them out worse than they are; Dulwich possibly."

"Well, Dulwich then. Your Miss Garland never went to Dulwich. So she's uneducated, purposeless, sterile—and all for them. And there she is, waiting, waiting, and, now she's done for, has to console herself with committees and crèches, having lost all hope of ever being turned into a Mrs. Brown, and burying four out of five and a husband. And she'll be expected to envy her younger sister when she's chosen to satisfy the desires of a middle-aged clergyman."

Harry laughed again. "You're a prophetess, Camilla. Why, that's just what is happening, I believe."

"Loathsome, horrible! I think I shall go, Harry—into a nunnery. I can creep off by a back way."

"I'll come with you—even into the nunnery. We'll walk over the common to Silvertown, and then you can take the tube from there."

Gwen listened to their footsteps as they walked away. She did not move. Her face was still hot with shame and pain. How could people be so horrible, so cruel! She hated Camilla, she hated Harry, but still more she hated Mr. Macausland. They must have known that she was there and could hear them; they had done it deliberately in order to hurt her. And she had liked Harry! He had seemed more than usually kind to her on the lawn not an hour ago. She wanted to cry; it was with an effort that she kept her tears back. She sat numbed, weary; her head ached. It wasn't true what they had said, she wouldn't have it true—and then every now and again came a horrible sinking sensation in her heart. Was it perhaps true?

She heard footsteps and voices of people approaching. It was getting late; she would have to go and find her mother and Ethel. She got up and walked out of the shrubbery on to the lawn. Mrs. Garland, Janet, and Ethel were waiting for her.

"Where have you been, my dear?" said her mother. "It's time to go, and now where's May?"

For a moment Gwen thought she would give May away, but then why should she?

"May says we're to go on. She won't be long."

On the way back to St. Catharine's Avenue they came up with Mrs. Davis and Hetty.

The daughters walked on ahead, the two mothers followed.

"Where's May?" said Hetty.

"She's coming on later," Janet said decisively, after waiting for Gwen or Ethel to answer the question; but Ethel and Gwen remained silent.

"Oh." Hetty's intelligence was unmistakable. What she thought was: I'm glad I'm not Ethel or Janet Garland. I'm glad I'm not thirty-eight, or even thirty-three, waiting to hear that my younger sister is engaged. And fancy marrying Mr. Macausland!

If they had been a little more or a little less intimate they would have spoken of this subject which made the gentle atmosphere of a summer evening so exciting; but, as it was, they did not know exactly what note to begin on, and so were silent.

The mothers were less delicate. Mrs. Garland was visibly excited.

"My dear," she began at once, "my dear, I believe he is going to ask her this evening. I think he must have asked her to stay behind."

"Oh, I am so glad. My dear Mrs. Garland, I *am* so glad. I *do* congratulate you heartily, very heartily. She will be happy, I'm sure."

Mrs. Garland wiped her eyes. "I feel he will make her a good husband, but—"

"Of course it's a wrench, parting, I mean, and all that. But you ought to be very happy, my dear, very happy."

The two ladies squeezed hands, and were silent. It was a solemn moment in the life of a widow with unmarried daughters that was drawing near; one of those moments of life which, like births and deaths, mark the beginning and end of periods, the fulfilment of effort and purpose, the consummation of desires. It is in such moments that a whole generation dies or is born. "Poor Ethel," Mrs. Garland had got to after a few minutes.

"After all, Hetty's only twenty-six," Mrs. Davis was saying to herself, "and ever so much more attractive than May Garland. I really must ask young Bernstein to dinner again."

They all stopped at the gate of the Garlands' house, and Mrs. Davis and Hetty were for saying good-bye. But Mrs. Garland insisted upon their coming in for a quarter of an hour at any rate. Gwen, who had longed for this moment to get away to her bedroom and cry in peace there, found herself sitting in a deck chair and listening to a halting conversation, and waiting, waiting with the others. They were waiting for the click of the garden gate. Only Ethel seemed to be unmoved and unexcited. On her lap lay a long paper covered with accounts showing the takings of the garden-party in aid of the Poor Dear Things. Unconsciously she was adding up the figures again and again: "Six and six is twelve, and five is seventeen, and six is twenty-two; twenty-two is one and ten, ten and carry one." She was not good at accounts.

Mrs. Davis knew that she ought not to stay, and at last she got up. Two minutes after she had gone the gate clicked. May appeared, very red in the face.

Mrs. Garland got up, and waited for her; her hands were trembling. "My dear," she said, "my dear!"

May put her arms round her mother and kissed her. "He —he—asked me——" she began.

"I'm so happy, my dear, so happy."

"He's coming here to-morrow to see you. He wanted to come before, but it's impossible; he can't. Such a bore."

Janet was standing just behind May. She gave her sister's back a quick glance in which only the most acute observer could have read the amused tolerance and placid understanding. She patted May's shoulder and said:

"Well, good luck, old girl, good luck."

Ethel put her accounts down carefully on the wicker table, and came over and kissed May. "I'm so glad," she said, "I congratulate you."

Gwen burst into tears and rushed out of the garden into the house.

"Well, I say!" said May. "Did you ever? What on earth is up with her? Is she jealous, I wonder?"

Mrs. Garland had got up as if to follow Gwen, but she thought better of it and sat down again. "I don't think Gwen's been quite herself lately; and then you know at these times with her . . . I expect this has excited her. We had better take no notice, or perhaps after a bit Ethel might go up and see how she is. Sit down, May, and tell me about it, my dear."

"I should think I'm the one who ought to be excited," May began to grumble. "My word, I shouldn't like to be proposed to often. I feel all of a tremble. Well, you know, he—Angus—I don't think I *can* call him Angus—he asked me to allow him to accompany me home. I suppose Gwen told you, though I asked her not to. It was rather awkward," May's voice showed that she took pleasure in the recollection; "we walked slap into the whole Lynton and Thompson gang, just as we were going out of the gate. I'm afraid I went as red as a peony. However, I don't think he noticed, he was pretty jumpy himself. We walked by the common and I talked hard the whole time. When we got to the old seat by the trees, you know, he said quite suddenly: 'Do you mind sitting down here, Miss May? there's something I want to say to you.' I was all of a tremble at once, so I sat down. It sounds like a book, doesn't it? He looked at me quite different from ordinary, and was very red and breathing hard. 'May, Miss May,' he said, 'I want to ask you a very serious question, very serious for me, at any rate. I want to ask you whether you will be my wife.' I simply *couldn't* say a word. I believe I held out my hand. I know he kissed it, and then—well, I think that's all."

May was evidently thinking of what happened after that: it had certainly surprised her a little. Mrs. Garland came and kissed her again.

"I'm so glad, May," she said, "I'm sure he will make you a very good husband. Don't you think you ought to go and see how Gwen is, Ethel dear? Oh, and while I think of it, you ought to get a few things for tea tomorrow morning, if Mr. Macausland is coming to tea."

"I really *can't* call him, Angus," Ethel heard May say, as she went into the house.

IX

CAMILLA MAKES UP HER MIND

Harry and Camilla walked over Richstead Common to Henalarg, from which place she was to get an omnibus to Silvertown. Like most places in London, this little patch of down-trodden grass, with its black bushes and blacker trees, and its manful blackberry brambles, has the power of covering itself in an individuality quite apart from its immediate surroundings. In the fringe of streets on the Richstead and Todmere side one is in communion with the spirit that built Broadstairs and Littlehampton and is now embodying itself in the more modern manifestation of Bexhill-on-Sea and Seaford: two steps on to the common, and with the haze of a glowing red sunset in their eyes, Harry and Camilla seemed to be in communion with the spirit which created the desert and the wilderness. The swarm of small boys who play cricket between the bramble bushes had scattered to their homes and beds; the place, empty except for one or two melancholy couples of lovers, seemed to stretch with its coarse grass and tangled bushes as far as the sunset itself.

"I always wondered," Camilla said, "whether London ended anywhere suddenly and the country began. I suppose this is it."

"It begins again, I'm afraid, on the other side," said Harry. "This is only a little patch that has escaped us—at least alive. In revenge we creep into it when we're dead. We've made a cemetery of it over there, in that corner."

They strolled slowly. Harry quite suddenly was aware of the keen pleasure that he was feeling. This sudden consciousness astonished him, though it was what he had before occasionally experienced when alone with Camilla. They had hardly spoken since leaving the garden-party. Was it only the pleasure from her physical presence? Would he feel it, he wondered, if she were just as she was in everything spiritual and mental, but instead of that glow of red and gold in her face there were the little red netted veins of Ethel? Was he feeling this? Wasn't he feeling still more the pleasure of being alone in all the world with her? And what was she feeling?

"What are you thinking about?" he said before he knew that he was saying it.

"Myself," said Camilla, laughing. "And you?"

"Ourselves." He shied off. "But what were you thinking about yourself?"

"Am I only a silly, vain woman, Harry? What right have I to look down on those people? Am I really any better? Is it any better to paint pictures and read books and gossip and—and live as we do, than to dole out bibles and soup to broken-down governesses and look forward to marrying a straw-hatted bank clerk? I suppose I'm more intelligent. Am I?"

"Yes, I think you may say that."

"And more beautiful, I suppose?"

"Yes, more beautiful, certainly."

"It isn't much, is it, Harry? Camilla Lawrence is a little more intelligent and a little more beautiful than Miss Garland. Oh, vanity of vanities."

"You might substitute great deal for little, and still be speaking the truth."

"It is not much. It rather horrifies me. Only a little better mind or education or body separating me from what's so obviously wrong. And then there's a nobility about them which I haven't got. None of us have. We're rather petty with our vanities and frills, intellectual and moral. Isn't it finer to be a monument like Mrs. Brown, or a whited sepulchre of resignation like Miss Garland?"

"You're happy, aren't you, Camilla? It's better to be happy."

They had just reached that row of "bijou residences," from the upper windows of which, one imagines, actresses look down upon the aristocrats and the polo grounds of Henalarg. Camilla stopped, and turned to look back over the melancholy, blackened little common.

"I suppose I am," she said; "sometimes, I think, I'm like a person walking in his sleep. I might wake up suddenly to find that I'm not—not happy at all."

For the moment the feeling of things happening without any sort or kind of meaning overwhelmed her. As she walked in silence by Harry's side between the row of tiny brick-built boxes, with their curtained windows, and the high wooden fence, it seemed to her as if she could almost feel the earth whirling round under her feet. Can anything be more senseless and meaningless than this perpetual revolving of the earth under us? She had a vision of an enormous orange suspended in the twilight of the stars, and two little matches stuck ridiculously upright, turning round and round with the meaningless turning of the orange. And she and Harry, between the houses and the fence, were only two out of the millions of ridiculous little upright matches spattered over the revolving earth. The need of sympathy from something human in this inhuman universe came upon her, the desire to lean upon and be protected and comforted, to be soothed of some nameless fear. Harry was nearer to her, in the emptiness of the street and the settling dusk, than he had ever been before. Instinctively she touched his hand; his closed upon hers, and they walked on in silence, hand in hand.

She felt the comfort that a tired child on a long walk feels when it takes the hand of some grown-up, and hears the words come down to her: "We'll soon be home now, dear," with a vision of the nursery fire reflected in the brown tea-pot waiting over there for her. She just resigned herself to be led home by Harry. To him for the moment it was overwhelming because so unexpected. His heart beat violently when he first felt her hand in his; he half turned to take her in his arms, but something impersonal in her face stopped him. He did not know what she meant or what she was feeling. He wanted to speak, but it was impossible to think of a word to say. It was ridiculously, intolerably awkward now. At one moment the blood buzzed in his ears and his heart thumped as he felt her hand in his, at another he had that unpleasant sinking sensation in the pit of his stomach which overtakes one when one has said something peculiarly stupid. He began to wonder whether he ought to let go this hand which now seemed an enormous dead weight in his. Then he began to get pins and needles in his fingers. What on earth was to happen when they reached the 'bus?

When they got to the 'bus Camilla gently and quite naturally took her hand out of his. She smiled at him. "Don't come any further, Harry, I'll get into the tube at Silvertown." Her voice seemed exquisitely gentle.

"Are you sure?" was all he could say.

"Yes, quite,"—the 'bus came up—"good-bye, and thanks so much; you're very comforting, Harry."

Harry stood and watched the omnibus disappear into the dusk. Once Camilla waved to him, and he waved back automatically. He stood on the curb for a minute or two, relieved to find himself alone, eager to recover himself and the habit of watching and understanding himself and his feelings. He started to walk at a great pace towards the common, stamping his feet on the pavement, beating the ground with his stick, blurting out odd, almost meaningless, sentences. He was thinking of Camilla, her beauty and brilliance and lovableness; wherever he looked he saw her face and that half-ironical, half-sad smile—among the trees, in the windows of houses and the grey mist that hung like a curtain of stillness over the common.

He knew now that he was in love; it amused him to think that he had been in love for weeks without acknowledging it to himself. "How beautiful are thy feet, O beloved!" he shouted, to the dismay of a passer-by, as he tore along. "Damned fool! Oh, damned fool!" He stopped suddenly and looked round him. He was in the middle of the melancholy little common again; a short distance from him two lovers sat on a seat, she lying almost in his arms, his face bent over hers. He smiled at odd recollections of how such sights used to infuriate him with envy that those damned little clerks and shop-keepers had what he perhaps would never have, had each a girl to go out with and kiss and cuddle and God knew what. He remembered those thoughts that plague youth with desires and haunt it with romance, sordid and exquisite, most earthy and most ideal. Sometimes he had thought that it would never come to him, neither woman nor love. It had come to him now, so different from anything he had ever imagined, what everyone said was the greatest thing in life. If he died that instant, at any rate he would have died after walking by those famous elms with Camilla's hand in his.

He felt more of a man; there was a new pleasure in feeling the power run through his veins and limbs. How different the great things of life were from what one imagined they would be. Was he a fool, a damned, sentimental fool for feeling like this because he had held Camilla's hand in his for two minutes? He laughed at the memory of an incident—the incongruity of life, of one's hopes and desires and reality! It had happened to him almost on that very spot; before the remembrance of it had always made him hot with shame. He had started to walk from the omnibus home across the common one dark autumn evening. He had been thinking of women, furious that he was missing what so many around him were enjoying. He stared into the face of a woman passing him. "Hullo, darling!" she said. He stopped, his heart beating violently. She came close to him. "Shall we go for a walk on the common, dearie?" she said. She took him by the arm and led him speechless on to the damp common behind the cemetery. There she sat down, and pulled him down by her side and kissed him. And he—how often had he dreamed of lust and women's kisses!—he felt nothing but a trembling disgust and cold and the dampness of the ground striking through the seat of his trousers. In the end she abused him in amazingly foul language, and he escaped, leaving in her hands three shillings and twopence, which was all the money he had with him.

And all the time he saw Camilla's face looking down on him from the top of the 'bus. Could she really be in love with him? What did she mean by taking his hand? Then he remembered the look on her face as he had turned eagerly towards her. It was like the face of someone walking in his sleep. She had said that she felt like that, and hadn't Katharine said the same of her? He was quite certain now that she had meant nothing by it, that she felt nothing for him. She had taken his hand just as she might have taken Katharine's—that is what he had read in her face.

He lay down on the grass and for half an hour watched himself give himself up to despair. Then he began to think again that after all it was a strange thing to do, to take his hand, if she had not felt anything for him. Then doubt again; then another rift of hope; and so on up and down until the consciousness of stiff and rather chill limbs made him leap to his feet cursing. He hurried home to find his mother and father and Hetty already at dinner.

"Where have you been, Harry? You're very late. It's so hard on the servants, such irregularity, and dinner having to be kept. Did you go home with your friend?"

His mother's words and the smell of roast mutton, and his father's eyes looking at him as if he were a piece of furniture which he had looked at every day for a quarter of a century, and that abominable way Hetty had of making little digs at her food—cabinet pudding again— filled him with intolerable, almost physical, nausea. He sat down without a word, and began to crumble up the half-stale piece of bread in front of him. Mrs. Davis shook herself.

"Nice manners, I must say!" she said. "I think when you come in late you might at least have the good manners to answer your mother's questions civilly."

"Can't you behave yourself, sir?" said Mr. Davis in an authoritative voice, and then went on as if his wife were a child and not present: "You had better answer; we don't want a row over nothing."

Mrs. Davis turned on her husband, still more exasperated. "I wish you wouldn't always adopt that tone, Charles. You encourage the boy in his rudeness. I'm not in the habit of having rows. I suppose I can ask my own son a question, if he lives in my house. I'm sure I don't interfere with him—he comes and goes exactly as he likes."

"Isn't that just what I told him? What have I done wrong, my dear? I only told him that he had better answer you."

Harry groaned, seeing all the old signs blowing up for a storm. At this moment the parlourmaid came in with a piece of tepid codfish on a plate. Her entrance stopped the discussion for the time, and Harry took the opportunity to say:

"I didn't take Miss Lawrence home. I went for a walk on the common."

Dead silence followed.

"Did you see Mrs. Parkins?" said Hetty, for the sake of decency and the maid.

"No, dear," said Mrs. Davis in a voice which suggested the cruelty of her son and the angelic nature of her daughter.

Harry gulped down the tepid fish. The see-saw of doubt and hope, hope and doubt was still going on in his mind. He seemed to be divided into several consciousnesses, one watching the other, one walking hand in hand with Camilla, one half afraid to believe that she would love him, one convinced that she never would, and one entangled in the intolerable atmosphere of family sores and lifelong irritations. He himself at moments stood outside these warring, jangling selves.

"Did you play golf to-day?" he said to his father.

"Yes, and couldn't hit a ball. Tore up my card. I get worse and worse. And yet I have moments—I did the third in three to-day."

Mrs. Davis felt that she had been extremely badly used. She looked at Harry's gloomy face and Mr. Davis's impassive eyes. She loved them, there could be no doubt of that in her mind, because she was the wife of the one and the mother of the other. And yet how unfeeling, how unseeing these males were! What she had gone through for Harry's sake, merely to bring him into the world! All the pain, and then all the worry and expense! And for years she had been everything to him, he had depended upon her absolutely. And now, instead of the son she had dreamed of and—when he was not there—even now imagined him, a gentle, tender-hearted man who adored his mother, she saw a strange, hard young man who objected to being asked why he was late for dinner. Surely she must still have some share in him, he still must need her in some way. There must be something wrong with him, if he couldn't see that.

"It's just as if you had no affection or respect for me at all," she began as soon as the table-cloth was removed, and the maid had withdrawn for the last time.

She wished to be contradicted, but nobody spoke. Mr. Davis breathed heavily, and looked at his wife sorrowfully and resigned, like an old gentleman watching a child "have its cry out," quite convinced that there is no reason whatever for the uproar, but that it saves trouble in the end to allow the irrational creature to open its mouth and roar.

"I think you might at least say something," said Hetty desperately.

"Now, Hetty, there's no need for you to interfere," said Mr. Davis, eager for a distraction. "Besides, what is there to say?"

Harry could bear it no longer. He got up and kissed his mother. "I'm going to bed," he said, "good-night."

"Going to bed? At a quarter to ten?" he heard Hetty say, as he shut the door.

For seven hours Harry's thoughts continued to revolve in his brain in the same circle of hope and despair, like a squirrel in a cage. At five o'clock, to his amazement, quite suddenly a new thought occurred to him: he would go to Camilla next morning and ask her whether she loved him. He turned over on his pillow with a sigh, and immediately fell asleep.

As he dressed the next morning he seemed like some person watching himself, sick and depressed at seeing what a poor figure of a man he was cutting. His head was hot and ached dully, his hands and feet were very cold. He tried to think of what he would say to Camilla. He was quite certain now that she would refuse him; and yet, as he constructed the scene, cleaning his teeth a little longer than usual, he imagined it ending in kisses. Mr. Davis was already at the breakfast-table, solidly and solemnly intent upon his food and paper; the morning mist of a hot day seemed to be hanging in the room itself and innumerable and invisible bees made an intolerable and distant buzzing in Harry's ears.

"You were the cause of a nice row here last night, sir," said his father to him.

"I'm sorry. Didn't it stop when I went?"

"Stop? It went on till past twelve. You shouldn't behave like that to your mother."

There was a silence. Then Mr. Davis remarked as casually as he could: "I don't think I shall be back to dinner to-night."

"Nor shall I."

Mrs. Davis came in, bringing an air of gentle martyrdom with her as she kissed Harry. This is what we are driven to, he thought; this is what, thirty years hence, almost certainly will be the result of my desires succeeding. I am no more a rational creature now than a mad dog. Whoever thinks of acting according to reason or because of reasons? It is just desires that move us along: caught like a rat in a trap.

"I shan't be able to get home to dinner to-night, my dear," said Mr. Davis. "I'm going to play golf, and I promised to go back to supper with Holmes. I'm playing with him."

"I shall be out for lunch and supper too," said Harry.

"Oh, very well," was Mrs. Davis's reply.

"I can't stand this," said Mr. Davis audibly to himself, and left the room.

Harry followed him quickly. He started at once for the Lawrences' house. Walking to the station, in the train, and on the doorstep in Horton Street he felt more and more like a man in a trance, driven along by something over which he had no power. He asked for Miss Camilla, and the maid showed him into a room in which Mr. Lawrence was sitting alone reading the Sunday paper. Harry had expected to find himself at once alone with Camilla. He felt as if he were being bullied, tossed up and down and beaten by excitement, misery, and these intolerable circumstances.

"Hullo!" said Mr. Lawrence. "I didn't know you were coming. Do you want Camilla?"

"Yes," Harry answered and sat down in a chair opposite to Mr. Lawrence. Mr. Lawrence looked at him reflectively over the top of the newspaper for some time. He did not say anything; the silence did not worry him; he rather liked just looking at Harry, who seemed uncomfortable.

The door opened and Katharine came in. "Oh, it's you, Harry. Do you want Camilla?"

"Yes. We were going for a walk," Harry said desperately.

"I expect she's forgotten, but she's certain to be down presently," said Mr. Lawrence.

"Yes—" Katharine began, but seemed to have a second thought. "You had better go up, she's in the studio."

Harry heard and saw these two people with extraordinary clearness, and yet it was as if everything was happening at a great distance from him. They dwindled away from him like things in those most terrible of nightmares in which everything is seen as if down the wrong end of a telescope. He found himself out of the room and walking upstairs, counting the stairs as he went. He opened the studio door: Camilla was standing by the fireplace.

"Hullo, Harry," she said. He shut the door and walked over to her without saying anything. He saw her face flush red and her lips tremble. She sat down in a chair and looked up at him. His mouth was dry and he had to gulp before he said:

"I suppose you know I'm in love with you. I have been for weeks."

She did not say anything. He noticed a curious movement in her throat.

"I can't stand this any longer," he said. "The suspense —doubt—I can't stand it any longer. You must end it, one way or the other."

He stood over her, looking down at her. To her there seemed to be in him something threatening almost, and alien. His whole body trembled slightly. As he stood there in that attitude of desire and waiting and excitement, beaten down under his short, sharp words, she realised to the full that he left her completely cold.

"But I'm not in love with you, Harry. I'm not in love with you," she said suddenly.

For the moment her words had no effect on him. He stood in the same attitude of expectancy looking at her. Then slowly she saw the eagerness die out of the eyes; a look of pain like that of a suffering animal crept into his face. To him it seemed somehow something that he had expected, this sudden drop from excitement and hope to a dull sense of utter failure. There was nothing more to say. He watched her face vaguely, noticing the shape of her lips and the quickness of her breathing. It was extraordinarily painful to him to do this, but he liked to be fully conscious of the pain.

"I'm so sorry, Harry. I like you so much," he heard Camilla say.

He walked to the empty fireplace and stood, his head against the mantlepiece, looking into it. He wondered what he should do—not in the far future, but this day, this Sunday—all Sunday to get through! There was nothing now that he wanted to say or hear in this room. A certainty of what, he felt now, he had through all the past week suspected was in him, had struck him like a blow with Camilla's words that she could never love him.

When he looked round she was shocked to see how pinched and tired his face looked. "Oh, Harry," she began, and stopped.

He felt that he must say something, if only to get himself out of the room.

"Don't worry about me," he said, and the whole

situation suddenly seemed absurd. That two human beings, moving masses of matter—after all, that was what he felt himself to be—should act upon one another so ridiculously! "I believe I always knew that you could feel nothing for me—not in that way. But, Camilla, I do love you so and I wanted you so much, and then—do you understand?— one thinks, and thinks, and thinks, and one begins to hope—doubt. I couldn't think of anything else, or sleep."

Camilla shuddered. It was as though something she could not understand were being demanded of her, as if she were at fault in not being able to give. At that moment there seemed to her to be something ignoble in not being able to give, in not being able even to feel anything of what Harry was feeling. Love, passion, what did it mean?

"I think I shall go now," Harry said.

"No, Harry, don't go like that. It's my fault—I suppose. I've behaved very badly. But—oh, can't we go on as before? There is no one I like better, or even so much as you. Yesterday I remember thinking how comforting you were."

"Yes, I remember that," Harry said, rather bitterly. "I shan't disappear. But I'd rather go now—I'm rather tired. I should like to walk somewhere."

He turned towards the door. An absurd hope started up that she would call him to her. She lay back in her chair; he saw that, as he turned his head for a moment before opening the door. There were tears on her cheeks, but she made no movement, said nothing. He went out, closing the door behind him as one closes the door of a sick-room, very quietly. He stood still on the landing outside. He noticed that his head was aching, the blood throbbing in his temples. He crept down the stairs quietly, afraid that he would meet someone. The house was curiously silent and dark, as if, he thought, it was a house in which some-one had just died. He smiled; they might pull the blinds down perhaps after he had left. Outside the glare of the sun dazzled him. He knew it must be very hot, and yet he was icy cold, almost shivering.

He walked slowly down Oxford Street. It was rather like going out for a walk for the first time after influenza. His limbs were heavy to move and ached a little, the sun hurt his eyes, the noise in the street jarred his brain. It gave him a moment of rather bitter amusement to catch himself feeling important and wondering that these strangers streaming by him did not notice anything odd in him, or turn to look at him as he passed. He was a man who had just proposed and been rejected. Wasn't that something? It didn't happen every day to a man; it hadn't happened to-day to that man, or that, or that. Suddenly he noticed the ugliness of people, as a woman laughed and showed a gleam of gold and a very red gum, and a row of false teeth. And the young men with straw hats at the back of their heads, and bluish whites to their stupid, lascivious eyes, and lips that did not end clear-cut and red against the skin of the cheek, but spread out at the corners into a pink, chapped-looking kind of sore. This last fact began to interest him; it had never struck him before. He counted how many of the people passing him had this blemish. It was disgusting; they nearly all had it, all the young men and young women.

He saw the women as he had never seen them before—ridiculous, grotesque, repulsive. The monstrous shapes of them in the bundles of clothes, if you just watched the outline of the two walking in front of you! One imagined that "forked animal" woman—a poor, thin, soft white body, forking out into two long, weedy white legs like one of those white clammy turnips, which you sometimes see forking grotesquely into two legs—one imagined her thrust into that sort of bell-like cover of clothes, like an egg into a ridiculous egg-cosy. It was very easy to see for what purpose man kept these creatures, very easy to see it in their giggles and their flauntings, in the way their escorts of males shepherded them, and fussed round them and strutted before them, like a ridiculous farmyard cock with his troop of foolish hens.

Without thinking of what he was doing, Harry made for Waterloo. In the station he stood undecided for a little. He could not go home; the length of the day that remained to him to be got through, before the sleep which he longed for, appalled him. He remembered he had told Camilla that he wanted to walk! Well, he would walk. He took a ticket to Horsley. It was only when he sat down in the train that he realised how tired he was physically as well as mentally. He was simply deadened, feeling nothing.

At Horsley he climbed slowly up through the woods to the top of the down which looks over the valley to Gomshall. He lay down under a tree. He wanted to be alone, to think. It was very hot and very silent, except for the buzzing of bees. He made a pillow of bracken for his head and closed his eyes.

At about half-past three in the afternoon he woke up. Ah, he remembered, of course, he had been refused by Camilla. It was odd that after the first shock and sinking feeling of remembrance there was no sharpness of feeling in it. Only everything seemed horribly flat; there was nothing to break the monotony, no moment jutting up to look forward to in all the seven days of the coming week, and that level expanse of time which was waiting to roll up and over one.

He got up and started to walk aimlessly westward towards Guildford. As he walked he began to feel the first and divine gift, self-pity, and gradually a gentle, almost pleasant, melancholy descended upon him.

Near Newlands Corner Harry stopped. Half-past five. He was hungry and tired. Guildford with its sunny streets, and its gloom of Sunday dressed people, he could not face. He turned to walk back to Gomshall. For the hundredth time he turned over in memory what had happened in Camilla's room. It seemed ridiculous that one human being could affect another human being like this. Love? Was it all imagination, a fantastic dream of this absurd little animal, man? It was impossible at moments to believe that he felt anything for Camilla at all. After all, what had he asked of her? To say: "I love you." Would that have thrown him into ecstasies—for twelve hours, or at most, to judge from what seemed best among others, for a few hours spread over twelve months? Camilla herself had lost all reality for him: a shadow figure seen down the wrong end of a telescope, minute, infinitely distant in a world of ridiculous dreams. There she was, that tiny little figure, sitting in the great chair, her head lying back, the lips moving: "But I don't love you."

And here he was with a feeling of absolute failure, of something irretrievably lost, of dreariness and emptiness and hopelessness. He was different from what he had been twelve months, twelve weeks, twelve hours ago. Something must have happened. And nothing was to happen: that was it. There was nothing to happen, nothing to look forward to to-morrow, or for the next day, or all the seven days of next week, or all the months and years to come. It was like standing on some momentary peak of time in one's life, and seeing before one a blank, dark, unbroken slope of nothing to happen before one.

As he walked down a lane into the main road at Gomshall an old man, a tramp hobbling along on a stick and a crutch, stopped him and asked him for twopence to buy a loaf of bread. It was pleasant to hear the sound of a human voice break into one's thoughts. The old man was dressed in a long, thick frock-coat and black trousers, and a coarse, heavy, workhouse shirt.

"You've got your winter clothes on," Harry said.
"Pretty hot for this sort of day."

The old man looked up and smiled a curiously knowing
and yet childlike smile. His eyes were very light blue, and
reminded Harry of the eyes of a new-born kitten.

"Hot, is it?" said he. "Mebbe. But I don't travel very
fast on me old pins."

"How old are you?"

The old man laughed. "I dunno as I rightly know, sir.
I suppose I be nearer seventy nor sixty, but that don't
matter much do it, sir?"

"I suppose it doesn't; but where have you come from?"

"Guildford. I were a month there in the workhouse,
what with me old pins what have gone, you see, and all.
But, Lord, I got tired of that, so when the weather come
over fine like, I comes out. I be going now to a bit of a
wood I knows up yonder—a fine place for sleeping out.
I've a little tea in this that they give me at a shop this
morning, and if I had a bit of bread now . . . If it wasn't
for me old pins I could do a bit o' work still, but they're
gone, you see."

He looked down at his legs covered in their black
trousers, ridiculous little twisted legs, and smiled cheer-
fully at them.

Harry gave him twopence.

"Thank you, sir. If it wasn't for me old pins I wouldn't
stop a gentleman like you. Now I can get me bit o' bread,
down yonder at a cottage I knows."

Harry looked into the pale blue eyes. It struck him that
there was no thought of the future in them, only perhaps
of getting and having got twopence out of himself.

"Good-night," he said, smiling at the old man.

"Good-evening to you, sir."

Harry walked down quickly to Gomshall. It was as
if something had fallen from him during the talk to the

tramp. He was neither cheered nor sad. It was all too meaningless and absurd.

"Inextricabilis error," he burst out with, to the astonishment of a passing cyclist. "Nothing matters, nothing matters."

X

CAMILLA'S MIND

Camilla did not move when Harry shut the door softly behind him. A momentary storm had passed through and stirred the room and her life. It is so rare to see anyone moved by violent feelings, that at the sight our own begin to surge up and toss and tumble in a sympathy which for want of a better name we vaguely call excitement. And she had been the centre and cause of this storm. The room had grown very quiet, full of the heavy hush of Sunday. She closed her eyes. She was not depressed, only physically rather tired. After all, had she anything to regret, anything to reproach herself with? This was life, surely, the romance and fire of it, these strange meetings and partings of human beings, one caught and entangled immediately with another only to be torn apart and washed away in the turmoil of incompatible, unsatisfied desires.

Desires! How strange they were! Harry—she pitied Harry —had a desire for her, but she had no desire for him. There it was in a sentence. It was pleasant to be with him, to talk to him, to know that he was in love with her—that was exciting too; it had pained her to see his pain, but all this was not love; there was no desire. Perhaps she was incapable of love, perhaps she did not wish this odd convulsion, passion, to overthrow her life. Her life was an adventure, the joy of roving among experiences that were ever new under the shifting and changing of chance. These passions and deep desires only cribbed and cabined one from the romance of life.

The door opened and Katharine came in. Camilla looked up but did not move.

"Well? I suppose he has proposed, as I said he would."

"He has proposed."

"And now you're inventing a justification for yourself, an explanation for your own satisfaction that you've acted rightly all through."

"No, I was thinking of the romance of life. I expect I ought to have been one of Hakluyt's adventurers, but being a beautiful and respectable woman in London, my traffics and discoveries are in——"

Camilla stopped and closed her eyes again. She remembered suddenly how pinched and worn Harry's face had looked when he turned round.

"You are brutal to me, Katharine," she said.

"You need it. At bottom you're not an adventurer but an adventuress. That's what you mean by the romance of life."

"Good Lord! Perhaps they're right. Who are you to judge them? They take their risks. There is something noble in taking risks."

"You know how they end."

"I won't look at the end."

"No, that's just it. It isn't bold, though; it's cowardice, pure cowardice, not to look at the end. You could have stopped this weeks ago; you know you could."

"But why should I?"

"Why? Really, Camilla, you are either heartless or brainless, I think, sometimes. What about the wretched Harry?"

"Harry? Risks again, Katharine. His risks are his risks, not mine. Besides, I don't suppose it's done him any—any harm falling in love with me. I'm not heartless, Katharine; I suppose really it is my brain. But it's too clear, that's what you don't like about it. Love—passion? You haven't felt it, my dear, any more than I, but if it's the greatest thing in the world—and doesn't everyone say that, say it until one's sick to death of hearing it?—then I've done no harm to him. There's pain—I've seen it here just now, and Katharine, I hate to see pain—but—but I'm not God, am I?"

There were tears in Camilla's eyes and on her cheeks, but she looked up with a half-smile at Katharine. Katharine, watching her with a wrinkled maternal forehead, sat down in a chair with: "I believe you're the devil, Milla." The next moment Camilla was sitting on her lap.

"Comfort me," she said.

"Tell me the truth."

Camilla told it. "You don't believe me," she said at the end of it, "but I hate the pain of it."

"You've behaved badly to Harry. Everyone would say so. If we knew respectable people they would call you a flirt. And what's to become of you?"

Katharine's voice was half-reproving, half-affectionate. And to each, as they sat there silent, the future seemed nothing but a dream.

XI

HARRY'S OPINIONS UPON LIFE

On some very warm day in June, when the smell of trees and the few blades of grass in the garden succeeded in making themselves felt through the smell of eggs and bacon, Mrs. Davis would look up at the patch of blue sky between the lace curtains, would nod her head at it, and say: "We shall have to be making up our minds where we're going to this summer." Hetty's "Well, not Deal again, I hope; I'm *sick* of Deal," would be the beginning of many hours of discussion, very often trembling on the verge of acrimony.

"Not a bad place, Deal," said Mr. Davis, thinking of the golf links.

"I expect it's all right if you play golf, papa, but everybody doesn't," retorted Hetty.

"I wasn't thinking of golf; I was thinking of Deal. When we first went there I remember your saying that you'd never get tired of it."

"Mamma may have said that; *I* certainly never did. Besides, the rooms were nice then, and last year they were beastly, everyone said so; Mrs. Parker so unobliging, and that horrible maid with the two thumbs. We all agreed that we wouldn't go back again to Deal."

"Well, that's true," said Mrs. Davis. "The rooms were very disappointing after the two previous years. Mrs. Parker seemed quite a different person. And the service very bad. And you remember how often we found hairs in the food. Besides, it doesn't do, in *my* opinion, to go too often to the same place. After all, one goes away for a change."

"Then why go to a seaside place at all?" asked Harry. "You might just as well stay in Richstead. Why not go to a small place right in the country."

Mrs. Davis thought of the monotony of green fields, green woods, and green country lanes which cannot listen or reply to conversation about the eternal subjects of interest, such as the human soul, servants, literature, and children. No band and no parade, no shops and no middle-aged ladies! After all, one doesn't go away for that! A small place right in the country is all very well if you're young, and can "get about," but it is too much of a change if you are more comfortable in a chair than upon your feet.

"Isn't that rather exaggerated, Harry," she said, "to say Deal is exactly like Richstead? You have the sea there, and bathing, and that picturesque old town, and the walks are delightful; that village—I forget its name—you walked to, don't you remember? when I drove in the donkey-cart. I'm sure we all enjoyed Deal. Not that I'm saying that a change isn't sometimes a good thing. I'm not thinking of myself. As far as I'm concerned I should be as happy, I'm sure, in my own home. All I want is to go to a place where you young people will enjoy yourselves. But if you take *my* advice, you'll go to a place where there's some life, some people you know and can talk to."

A similar question had been debated with more or less acrimony, varying with the family level of strength of will, and convention of affection, in all the other respectable houses in Richstead, including that of Mrs. Garland. To "go away" during August, at any rate, is the last sign of respectability which one can afford to lose. Mrs. Brown may have difficulty with her h's, Mrs. Smith—so the gardener told the parlour-maid—may be too familiar with her coachman, Mrs. Robinson may hide the ravages of whisky under a thick layer of liquid rouge and face-powder, and the smell of it under Violette de Parme—all these things will be forgiven them by someone else who has a banking account. But who will forgive anyone who has two servants and does not at least for three weeks every year pull the blinds down, back and front, and disappear, if it is only into an uncomfortable bed and two rooms in a lodging-house at Broadstairs? The story is still told in Richstead of how the Daltons, who lived in the very house where Mrs. Davis is nodding her head to the June sky, and thinking of apartments, preferred to sit behind drawn blinds all one August, and to sally forth on September 1st, their faces bronzed artificially to simulate the suns of Bognor, rather than to confess that circumstances made it impossible for them to go away for the summer. No wonder that Mr. Dalton went bankrupt early in October and that the family, accompanied by nocturnal removal vans, left the neighbourhood!

Early in July Mrs. Garland and Mrs. Davis put their heads together. Why should not the two families—the young people got on so well together—go away to the same parade, the same sea, the same pier, and even the same apartments? Mrs. Garland had thought of Eastbourne. Mrs. Davis approved of Eastbourne; there was plenty of life there, people said, and the Devonshire Park was a great attraction, and there are fine walks on the downs for the young people. And the young people approved, except perhaps Harry, for in their hearts they knew that Mrs. Davis spoke with wisdom and experience when she said: "If you take my advice you'll go to a place where there are some people you know and can talk to." We say jauntily: "Let's go right away out of the beaten track, where we shan't meet anyone we know"; but how our spirits quicken and the morning air is filled with the song of birds, when, after two weeks with our family, the figures of all the Joneses suddenly appear in the empty landscape. Jones was a bore in Richstead, and Mrs. Jones so vulgar, but we don't find them so in a fishing-village in Cornwall.

So it happened that three days after Camilla had told Harry that she did not love him, he found himself sitting in a railway carriage at Victoria station with Hetty and Mrs. Davis, Mrs. Garland and her four daughters, all bound for the same Family Hotel at Eastbourne. Mr. Davis, whose comings and goings were decided by mysterious persons called generically clients, and by several thousand miles of those inanimate parallel steel lines lying on the bosom of America (visualised by him only as figures rising and falling by fractions), was kept in London by one or the other, or both, but would follow in a day or two. Mr. Macausland, whose comings and goings were decided only by Sundays, had promised to run down for a fortnight on Monday, having procured by the payment of four guineas, for two Sundays, the services of the Rev. John Tucker. This gentleman was undoubtedly a clergyman; his red nose and the causes of it had made it difficult for him to be a minister of Christ for any long time in one place, but were no obstacle to his earning a precarious livelihood by preaching Christ's word at two guineas a Sunday in the churches of such of his brother clergymen who wanted a holiday. His life had its advantages, he used to affirm in his more secular moments, because he never had to write a new sermon; one congregation after another listened to the same four which had escaped the wear and tear of wandering with their author up and down England.

In the railway carriage the spirits of all, except Gwen and Harry, were high. Mrs. Garland had remarked that Gwen had never "been herself" since the day of the garden-party and May's engagement. She was depressed and irritable. May put it down with some pleasurable self-satisfaction to jealousy. The irritability had taken the form of a violent dislike to the Davises: Mrs. Davis was a bore

and a snob, Hetty vulgar, and Harry disgustingly conceited
and bad-mannered; it was intolerable that their holidays
should be spoilt by being cooped up in the same place with
these people. She told herself bitterly again and again that
she never wanted to see Harry any more; but when they all
met at the station it was with some eagerness that she had
looked at once for him. Something in his face, in the line
of the thin lips which always seemed to be pressed together with uncessary strength, made her look at him more
closely now that they were in the same carriage. She was
quick to see that he too was unhappy: his face was older,
heavier, more sallow than she remembered it. He was
sitting forward, his hands on his knees, listening to Mrs.
Garland, only raising his eyes to say from time to time
"Yes" or "No" or "Really." She wondered what he was
thinking about; it was clear that it was not Mrs. Garland's
description of Eastbourne as she remembered it when she,
not yet a widow or mother, visited it forty-five years ago.
Once his eyes wandered round the carriage, and passed
over her in the unseeing manner which showed that he did
not distinguish her from the other animate and inanimate
objects which happened to be surrounding him. It
deepened her sense of oppression.

> "Good-bye church, good-bye steeple,
> Good-bye all you London people,"

Hetty chanted with a laugh as the train began to move
slowly out of the station. Harry looked up quickly, half
smiling at his sister. The words, and the grey pavement and
cabs and domed glass and girders gliding slowly backwards
past the windows, and the gloom in the carriage gradually
changing to glare, jerked him back, not in memory, only
out of the present. Faintly and confusedly there stirred in
him the feelings that he had had as a child, when the train
gave the little lurch, a crashing and grinding together of

steel, and all the outside world started to glide backwards, and some visionary nurse chanted to him: "Now, Master Harry, wave your hand. Good-bye church, good-bye steeple, good-bye all you London people." It was like one of those troubled dreams which one has in the early morning, when all sorts of things happen to one, and yet through it all one knows that one is lying in bed dreaming. There was Hetty, sitting upright and smiling in her corner seat, a well-set-up, fashionable young woman; but he half saw her through a faint vision of a little girl, looking out of the window and waving her hand, a little girl with a long curl of black hair hanging down her cheek. "Now, Miss Hetty, you must not lean out of the window," that visionary nurse spoke again out of the past. There seemed to be a faint smell of egg sandwiches in the carriage, which faded away with the rest of the vision as Battersea Park came into view.

"You look very serious, Master Harry," said Ethel to him, smiling to carry off the familiarity and the mildness of her humour.

"Do I? I was thinking of egg sandwiches."

Hetty laughed. "I know what made you think of that, Harry. I wonder why we always had egg sandwiches when we went on a train journey? We never had them at any other time."

"I expect because they produced a fine sickly smell in the carriage—which often materialised, I remember—and also because they squashed so well into the cushions."

"Egg sandwiches," said Mrs. Davis, rather nettled, "are very sustaining."

"Delicious, too, I'm sure," said Mrs. Garland gently, "delicious."

"They are the best thing for young children on a long railway journey. They're sustaining and light; they don't lie heavy like meat. One has to be so careful not to upset young children travelling."

Harry looked at his mother. He tried to recall the vision of what she was too in that visionary carriage of fifteen years ago, with the little boy waving his hand because he was told to, and the little girl with the curl of black hair. The little boy was practically a stranger to him, only memories of those dim and flickering ghosts of feelings, rising suddenly out of and vanishing again into the past, bound them together. What bound him in the past to the elderly lady in the plumed hat, now sitting opposite to him and talking about egg sandwiches? The little boy he remembered had known a very tall grown-up, very beautiful, whom he had loved, of course! She must have been sitting opposite to him in that carriage too, providing him with egg sandwiches because they were sustaining. For twelve, perhaps fourteen years of his life he had been tied to her, and moulded and ruled by her. He could remember the vivid world in which he actually lived in those days, and the vivid presence of her who was more powerful than God because more present; and outside that vivid world of things which she made him do, or suffered him to do, the dim world of things in which he was allowed to have no part, through which she moved him inevitably and inscrutably. It was strange that no finest strand of that relationship, one could hardly call it love or affection, remained to bind him to her. He wondered whether perhaps he was merely without human feelings.

In the train, where conversation was general and broken only by the reading of books and papers, Harry noticed nothing of Gwen's depression. They did not talk together. In the hotel omnibus he recalled for the first time with irritation his last conversation with her. "A silly schoolgirl!" The discomfort of arriving at the immense red building which seemed to be all gold letters and windows drove all other thoughts and feelings from him. They stood huddled together for comfort, like nervous sheep, in a large, gloomy lounge under the supercilious observation of five people drinking tea at two wicker tables, and of an obviously disapproving, florid, gold-laced hall-porter. A young woman, apparently very proud of her bosom and black silk bodice, gave the number of their rooms from below a glass window in a voice that clearly showed that the hotel regretted ever having agreed to allow Mrs. Davis and party to take them (at a reduction of fifteen shillings per head in consideration of the largeness of the party). Thoroughly ashamed of themselves and eath other, they packed themselves into the lift. They only recovered their ordinary feelings of naturalness and composure when each found himself or herself alone in their bedrooms, which Mrs. Davis pronounced immediately to be very comfortable. A knock at Gwen's door, and the entrance of a red-cheeked maid bringing into the room a strong smell of cotton print dresses and inquiring: "Will you require any hot water, miss?" immediately brought back the feeling that she was not the sort of person who had any right to be in the hotel, and that the young woman standing offensively subservient in the doorway was registering the fact against her. She wanted to sit quietly on the side of the bed and think; she did not want to wash her hands, but she said apologetically: "Yes, please."

When the maid returned with the shining brass can, to Gwen's annoyance she again stopped in the doorway.

"Can I unpack your box for you, miss?"

"Oh, don't trouble. I can do it," she answered.

"No trouble, I'm sure, miss. I'll do it at once." She started to take out dresses and underclothing. "Is this your first visit to Eastbourne, miss?"

"Yes, I've never been here before."

"Well, I do hope you'll enjoy it. People do say it's the best place for a holiday anywhere hereabouts," she said with a little sigh. The sigh and something in the strange softness of the girl's speech made Gwen look at her with more interest and ask:

"Don't you live here?"

The girl looked up with eagerness. "Oh no, miss. I don't come from these parts. I'm West country, so they call it, Cornwall. I've only been here these two weeks. But I oughtn't to be talking like this, I know I oughtn't."

The conversation had made Gwen feel more like a human being, but her own thoughts pressed in and she did not answer. For the first time since the garden-party she was happy and excited. All sorts of things were going to happen. She would have to talk to Harry: should she tell him that she had overheard his conversation with Miss Lawrence? She had several times in the last week imagined her attitude of cold indifference to Harry when they met again: she would never speak to him unless he spoke to her, and then he would notice it and ask what was the matter, and then—and then—well, Harry's face in the train had made her less certain of the stinging words she had composed for the occasion. Poor Harry! He—

"Have you ever been to Cornwall, miss?" broke in the maid.

Gwen smiled. "No. Is it nicer than Eastbourne?"

"Oh, miss. It's— Oh, I don't want to say anything, because I hope you'll enjoy yourself, miss, and I expect for those who like it this is a very nice place. But, oh, miss, I do wish you could see Cornwall. If I shut my eyes I can see our place down by the sea. The sea's so different, miss. I don't call this the sea, somehow. When I took this place, my old father—he hurt himself fishing, you know, miss, and so I had to go out to service—he says: 'Jenny,' he says, 'you'll be down by the sea, yonder; it'll make you feel homelike, my girl.' But, oh, miss, when I went out on what they calls the parade, and see the sea, so shallow and flat, and all the houses— I daresay it's very nice, I'm sure, for those who like it, but 'tisn't somehow, miss, what we calls the sea exactly. I suppose there's seas and seas, just as there's peoples here and peoples yonder; it wouldn't do for all to be alike. 'Tis as my father said: 'Jenny,' he says, 'if you find things different yonder, remember,' he says, 'there's plaices,' he says, 'and there's herrings,' he says."

The girl stopped and looked at Gwen with round eyes, nodding her head. Gwen waited for the conclusion. The girl nodded her head again, and said in a lower tone, almost to herself: " 'There's plaices,' he says, 'and there's herrings,' he says." Gwen began to laugh, but she stopped herself, because the girl looked so sad; it was on her lips to say something kind, but the thought that she was a servant whom she had only seen for the first time, and that it does not do to encourage familiarity at once, checked her.

"I beg your pardon, miss. Is there anything more, miss?"

Gwen sat still for some time after the door closed. Was that, she wondered, how people became clever and wrote books? She had had a vision of an old fisherman teaching his daughter wisdom by the side of the seas that lay deep and green and murmurous in the lap of enormous rocks. A flush of pleasure ran through her to think that she had come nearer to a life so outside her own, so far away. "The mystery of things"—she remembered that line in Hamlet, was it, or King Lear? which Harry had made her read. The mystery of things, the mystery of things, she murmured to herself, pleased a little to hear herself do it; she was different from May and Ethel, because surely they did not even recognise the mystery of things. Her eyes had at any rate been opened to it, and might she not learn some of the secrets now? Harry—it would be pleasant to talk to Harry. She got up to go downstairs.

The lounge was empty, except where it became one with the hall, and there stood, like a conductor before the crescent of his orchestra, the hall-porter, and watched her critically over his florid moustaches. She found a *Strand Magazine,* and merged with it into the gloom of a corner made gloomier by a dry and drooping palm. She had never before stayed in an hotel, or she would have recognised working in herself the restless spirit of those restless worlds. As soon as she sat down in the wicker chair she began to wonder whether the other chair next to her was not more comfortable. She changed, and opened the magazine; but the light fell better, or the gloom was less, upon the first, and she changed back again. She looked at a page: would it not be better to go and try to find the others? She got up, only to sit down again, with the thought that she did not know where to look for them, and that someone would be sure to "turn up" soon. It was impossible to read: the twilight, grey and heavy with the smell and smoke from many dead cigars— the frayed ends of some of them still lay lugubriously upon the tarnished ash-trays—the twilight spread like a film over everything within the room. It hung over the little tables, each with its white matchbox, over the rickety wicker chairs, over the two cavernous, velvety arm-chairs, over St. George, stiff with blobs of lustreless paint and towering up above the distracted green coils of his diminutive dragon from floor to ceiling, with the enormous gold frame which refused to glitter. One felt somehow or other that outside the sun was shining brightly, intensifying within the room this sullen twilight. The black ends of two passages, like two enormous mole runs, one on each side, marked the point where the hall became the lounge and the lounge the hall; and from these the head of some maid, or the small lift-boy, would show itself suddenly and silently, would peer sadly and hopelessly round the lounge for someone sought or something forgotten, and would then, with a whisper to the grim figure of the porter, disappear again into the darkness. Out of that darkness the silence was at intervals startlingly broken by the far-off crash of slamming doors or the rattle and crackle of plates and dishes, knives and forks.

Every moment she glanced up from the soiled pages of her magazine, expecting something to come or to happen out of the dark ends of those two passages. She sat very still, and waiting a little breathlessly and nervously, when in one of these glances she saw that Harry had emerged from the darkness. He had stopped before the gloom of the lounge, clearly undecided, not what to do, but where to finish the thoughts that wrinkled his forehead. As at last he moved slowly forward, his hands in his pockets, his head bent slightly forward, frowning, and his eyes upon the floor, she saw that the palm and her stillness had prevented him from noticing her in the deep shadows of her corner. He stopped at the table on which the papers lay, and stood over it, looking down at it, and certainly not seeing an opened magazine. One finger tapped softly and regularly upon the table as if to mark the monotonous passing of time. She sat very still, feeling that something depended upon her making no movement and no noise. An odd warmth of pity and almost tenderness for that face, so white and impassive in the shadows, rose in her. It was almost painful to watch the eyes raised and staring at the great dark hangings that cut off all light from the long line of windowed conservatory or "winter garden," and the finger silently tapping on the table.

Some movement of hers must have attracted his attention, for he turned slowly, and—it pleased her—without any start in the same rhythm of thought he walked slowly over to her.

"A sad place," he said in a low voice.

"Yes, a sad place," she repeated, as if she were answering in church.

"One feels the sun shining outside, doesn't one? It's as if one heard it too."

She could think of nothing to say. He sat down in the chair next to her; he was so close to her that she could feel his knee against hers. He sat forward, leaning with his arms upon his knees, and his hands touched her dress; his fingers began to twist and untwist the fringe of a long, soft scarf that she had put over her shoulders.

"Oh, Harry," she began, without meaning to, "is anything the matter? You seem— Has anything happened? to—to make you, I mean, so unhappy?"

Harry sat quite still, the fringe of her scarf twisted round one motionless finger. He seemed to be undecided, taking his own leisurely time to make up his mind.

"Why do you think something has happened, Gwen? Nothing ever happens, you know—you said so yourself— to people who live in Richstead."

"You *are* different. You seemed so—so depressed, in the train. I saw you were at once. And just now—what were you thinking about?"

"Monotony. The secret of life; doing the same acts, and feeling the same feelings day after day. If one could only get to love it one would be so happy. I was thinking that one might in the shadows of this room. Don't you feel them resting on you somehow, like soft bedclothes on you in bed, soothing you? If you'd only sit as you are now, half-asleep, I could go on twisting and untwisting your scarf for hours, for ever—quite happily. It's like opium."

"You remember the garden-party, Harry. I've meant to tell you. I overheard what you said to Miss Lawrence in the shrubbery place."

Harry sat very still. The blood rushed to Gwen's face. She felt she had done something absurdly stupid. He was angry with her.

"What did I say?" he asked after a long pause. It was

impossible to tell from his voice what he thought of her, and this increased her nervousness.

"I ought not to have told you. You said—oh, I can't tell you—it's all too silly."

"Out with it, Gwen."

"You laughed at us. You said we were uneducated, and stupid. You said we just wanted to be married to—to—gross clergymen, and—and—young men in straw hats. At least she said that. You said we were quite happy, and that was the worst of it."

Harry looked up in her face, smiling. The queer, tense look about his mouth seemed to relax, as if her words had come as a relief to him.

"Poor old Gwen," he said gently.

She shrank away. "Don't, Harry. I hate people to say that."

"Poor old Gwen," he said again, and patted her hand with his. "Come on out of this gloom, and let's explore the garden. We'll have this out in the open air."

She did not shrink from the second "Poor old Gwen." There seemed to be, with the momentary feel of his hand on hers, no suggestion of "Poor old Ethel" in it. She got up with a feeling of happiness and excitement. They went through the curtained glass door into a long conservatory in which were ranged in orderly alternation palms, wicker chairs and tables, an old lady, and pots of geraniums. The old lady, who fully filled one of the small wicker chairs, was the only occupant; by her side upon the table lay an open novel which she consulted from time to time, breathing heavily over her knitting. She examined Gwen and Harry so carefully that they quickly passed through the conservatory into the garden.

Gwen and Harry had seen, several times, among the advertisements on railway stations, pictures of the hotel and its gardens. Standing now in the evening sun upon the gravelled path they recognised the rudimentary signs of the large pleasure grounds upon which the artist's imagination had worked. The little wedge of sea between two small trees had grown in the picture into a long line of deep blue water upon which a battle-ship, rowing boats, and a pleasure steamer, alive with small black heads and waving handkerchiefs, mingled indiscriminately. The thin borders of geraniums and calceolarias had widened into great beds of flowers. A seat screened by two laurel bushes and three trees had begotten many other seats, and a little forest. Only there was no trace of the romantic little ladies, wearing bustles and carrying parasols, and the little gentlemen in long brown tail coats and light brown bowler hats, smoking cigars and strolling with the little ladies up and down the yellow paths.

When they sat down on the seat Harry seemed to go off into a train of thought of his own. Gwen waited patiently, but began to think with disappointment that he had forgotten her and all that they had come out into the bright deserted little garden to clear up.

"Did it make you wretched?" he asked at last.

"I made a fool of myself that evening. When May came back and said she was engaged to Mr. Macausland I cried."

"Poor old Gwen."

"The worst of it is I felt it was true. How *can* May? I hate the way we live. I hated it before you came, but there was no one to talk to—no one would have understood." She stopped and smiled. "Do you know, Harry, I had prepared an awful stinger for you instead of this?"

"Well, let's have it, Gwen, all the same."

"I can't now. It seems too silly. Besides, it was true, what you said."

"It wasn't true, what *I* said. *You* aren't happy. You see the beastliness of all that and the intolerable monotony. You aren't like Ethel and May, and all the rest of them.

Isn't that why we're talking here. I couldn't say all this to them, could I? It's only if you're happy that you're damned."

"I think I *am* different, somehow. But what can one do?"

Harry bent forward, looking down at the ground and frowning, scowling almost.

"Do?" he said violently. "Anything. What the devil does it matter what one does? Nothing matters, that's the first thing to remember in life, Gwen, except about two things."

"But what are they, Harry?" Gwen asked almost timidly.

Harry laughed. "You'd be shocked if I told you."

Gwen flushed. "Don't say that. You know I wouldn't be. Do talk to me as you would to—to anyone."

Harry looked up at her. "Do you mean that?" he asked slowly.

Gwen was hot with excitement. "Of course I do. I want to know about things, about everything. I know nothing now."

"Well," Harry began and stopped. He remained silent for a little while and started to play with the fringe of her scarf again. "I often think," he said, as if his thoughts were slipping gradually into words, "that the curse upon us is that we take everything which concerns ourselves so damned seriously. Really, of course, it doesn't matter twopence-halfpenny what we do. It hardly matters, you know, even to ourselves. One thinks: 'Good Lord! how awful if I did that! What would people say of me? My whole life would be ruined!' And if one did it no one would notice it as much as a foggy day or their own little stomach-aches, and two days afterwards the only effect on oneself is a slight feeling of depression which makes one sleep all the better. I say, this is pretty boring."

"No, no. It's true, I'm sure it's true, Harry, and nobody ever talks to me like that."

"Well, in Richstead they rule their whole lives like that, or at any rate their women's lives. They've stuck up sign-posts and notice boards all over the place to say: 'This is the path for you,' 'You may sit on this seat,' 'You must marry anyone found in this enclosure,' 'You must not walk down this lane,' 'No children to be born here, penalty death.' And then they, Ethel and May and all the rest of them, your mother and mine, and Hetty too, in her cold, calculating way, think that the only things a person can do are contained in those damned notices. They think there really is a penalty of death. They don't give themselves a chance. If they'd only follow their own instincts, instead of death they might get the only thing in the world worth getting. Look at poor old Ethel. She has never given herself a chance. There isn't a real thing that she could do, because it would be too terrible not to be allowed to live the dreariest, emptiest life imaginable. And if she did the very most terrible of all those terrible things it wouldn't matter—it wouldn't matter a brass farthing to anyone in the world. Good Lord! why hasn't she had a child?"

Gwen's face became scarlet.

"There now, I've shocked you. I knew I would. I'm a fool. But it was your fault; you told me— O Lord!" he sighed with disgust.

The tears came into Gwen's eyes. "Don't be angry, Harry. It was my fault. Only—it's strange at first, because — Oh, I told you no one ever talks like that. And it's exciting. I want to know things. Don't spoil it all at once."

"Well then, why hasn't she? Wouldn't it be better for her and everyone than the sterile life she's lived? At any rate she'd have produced something for which she could have felt some human feeling."

"But Harry, isn't it all rather horrible, that? Don't be angry—I may be silly—but it does make me shudder rather. Those women——"

"Well, you can have a child without being one of 'those women.' "

"But—I don't know. All that seems so—so disgusting."

"So it is. But when all's said and done, I'd rather be any kind of woman than Ethel. And what about May? Isn't that disgusting? What's her attitude to Macausland, whom she's marrying? Love? Bah!"

Gwen tried to collect her thoughts, to find out where exactly she had got to. It was as if she had suddenly slipped off a safe bank into an icy cold stream, to be swept away immediately. Only she wasn't cold; her face was burning, the blood throbbed in her temples. Suddenly, almost before she was aware of it, she began to cry.

"I say, Gwen, I *am* sorry," said Harry, moving close up to her. "What a damned fool I am. I didn't know—really—Gwen, dear, don't cry, don't cry." He took her hand and began stroking it awkwardly. "I—"

"It's my fault," Gwen said, half laughing. "It isn't yours. You're so kind."

Harry's face was very close to hers. He kissed her twice, very awkwardly, it seemed to him, on the corner of her mouth. It at any rate had the desired effect, if that was his object, of stopping her tears. He let go her hand, and they sat stiffly and uncomfortably close together.

It surprised Gwen to feel the keen pleasure which Harry's unexpert kiss gave her. A sort of thrill passed through her body, which was followed by a sense of relaxing and resigning herself to comfort and soothing. It was like getting tired and with stiff limbs into a very soft bed, when the fine, cool sheets and the deep down of the mattress seem to rise up very slowly and gently to receive one's body. Harry was so strong and certain and gentle; life was so difficult, such a horrible tangle as soon as ever one began to think of it, and it became so exciting and so pleasant to resign oneself to him. It did not seem strange to her to be kissed by him, but only a little uncomfortable now, a little awkward to know what exactly they should do next. Harry began to fidget about with his feet, and managed to edge away from her down the seat.

"Well, Gwen," he said, with rather exaggerated impersonal bluffness, "we can't settle the universe before dinner. But we may in the next two weeks."

Gwen was a little disappointed. She came down out of those rare regions, which novels had opened to her in imagination, and Harry in real life, with something of a run, into a dishevelled corner of a garden with an old tin which had once contained golden syrup lying battered on the worn and weedy grass. The glamour of those romantic places, the promise of life beating with a quicker pulse, of mysteries and tremendous things and great passions, did not fall from her completely; only a puff of chilly air from Richstead, that little chaste and ordered rose-garden, with its three bare walls and Ethel and Janet and May and her mother and Mr. Macausland, came gently by between herself and Harry. It reminded her that she had been thinking only of herself, that Harry had never told her why he was melancholy.

"You never told me what was the matter. Is there anything, Harry? I've told you all about myself. I think you ought to confess to me."

Harry got up and walked over to the old tin and kicked it behind a bush. The sound of the old thing bumping over the ground seemed to bring Gwen all the nearer to earth. Harry came over and stood in front of her, looking down and smiling at her rather cynically.

"I've lost my belief in God," he said seriously. "You believe in Him, of course, Gwen, and Christ and the New Testament?"

"Yes."

"And the immortality of the soul and the book of Habakkuk?"

"Yes," said Gwen rather doubtfully.

"And the Athanasian Creed and the doctrine of Intinction?"

"Now you're laughing at me. It isn't fair to laugh at people's religion."

"I'm not. I want to explain to you the cause of my not unreasonable fits of depression. Wouldn't you be miserable if you lost your faith?"

"Yes. But Harry, don't you really believe in anything?"

"Nothing. Isn't it appalling? I once thought for a few minutes I really might believe in Aphrodite, but even that passed off with the resurrection of the body."

"Whatever is Aphrodite?"

"Oh, one of the heresies. Yours is a low church, isn't it?"

"Moderate. Mr. Macausland is not really low or high."

"Well, you wouldn't come across it there."

"But, Harry, why don't you believe?"

"But, Gwen, why do you?"

"There's the—oh, it's so difficult to put it at once. There's the Bible."

"Why do you believe in that?"

It seemed absurd to give Mrs. Garland as a reason; her mother no longer seemed an adequate reason against Harry.

"I find," Harry went on, as if he guessed her thoughts, "that the tragedy of life is that there are more and more things that I can't believe merely because my parents told them to me."

"But Harry, is there nothing afterwards? Do we just go out?"

"Nothing, absolutely nothing. Puff and—hello, here's May and Hetty.

Gwen sighed and looked round. They watched May and Hetty come towards them.

"Hello," said May. "Wherever have you two been? We've all been down to the sea."

Since her engagement May had begun to change. To Hetty and Gwen, even to her mother and Ethel, she had become patronising, almost dignified and matronly. She had passed, it seemed, already out of the ranks of maidens who wait, timorous, ignorant, and in doubt of themselves, for the marks of merit and the gift of wisdom descending in the form of a man—that may never come. She forgot even that all this had come to her mother, in the form of her father, a large fat man, who suffered from and died of diabetes, and whose photograph hanging in a broad black frame above her mother's bed still recalled his weak and watery eyes. Poor Ethel! Poor Ethel! One had to treat her gently as one whose mind had never fully developed, or who suffered from some sad physical infirmity. And Gwen, of course, was a mere chit of a girl who did not know anything of the seriousness of life or of the flood of light that the kisses of Angus Macausland could pour into one on Richstead Common.

Something of all this May managed to convey even into her statement that they had been down to the sea. Gwen felt it, but after the conversation with Harry May did not irritate her as she had done in the last two weeks. She pitied May now.

"The maid who does my room," she said, "told me that the sea isn't like the sea here."

"What cheek!" said May. "It's a very jolly place, with a splendid pier."

"And Harry," put in Hetty, "I heard the voice of one singing on the sands, and he sang:

> 'Ev'ry night
> 'Twas my delight
> To go round and spoon with Nell,
> Tales of love to her to tell,
> Call her charmante ma belle.' "

Again Hetty succeeded in giving Harry a curious shock,

of throwing him back into the past. This time, half-pityingly, half-mockingly, he saw a little boy sitting on the sands listening to a man in a top-hat with a hole in the crown, through which a long lock of yellow hair had been pulled, singing on a square wooden platform. He felt again dimly the mystery of that world through which passed visions of Nell, in the form of a red-cheeked girl with one of those cascades of yellow hair down her back, doing exercises in a gymnasium. And then the mysterious and sinister figure of the Man that broke the bank at Monte Carlo! He answered Hetty with:

> "Yesterday I was sad
> But I'm blithe to-day,
> For the artful minx has sloped away
> With the Man that broke the Bank at Monte Carlo!"

Something of the meaninglessness, of the absurd broken inconsequence of the world of his childhood—the passionate beliefs and desires and hopes—seemed for the moment so clearly distinguishable in this sordid little garden, in Gwen and himself sitting on the seat together, in that ridiculous kiss, in Hetty laughing at an old song, in May standing four-square in patronising dignity and digging the ground with a white parasol. It seemed just the same, except that the red-cheeked girl with the yellow ripples of hair had become Camilla! A wave of irritation and disgust passed over him. Without saying another word he walked quickly away into the hotel.

The others were left rather awkwardly standing together.

"That's the way things always end," thought Gwen, as the wave of ordinary life closed over her head with Hetty's next remark:

"I suppose we must dress for dinner here."

XII

HARRY'S OPINIONS ON LIFE CONTINUED

The whole party found that life in an hotel, certainly the first evening, is not ordinary. There is the solemnity of un-accustomed evening dress, the great room glaring with electric lights, red wall-paper, and innumerable white and gold candles. It is difficult to sit at a small round table and try to converse under the critical eyes of a waiter and head waiter and twenty other guests as if you were com-fortably shielded from all the cold, superior outside world by the four walls of your dining-room at Richstead.

It amused Harry to notice that at dinner the only one to be really natural and comfortable was Ethel. She was not more talkative nor more silent than usual; always ready with her gentle smile and a few words to any re-marks addressed to her, she sat as she would sit through a family meal in St. Catherine's Avenue, in a silence infi-nitely more easy and reassuring than the rattle of Hetty's conversation. Her eyes never wandered, horribly fasci-nated by the forty eyes at the other tables; they never had to drop hastily or turn away flurried only to catch and drop before another pair of strange eyes; they were fixed in quiet abstraction upon—what? What curious visions passed before them? What shadowy forms were mirrored when she gazed upon the white tablecloth: of the past, or the present, or the future? Or had she some world of her own, a white and virgin world of her own meditations? Or were those eyes fixed merely upon nothing in the gentle trance of some soft-skinned doe, lying up in long grass and chewing the cud all through the dreary length of a hot day?

"What are you thinking about?" he said to her suddenly.

"I? I don't think I was thinking about anything."

"But you must have been thinking about something."

She still smiled, but a very faint suggestion of fear or pain came into her eyes.

"No—no; not anything in particular. I expect I was listening to the conversation."

Harry stopped, feeling that to press her further would be like torturing some dumb animal to try to make it speak.

Mrs. Garland and Mrs. Davis sat next to one another. Both were nervous and a little flushed. Mrs. Garland was frankly confessing to herself that she wished she was carving a leg of mutton with Agnes breathing down her neck in St. Catherine's Avenue. It made her miserable to have to tell the waiter whether she would take vol-au-vent or tournedos, and when she was miserable she became silent. The effect upon Mrs. Davis was very different; she wanted to convince both herself and others that she was as much at her ease in an hotel as in her own home, and the only way to do this was to talk continually and to address the waiter in a sad, slow, and very dignified voice. The train of her thought was at the same time continually being broken by the necessity of watching the people at the other tables. Hetty across the table pursued the same method with rather more lightness, being in the twenties instead of the fifties. May lumbered along awkwardly in the rear of the conversation.

After they had eaten and waited, and eaten and waited, and eaten and waited again, for an hour, Gwen found that most of the feelings of an ordinary human being had left her. From time to time she looked at Harry sitting moodily on the other side of the table. Then Mrs. Davis's voice would begin again:

"Excellent taste they do everything now in a place like

this. Flowers on all the tables; really very well managed.
No, thank you, I won't take a savoury. And the decora-
tions, if—" she turned her head to watch a young man
and woman walk out of the room. "On their honeymoon,
evidently. A nice-looking girl, very good style. She reminded me so much of someone I know. Hetty, dear, who
is it we know exactly like that girl who just went out?"

"She was rather like Ethel Tilly."

"Yes, of course, dear Ethel Tilly. How funny! We
haven't seen her for quite an age. She's Ethel Parker now,
of course, and has a child. She was really an angel, a
beautiful nature, one of those characters, you know, who
always think of doings things for others, and of very good
family, but not well off. She became a hospital nurse; her
work was everything to her. Do you remember, Hetty,
going to tea with her at the hospital? It really was beautiful to see her with those poor things. And then she became
engaged to one of the doctors. It must have been a wrench
to her to give up her work so soon too, only a year. But
then—"

The conversation flowed over to the lounge, where they
gathered again round two small tables for coffee, a little
closer to and a little more closely observed by the other
guests, who could now not only see them but listen to
what they said. The result was that only Mrs. Davis and
Hetty were equal to sustained talking in a sufficiently impressive key. Harry wandered away to get a book. Gwen
waited, longing for the moment when she could let herself go in thought alone in her room. Silences became
longer and yawns more frequent in all the scattered
groups. At half-past nine the old lady with the knitting and
the novel fell asleep and caused some increase in conversation by snoring, for while the less well-behaved smiled,
a retired colonel and his wife showed their good manners
by trying to raise their voices sufficiently to drown the

noise. At a quarter to ten she woke herself up by allowing her book and knitting to slide off her lap on to the floor. After reading for five minutes to prove that she was awake, she looked severely round the room and went sailing out to bed. It was a welcome signal for the groups to break up, and Mrs. Davis's was one of them.

As Gwen passed the door of the smoking-room Harry came out. "Here's a book for you to read," he said, giving her "The Master Builder." "You've just reached the pinnacle of life to like it."

The others had gone on ahead; they were alone in the gloomy passage.

"What are the two things, Harry? You never told me."

"I will to-morrow. Perhaps there's only one. Hilda may tell you, in there."

She took the book and hesitated. She felt that there was something else she wanted, though she could not have said what it was.

"Is being in love one of them, Harry?"

"So they say."

"But do you believe it? You do, don't you?"

"Yes, I do."

"And—and—all that, you know what I mean, kissing and all the other things—and—and—having children—is that it?"

Harry smiled. "Yes, part of it."

Gwen looked away up the long passage, and hesitated again. "Are you going to sit up, in there?"

"Yes, I shall for a bit."

"I must go, I suppose. I'm silly, Harry, I know, but I'm frightened sometimes. I don't know why, but I'm frightened now."

He took hold of her hand. "That *is* silly, Gwen, really."

"I know. Good-night, Harry. I'll go now. Harry, will you kiss me good-night?"

Harry put his arms round her and kissed her cheek.

"You are a child, Gwen; good-night." In the smoking-room he smiled as he lit a pipe. He was thinking of his relations with Gwen. They were rather ridiculous, and yet amusing and flattering enough to make the three weeks at East-bourne less detestable now. He had kissed her twice to-day: it would have seemed absurd if anyone had told him yesterday that he would do that. It gave him pleasure to think that he would probably kiss her to-morrow. She was only a school-girl; still, it was odd to think of her doing that. "And a damned good thing to open her mind a bit," he said to himself. He smiled. One learns a lot about women between twenty-three and twenty-eight, it seemed to him. He sat down at the writing-table and wrote the following letter:

"DEAREST CAMILLA,

"Do you mind my addressing you like this? You are, you know, to me, and it gives me some pleasure to see it down there, flowing out of me, out of my finger-tips in blue-black ink. I am not going to write you a letter, only in this dreary room, among these dreary people—now that they have faded away to bed and left me alone with the smell of their smoked cigars—the desire for you is so strong that if I cannot see you or talk to you I want at least to know that to-morrow you will know that I was thinking of you as dearest Camilla. And won't you write to me?—tell me what you are doing and that after three weeks I may at any rate see you again? I won't trouble you with vows or protestations. We will begin again from your words as the 'bus came up and the last wave of the hand down that long road from the elms to the bridge. I suppose if I were a 'strong man' I would refuse to take your 'No' as irrevocable, but somehow or other in those two 'I don't love you's' I heard something more than the mere temporary breaking of what I hoped for. Perhaps you were never made to be able to say 'I love you.' I've missed the greatest thing in life, but that is no reason for you to deny me the second and the third best, which are to love you and see you.

"HARRY."

"P.S.—The fourth best is to hear from you."

Gwen sat for a long time on the side of her bed, thinking. She wondered what Harry really thought of her. He must like her, or he would not have talked to her as he did, nor be so gentle to her, nor have kissed her in the garden. And yet somehow she felt that he did not take her quite seriously. A kind of hot wave of determination passed over her body at the thought. She would show him that she was not an ordinary person, she would make him admire her by some noble and courageous act. She would not go back to that dreary, unreal life at Richstead. It was true what Harry had said about Ethel: poor Ethel had missed all the wonderful things of life, which had begun to come to Gwen only in the last few days. It would have been a noble and romantic thing for her to have had a child. Harry was right: Harry was the only person who saw things as they were. She fell asleep going over again her conversation with Harry in the garden.

The next day was a disappointment to Gwen, for she had no opportunity of talking to Harry. In the morning he was taken off by Hetty, and in the afternoon they all went on one of those expeditions on which there is always a third and sometimes a fourth to ruin all rational conversation. She had, however, some consolation in sitting on the beach between breakfast and lunch and reading "The Master Builder." If Hetty, or even Harry two weeks before, had told her to read this book, it is certain she would have found it silly or un-understandable; but now the Harry of yesterday in the garden and in the dark passage, and her own state of mind, had prepared her to receive impressions. She went straight from the babble of the sea and children paddling in it, and the shouts of bathers and hawkers, and the thin voice of the singing, gesticulating, coloured clown upon the platform, into the world of Hilda and Solness. What exactly was happening there she did not understand. What these odd people said in their short sentences was so simple and clear, and yet there seemed to be in each sentence some meaning which was always not just within one's understanding, which was always just on the tip of one's brain. A little thrill of excitement crept into the world with Solness' whisper, "Kaia," which rose and rose and rose as she read on, until everything seemed to vibrate with passion. *She—she* was Hilda, surely. "Oh, it all seems to me so foolish—so foolish! Not to be able to grasp at your own happiness—at your own life!" "The wild bird never wants to go into the cage." Wasn't she the wild bird and Richstead the cage; wasn't Harry *her* Master Builder?

When she closed the book the sea and the children were still babbling, the bathers were still bobbing up and down and shouting, the little coloured figure was still gesticulating on the platform, through the confused din broken words of the song in the thin voice reached her: "Ev'ry burr burr burr burr burr round burr burr burr Nell." But there had entered into everything a curious vividness and reality: she saw things as she had never seen them before. It was like watching things happen on a cinematograph. Everything, even the sea and the seagulls, rising and falling as if they were worked by wires from the top of the stage, had an increased solidity, a mysterious meaning. It moved her strangely to watch this tremendous drama going on before her eyes. Figures of men and women and children ran out into the sea, waving their arms and calling unintelligible things to one another; an old man sat on a little wooden footstool under a white umbrella staring at his boots; a child with a spade in its hand, with naked feet and diapers wound round and between the top of its legs, was staggering about near the little thin white rims of waves that ran up the sand, and talking incoherently to itself. As she strolled back to the hotel the same intensity of life surrounded her, the same consciousness of some new insight into the outward show of things which, before acquiesced in and almost unseen, had now become mysterious. She stopped to look at the rows of solemn children sitting upon the sands, watching the man, now in a long black ulster, singing on the platform:

> "I've a sofa made to float about up in the air,
>   A work couch and a musical box and a chair,
>   The bones of a man, the skull of a cat,
>   A knock at the door that goes ratatatat,
>   A patent astrology medium hat,
> And a lamp with a gha-a-stly glare."

Why not? She smiled; his possessions seemed to fit in admirably with the scheme of things.

The next morning she came upon Harry alone in the lounge after breakfast. He thought of going for a walk, and suggested that she should come with him.

"Well?" he said as soon as they were among the evergreens on the parade.

Gwen laughed happily. "Well," she answered, "I call this a jolly day."

Harry looked round and smiled at her. "Good—then let's enjoy it. Let's talk like rational people."

"Haven't we before, Harry?"

"No. I've been thinking it over. We've got off the lines. I've been talking it over with May."

"May? Good Lord! You haven't given me away to May?"

"Yesterday I found myself next to your sister May, rather in front of the others. We were walking downhill, and she gets up impetus downhill. I felt I had to break the silence, so I asked her whether she had read 'The Master Builder.' She said she had read 'The Master Christian,' but it turned out upon investigation that it was only 'The Christian.' Then she said: 'I don't think you ought to lend those books to Gwen.' I asked her what books. 'I don't know,' she said, 'but Angus—Mr. Macausland—found one in the drawing-room and said it wasn't fit for a young girl to read!' 'Why not?' I asked. 'Mr. Macausland says,' said May, 'that they unsettle the mind.' 'Has your mind ever been unsettled?' I asked. 'I've passed through that,' she said. 'Everyone when they're quite young passes through it. It's like measles, Mr. Macausland says. It's not serious, but one shouldn't encourage it.' So we won't encourage it."

"Did she say anything more?"

"No, I don't think so. I asked her whether it didn't tend to settle one's mind to think of marrying a clergyman. She was a bit suspicious, but she admitted that it did."

They were climbing the great green hill to Beachy Head, a little breeze cool from the sea upon their cheeks. Turning round from time to time they saw the absurd jumble of red brick and grey roof falling away further and further behind and below them through the film of yellow air that hung over it. In front of them the green slope shot up, steep, bare, deserted, to nothing but a ribbon of pale blue sky and little fluffy white clouds. To Gwen came the keen pleasure of climbing, climbing, climbing, with a light heart and Harry by her side, out of something muddled and troubled, up into pure, uninhabited air upon rolling downs and windy spaces. She felt continually a desire to laugh or to sing; she had ceased to think. There were no perplexities, no dissatisfactions high up in this dancing, singing breeze, and her spirit seemed to gather itself together, just as one gathers oneself together for a great leap of joy to meet some strange and wonderful happening, some immense happiness.

"Do you hear the sound of harps in the air?" she said, laughing aloud.

"Larks?"

"Larks or harps—what does it matter?"

Over there straight across, perhaps only on the other side of that far-off hill that seemed to lean heavily upon the sea, Harry saw a vision of another down and Camilla walking by his side and a fresh morning breeze and the song of larks above.

"It makes all the difference in the world," he said gloomily. But Gwen's good spirits and the day were too much for him. He had started out to enjoy himself, and he turned away from his vision to Gwen. "You look as if you'd heard both."

"It's you, Harry," she half turned to him impulsively, laying her hand on his arm for a moment. "It's you— you've done so much for me, Harry; you've made me so happy. I feel you've turned me into a—a—Hilda."

Harry laughed. "By Jove, you look like it too. Youth knocking at the door. I'll call you Hilda after this, I think."

Gwen blushed with pleasure. "And you—you're the master builder."

"No, no. I'm not that. I'm the wandering Jew, the ever-lasting Jew. Only I don't wander—I wish I could. I wonder why the devil one doesn't. Wouldn't it be jolly just to go on day after day like this and never have to come back for lunch?"

"*I* would—now."

The ring in Gwen's voice made him look round at her. "You will, I believe, one day, Hilda. You'll have to set out one day, you know, put on a short skirt and pack your knapsack and set out on to the great road—that's the right word, what they call it in books—to find your kingdom. I hope we'll meet before you find it, on the great road— for that will be my place too, of course, that's where the everlasting Jew wanders, I suppose. And we'll sit down under a dusty hedge so white with dust that you can't tell where the clematis begins or ends—isn't that your idea of the great road? and we'll talk over old times and you'll give me a crust of bread and a drink of water out of your knapsack, and I'll tell you how just over the brow of the hill in a gale of wind is your kingdom. Good Lord! perhaps that's what has happened already."

"Hurrah! We're off now—we will never come back to lunch. But we'll go together, Harry. You're showing me the way—you're not that—that—oh, I don't like your calling yourself that."

"Jew? Why not? I am one, and proud of it too. And the everlasting one. And the point of him is, you know, that there never is any kingdom for him to find."

"Do you—do you mind being a Jew, Harry?"

"No, I like it—I'm proud of it. *You* don't like them, of course."

"I? Oh no, Harry, don't think that—it isn't true. I don't know any except you."

"But you'd rather I wasn't one," Harry laughed.

Gwen blushed. "No—no, that isn't true; not now—now that I know you. I remember——"

She stopped, remembering that afternoon in the garden at Richstead and the swifts screaming round the house and the little cold douche of disappointment at hearing that the Davises were Jews. A faint shadow from the past seem- ed to fall upon her. It was as if for one sudden moment she realised that she was at a dangerous point in life; she was vaguely conscious of being the same Gwen as that one who sat in the garden with May and Ethel, but broken loose, drifting to what? How far?

"You remember?" Harry broke in on her thoughts. "What? Out with it, Gwen."

"I didn't like it when I heard you were Jews."

Harry made no answer and they walked on in silence. On the crest of one of those long, shallow billows of soft turf in which the cliffs go rolling away to Seaford high up above the sea they lay down. The sea in great patches of pale grey, greens and blues, heaving gently, drowsily close in under the clear-cut line of the cliff, seemed gradually to

fall motionless asleep far out where tiny steamers lay
motionless too under enormous plumes of smoke. On the
cliff's edge sat five great gulls in a row; first one and then
another would rise up with a strange, melancholy little cry
and poise itself in two dazzling curves above the sea, to
sink with one last gentle, delicate wave of the white wings
down again upon the cliff's edge. Gwen lay, looking out
into the enormous arc of sky and sea; the immensity of it
entranced her, its delicate beauty, its tender purity. Some
spring of intense happiness seemed to be loosed in her so
that the tears came into her eyes and a lump into her
throat. And Harry by her side lay flat on his back, his two
arms stretched out with open palms upon the grass. She
would have liked to have touched his hair; unknown to
herself the wave of her tenderness was directed towards
him. She did not move, or touch him.

They lay with closed eyes, the wind waving in their hair
and touching their cheeks like little strands of cobwebs.
For a long time neither of them spoke; a delicious sense
of drowsiness came over Gwen. She glided gently away
into the garden of St. Catherine's Avenue, up the yellow
path of which she walked hand in hand with Ethel. Harry
stood in their path, stopped them, and said: "Nothing
matters. There's only one thing in life, and that's love."
Ethel uttered a strange, melancholy cry. Gwen opened
her eyes and sat up. The five gulls were still standing on
the edge of the cliff. Harry was asleep, breathing gently.

"Harry," Gwen called timidly. He opened his eyes,
looked at her, but did not move.

"Have you ever been in love, Harry?"

He closed his eyes again and did not answer. She waited.

"I suppose you want me to tell you the truth," he said
at last with a sigh.

"Yes, of course."

"Well, I've been in love, but I've never really been in love."

"I don't understand."

Harry opened his eyes and smiled at her. "It's just touched me. I've been in love for a day or a week. That happens to everyone. It's come close enough for me to know what the real thing is."

"And is that one of the important things?"

Harry closed his eyes. "The most."

"Why?"

"I—Lord! it's quite clear you've never been in love, Gwen. Why? I don't know. Perhaps because it's so exciting. Your past—everything—goes with a little click—out. Everything else except—except what you want, becomes stale, and you want—O Lord, Lord! you want such strange, wonderful things; you don't know what you want—except someone else absolutely. And so you go whirling away high up above your own flat, unprofitable past. But I'm afraid you won't understand all this, Gwen; you've never been in love. When you do feel like that, though, you had better come and tell me. It will be time for you to pack up."

A sudden desire came upon Gwen to throw herself upon Harry and to tell him that that was how she felt towards him, that she wanted him to kiss her again, that she wanted to feel his arms round her body. She got up, turned from him, and stood looking out over the sea, her face burning, tears in her eyes.

Harry stretched himself and yawned. "Lord, Lord! You foolish virgins!"

"What do you mean?" asked Gwen without turning round.

"Do you know what I mean, I wonder?"

"Yes—no—I don't know."

Harry explained. Gwen sat down with her back turned to him.

"That's what's wrong with you all," Harry went on.

"You are only half-baked. There's something wanting here and there"—he touched his forehead and left breast. "You are like village idiots, a little wanting. One half of life you never can understand, the male the female, and the female the male. The Greeks were wiser than we; they initiated their young men and women into the mysteries. Well, they lost what they lost and gained the whole world. There were no Ethels in Athens."

"But are you—have you gained the whole world, as you call it, Harry?"

Harry looked at Gwen's back, hesitated and then smiled. "Yes, thank God," he said.

They were silent, Harry thinking of himself and Gwen of herself. Gwen was frightened, frightened of the new violence of her feelings and of the way in which the veils seemed to be torn from life for her by Harry. She was frightened too this time to tell Harry that she was frightened. One of the gulls rose hovering into the air, and uttered the strange, melancholy cry. It was the same cry that Ethel had uttered in the garden. So vivid had been her dream that it really seemed to have entered into her life of the last hour, Ethel's hand in hers and Harry's words as he stood in front of them on the gravelled path, and then Ethel's cry.

"Quarter to one," said Harry suddenly. "We shall be late for lunch."

He got up and they started for the hotel. They did not talk much on the way home, and when they did it was about the country and the sea, about Deal and Eastbourne.

"Well, we're back for lunch," said Harry, smiling as they walked up the steps of the hotel. "Julian soup, whiting, sauce Hollandaise, cold lamb and mint sauce, caramel pudding and cheese. You've forgotten your kingdom."

Gwen did not answer. She was thinking how cruel people could be, when a chorus of "Well, you *are* late," greeted them.

XIII

GWEN AGAIN BECOMES EMOTIONAL

On Saturday Mr. Davis arrived, and on Monday Mr. Macausland. Mr. Davis's arrival did not make any great difference to the party. On Saturday afternoon he joined the golf club; Sunday and the following mornings and afternoons he spent upon the links. He read the *Times* steadily through breakfast, and at dinner and in the evening contributed sparingly facts, figures, and statements to the conversation. He was one of those persons who seem to give nothing to and to receive nothing from the atmosphere of the circle in which they find themselves, whose work in life is to make arrangements for other people, and to keep them right on matters of general information. As he had a habit of reading Bradshaw, the A.B.C., and Whitaker's Almanack, when another person would find relaxation in a novel, his arrangements and information were usually excellent, being based upon a firm foundation of knowledge.

Mr. Macausland brought an atmosphere with him which soon pervaded not only his particular party but the whole hotel. He had a habit of pushing back his final cup of coffee at breakfast, wiping his mouth with the napkin, and saying: "Well, what's the program for to-day?" For everyone the day immediately seemed to fall into little blocks of hours, divided by lunch, dinner, and tea. Mrs. Garland never had the courage to say that she wanted to sit on the beach and read Mr. Walton's "Life of Mrs. Humphrey Ward," nor Gwen that she wanted to go off with Harry, nor Harry that he wanted to go off alone and paint. Before they knew what had happened Mr. Macausland

and Mrs. Davis between them had filled up for each jointly and severally the three little blocks into which daylight is divided. They became pre-eminently a summer holiday party, bathing together, walking together, taking the tram together. And so the days raced gaily by under the skilful pilotage of Mr. Macausland.

Harry scarcely noticed that he very rarely in the next week was alone with Gwen. When he was alone with her he relieved himself of some of the bitterness of a rejected lover by opening the mind of a mere schoolgirl, but Mr. Macausland made them so much the members of a party that intimacy was bound to be spasmodic. Besides, the novelty of failure and despair, which mercifully mitigates the misery and first shock of such catastrophes, had worn off: he was left now with only the failure and the despair. He learnt that those short moments of intense desire for someone, which stab us suddenly to shut our eyes—only to see a visionary face in the revolving darkness—were not the worst symptoms of what men, following the shrill and passionate preachings of poets and other articulate and artistic sufferers, are agreed in counting the cruellest of human sufferings. However real and sharp these stabs are, there is always time for us to take a glance out of the corner of our eye at ourselves, to find some balm in self-pity, or in the sight of self in an heroic position. But neither happiness nor unhappiness consists in moments of intense anything, so much as in the effect upon every hour of the hope or despair of attaining happiness. When Camilla did not answer his letter, Time again seemed to Harry to flatten itself out before him into a level expanse of nothing to look forward to. He could not look forward to an excursion to Hastings, or a bathe in the sea, or a talk with Gwen; and that was what life meant in its fifty-seven thousand six hundred seconds of living between one unconsciousness and another. The truth was that he was bored, and it is difficult to find in such a condition that which is as important as air to the healthy life of each individual, the sentimental and secret contemplation of oneself as a hero.

Gwen, however, who had become during these days, according to May, disagreeable, and according to Mrs. Garland "difficult"—she always expected young girls between the age of seventeen and twenty-five to be difficult —both noticed and suffered from the sudden interruption of her short intimacy with Harry. She had lived her twenty-two years without any serious attempt to pry into her own thoughts and feelings; opinions were accepted, good feelings from time to time and on suitable occasions acknowledged and displayed, and bad ones, such as discontent, suppressed. It is impossible in twenty-two days to unlearn the ignorance and habits of twenty-two years. Harry had shown her a new world lying within herself, but without his hand and voice to guide her through the new world she stood mazed, fogged, frightened. She did not see that what she looked forward to was Harry, that from him emanated the vision of herself as a second Hilda, her revolt from the old life at Richstead, her longing to prove herself by some daring act or noble passion, and above all her fear. All that she was conscious of were thoughts that chased one another like clouds across her mind, bursts of irritability, a sudden welling up of determination, of joy and laughter, a collapse into misery, a clutch at the heart of fear.

Sometimes she looked at Ethel or May or Janet with the thought and desire to talk to them, but something in their faces showed her that she had no confidences to make to them. One afternoon, when rain had defeated Mr. Macausland's intention of leading them out for the third time up Beachy Head, and down again to Birling Gap, she saw through the glass doors that Mrs. Garland had escaped by herself with a book into a wicker chair under the palm-trees of the winter garden. She was near enough to her childhood to remember the time when she had carried her troubles to the little figure in black, which age and a life already passed seemed to have settled comfortably back in quiet knowledge. Gwen went through the glass doors and stood by her mother. Mrs. Garland looked up from her book, took off her glasses, smiled at Gwen, and said: "Well, dear?"

"I want to speak to you, mother."

Mrs. Garland glanced at the open page and sighed. "Very good. I've just got *two* pages to finish this chapter —really a very interesting book, dear—and after that we'll have a talk."

Gwen sat down in the wicker chair near her mother. There was no sound except the monotonous, dreary dripping of the rain upon the glass roof. It seemed to numb and dull her brain. What was she to say to her mother? Mrs. Garland went on reading quietly and slowly; she finished the chapter, took off her glasses, put them in between the pages, and laid the closed book gently upon the little wicker table by her side. Then she settled herself again in her chair.

"A very interesting book; you ought to read it, Gwen," she said. "Mrs. Humphrey Ward must be a wonderful woman. Dear me, how the time does fly! Four o'clock already, and I meant to write to your Aunt Jane before tea. Well, dear, what is it you want to tell me?"

Mrs. Garland still smiled; her hands, very smooth and round and fat, lay passively on the black lap. She watched the long grey lines of rain falling steadily across the trees in the garden.

"I can't go back to that life at Richstead," Gwen began desperately. "It's wrong; it's—mother, I'm miserable."

"I don't think you've been quite the thing lately, Gwen

dear," said Mrs. Garland very gently. "I've noticed it. Dear me, how it rains! I'm afraid the weather has quite broken up. When we get back to Richstead I should like Dr. Henson just to see you."

The tears came into Gwen's eyes. "Oh, mother darling, it isn't that. Don't you see? It's not—oh, I'm well enough. But—but——"

Gwen hesitated. What was it she could say? Mrs. Garland's hands lay quite still on her black lap. "Well, dear?" she smiled.

"I hate the way we live," was all Gwen could say. "I would rather be—I would rather be a——" It was no good. She could not say it to her mother.

"I think I know what you mean, Gwen dear. You are at a very difficult age. I remember it was just the same with Ethel and May, and Janet too. That reminds me: if they don't bring us those little rock-cakes with the tea, just ask for them, will you, dear? Angus does like them so. Well, I was going to suggest to you to take something up when we get back. It is *so* much better to have something to occupy oneself with. Cooking, now; I see nearly all young girls are being taught cooking, besides being an asset. Or French, say; you don't know French thoroughly. Or you might even do both—two days to a cooking school and two, or three even, to a French class. Dear, dear, what rain! Mrs. Ward must be a wonderful French scholar. I was just reading about it when you came in. They give a list of the French words used by her in her novels. Most interesting. And there were one or two that I'm ashamed to say I didn't know. En-en—no, I must find it. Yes, e-n-g-o-u-e-m-e-n-t. Now, what does that mean? It can't be enjoyment, I suppose. That would have a j, surely—joy, joie."

"I don't know," Gwen said in a low voice.

"You see, dear, what I mean? And then there's May's

crèche. Ah! I do believe it may clear up: there's a little
blue waistcoat. May's creche, yes. Crèche is a French word,
of course. It does add an interest to know foreign languages,
besides being an asset. I expect May will have to give up
that now, for a time at any rate. You might take it over
from her."

Mrs. Garland waited. Gwen could not resist the gentle-
ness and kindness in the smooth, old, childlike face, or the
passive, fat white hands. She smiled bravely, and said:
"Yes, mother."

At last one of the hands moved and just patted Gwen's
cheek. "That's right, dear. It's so much better to come to
your old mother and tell her your troubles. I know, Gwen
dear, what it means: I've been young myself and you're
my fourth daughter, remember. When one's young, that
sort of thing is only natural. I don't blame you."

They were silent. Again the tears came into Gwen's
eyes: it seemed to her that it was her mother who was so
clearly the child. She laid her hand on her mother's hand.
Mrs. Garland patted it gently.

"You get on well with Hetty Davis, don't you, dear?"

"Oh yes."

"A nice, sensible girl, and so clever. You might get her
to go to the cooking classes with you. And then there's
Harry. You seem to get on well with him. I expect you
know more about him than I do; he is so very silent at
meals. You like him, don't you, dear?"

"He is very clever, I think."

"Clever? Yes, I expect he is. They're a clever family.
But he's a young man and talks wildly sometimes, I notice. Young men do; it's only natural, when you're young
and you haven't learnt by experience. I suppose you talk
about all sorts of things that your old mother wouldn't
understand?"

Gwen blushed. "I don't know. I don't think so."

"Well, times change; but remember, Gwen dear, one lives and learns. Dear, dear, how it does come down, just as bad as ever; my little blue waistcoat quite gone! And you mustn't take too seriously all he says. He's clever, but young men do talk wildly nowadays. And now, my dear, we must go to tea—we've had quite a cosy little talk."

Gwen kissed her mother and they went in to tea.

The next time that Gwen was alone with Harry was some days later, when Mr. Macausland's expedition had at last come off. After tea he had stood out against following the road from Birling Gap to Eastbourne with the others, and Gwen's desire to be with him had made her bold enough to say that she too would go by the cliff. She had felt his gloom and silence increasing during the last days, and it made her uncomfortable and nervous to find that they did not lift now that he was alone with her. Half-way up the first rise, she said:

"Are you angry at my coming, Harry? Do you want to go alone?"

"No," he said in a perfectly toneless voice. "Do you want me to say I'm pleased you've come? I will if you like."

Harry had never spoken so unkindly to her, and yet she had never before felt such a longing for him. As she did not answer he just looked round at her, and then went on slouching along with his hands in his pockets and kicking at pieces of chalk which were scattered over the grass.

"My God!" he said suddenly, "I wish I were father."

"Why?"

"What do you think of father?"

"I don't know. I don't think I understand him."

"You wouldn't unless you understood God. What d'you think of Hetty?"

"Oh, Harry, what *do* you mean? I like Hetty."

"And Mr. Macausland, and Ethel, and the head-waiter.

So do I. You might do worse than marry someone like my father. Why don't you?"

"Why do you wish you were Mr. Davis, Harry?"

"To marry you, d'you mean? I wasn't thinking of that then. No, I happened to be thinking of myself—for a wonder. Father is what God intended the human species to be—he accepts his environment and the universe, absolutely. Consequently he is happy, consequently he is the fittest, consequently he will survive. Damn him!"

They had reached the top of the headland now, and Harry flung himself full length on the grass. Gwen sat down by him silently. It was a grey day, grey sky and grey mist on the grey sea. The sea and air were as motionless as the heavy, colourless curves of downs. "Thunder," the porter at the hotel had said, "I feels it in my head regular." Gwen felt it in her whole body, suddenly so conscious of the vastness and stillness and emptiness of the earth, high up there, alone with Harry, in front of that enormous, colourless curtain that lay upon the sea. She drew deep and long breaths to fight off the oppression and suffocation, but they seemed to her to turn into sighs. Once or twice she was near to absurd tears or to still more absurd laughter.

"Filthy day." Harry frowned at the dingy sky hanging a few feet over their heads.

Gwen put out her hand to touch his; but drew it back with an effort. Harry, who was looking away from her, did not notice.

"I can't stand this," he growled after a minute or two, "I can't stand it any longer." He thumped the grass with a great piece of chalk. "I'm off to-morrow."

Little electric shocks seemed to run all over her. She leaned towards him. "Why, Harry? where to?"

He did not look at her, but went on pounding at the grass.

"Twenty pounds. That'll last me months. I shall walk—wander—place to place. I shall try to get to Italy. I want to get away from this infernal place, these infernal people. Talk, talk, talk. I'm sick of it. All that silly talk about your kingdom. My God! what fools we are. You had better marry someone, my dear Gwen, or you'll be back in St. Catherine's Avenue inside of a month. It's the only way out of it for you, I'm afraid. But I'm off to-morrow—and I hope to God I'll never come back."

A sort of storm broke in Gwen's mind. She half flung herself upon Harry. "Don't, Harry, don't, you are cruel. I shall go with you, Harry. Take me with you."

Gwen's arms were awkwardly round Harry's shoulders, her face against his. He felt her body on his. He took her in his arms, and began to kiss her. She returned his kisses passionately, pressing herself against him. Her violence and her tears surprised him; he half drew away, but she held him to her. He allowed her to lie quietly in his arms. Her eyes closed; she seemed half-unconscious.

"What a child you are, Gwen," he said gently. "I believe you really half believe you could go off with me to-morrow."

She started back, leaning so heavily upon his arm that his elbow was painfully pressed into the ground.

"What do you mean, Harry? Don't you—surely— I must come, I will. You don't think I'm going back to all that now?"

Her trembling lips frightened Harry. Had he gone too far? He laughed, but the laugh sounded awkward and unpleasant.

"I say, Gwen, be sensible. You don't really think you could go off with me to-morrow. I shall be away months."

A sort of shiver ran through Gwen's body. "Oh, Harry, don't you see? don't you—I love you, Harry. I can't live without you. I love you. And just now you—you took me and kissed me like that."

This time Harry tore himself away from her. He stopped on his knees, looking at her half lying on her side. Catching himself in that attitude, with wide-open eyes and open mouth, he almost laughed through his sudden fear and horror. The world seemed to him too mad.

"But I——" he began and felt he could not say it. She had sat up, her eyes fixed on him, her lips still trembling, that curious movement up and down in the throat which he remembered he had seen before. She was so white that he thought she would faint. She just looked at him, and on her face he seemed to see that gradually, in the horrible silence, in the horrible situation, ludicrous, cruel, which nothing could end, the knowledge of what he was going to say came to her.

"You don't love me," she said in a low voice. "I know—but, Harry, why did— Oh, Harry, I am miserable without you."

"I'm a fool, a brute——" he began, but he felt too ashamed to go on.

"I won't go back, I won't," she burst out. "I'll go with you all the same. You like me being with you—you know you do; say you do, Harry."

"Of course I do, Gwen, but——"

"It's true what you said. I've known it the whole time. It's the greatest thing—and—and—*you* said it, Harry, *you* said it. You said it would be better for Ethel. I'll go with you, Harry."

Harry covered his face with his hands; everything seemed to be whirling round him. He could think of nothing to say. One sentence only kept on absurdly coming again and again into his head: "People don't *do* those sorts of things." Ibsen, of course—Hedda Gabler. People don't *do* those sorts of things. Could he say that to Gwen—now? Wouldn't it, after the last week, sound too contemptible, too mean?—people don't *do* those sorts of things?

"Harry, Harry," he heard Gwen whisper, "say something, do. What are you thinking now? I love you so much, Harry dearest. I can't live without you. If you make me go back home now I shall kill myself. It doesn't matter your not—your not loving me. We would be happy together—you said you would—just going on and on, and I would leave you, really I would, when you didn't want me any more."

She had taken hold of Harry's hand and had spoken passionately, imploringly. He still felt the same impotence, the same absurdity of not knowing what to do or to say, so he drew her towards him, took her in his arms again, kissed her.

"Gwen, dear," he began at last, as she continued to cling to him, "I'm so sorry. It is my fault, but I think you're excited. Let's go back now, and we—we will talk about it again to-morrow."

"You mean I can't go with you?"

"People don't— Surely, Gwen, you must see. Do try and be calm. Think what your mother would say."

Gwen got up quickly; she seemed suddenly to have grown very calm. Harry stood waiting, his face burning, his heart beating violently.

"You said being in love was the greatest thing, didn't you, Harry?" she said slowly. Harry didn't answer. "You said Ethel had missed everything in life! You told me I was going to miss everything in life! You said Ethel ought to have had a child, didn't you?"

Harry was still silent.

"You said one ought to lead one's own life, didn't you? Was all that untrue?"

"Yes—no. Oh, Gwen, don't you see? I never thought you'd take it so seriously about yourself."

Gwen turned very quickly and began to walk towards

Eastbourne. Harry allowed her to get some way ahead, and then followed her slowly. He wanted to think quietly, to recover himself. But the only thought that came to him sent waves of heat over his body. In life, in every crisis of life he had failed absolutely. Camilla—and now his mean, contemptible, ridiculous situation with Gwen. What was she thinking now? He quickened his pace and caught her up. There was nothing to say. They walked in silence. He heard her catch her breath every now and then. It almost made him cry out. What was she thinking now?

"Gwen," he said when the silence became intolerable to him.

Gwen did not answer.

"Gwen, do say you forgive me. I was mad, I must have been mad. Forget what I said. I'm fond of you, Gwen—really, Gwen, you know, don't you? You know that; I am very fond of you, I want to ask you something, but it's so difficult after this. If only you would forget it. I want—I want to ask you to marry me."

"Don't, Harry, don't!" she cried.

"But I love you, Gwen, I swear I love you."

Gwen began to cry. "Please, Harry, please don't," she said between her sobs. "I—I—know you don't love me. I've always known it, and—and—oh, not now—not any more now. To-morrow—to-morrow—perhaps—"

A weight seemed to settle upon Harry's mind. He had nothing to say. Gwen's sobs gradually quieted and ceased. She seemed to walk in the same kind of trance in which he had fallen. They walked in an unreal world, dazed. The heavy grey sky pressed upon them.

When they came to the hotel Gwen drew her hand across her eyes.

"It's late," she said; "I shall go straight up. Tell them I've a headache. I won't come down to dinner. And see that no one comes up; I'm all right."

Harry walked down the passage and into the dining-room without thinking of anything—even of washing his hands and brushing his hair, the hall-porter noted with disapproval. He stood for a second dazzled by the lights, dazed by the click clack of conversation all round him. It hardly seemed real after the last hour—the discreet gaiety of the lights and little tables and flowers and wine-glasses, the low-neck, soft evening dresses, and the smooth, black, white-fronted, red-cheeked gentlemen. Like a scene in an Ibsen play, he thought, and then saw Gwen's trembling lips, and again: "People don't *do*," and he was listening to "Hallo" from Mr. Davis, and a chorus of: "Where have you been?" "You are late!" "Where's Gwen?" and then Hetty's nasal: "You look like a ghost." There was a lull when he explained that Gwen had a headache, had gone to bed, wanted no food, and no one to come up. May or Ethel would go up after dinner—it was certainly the weather, thunder in the air; Mrs. Davis had had a slight headache all day. Click, clack, click, clack, knives and forks and words began again.

He was allowed to eat in silence, undisturbed. The sense of unreality persisted; it was a picture, a play on the stage. He felt enormously himself in a ring of automata, little figures, marionettes worked by wires—there they were jumping about in the gilded room, and outside the great world, wild, passionate, unrestrained. He felt Ethel, sitting silent on his right, a little marionette that would answer to the pull of the wires. No, that was his mistake before with poor Gwen. A few vague words, a look, a touch of the hand, a kiss, and Ethel too, poor Ethel, would kick up her heels, break the wires and plunge off wildly into the great world outside. He caught his breath with excitement, with a sudden rise of emotion as he looked round the table with new eyes. They seemed for the moment pathetic, noble, tragic, these straight, quiet figures each cut off from the other, pretending, pretending, pretending—and at any moment something inside, unseen, unthought of by the others, might bubble up, and off they would go—mad, mad!

The thought of Gwen suddenly made him clench his fists. She was crying up there in her room now, he was sure. He remembered her dry eyes as they walked home, and the childish, weak lips trembling. What a fool he had been. God! what a fool he had been.

"And the old king," he heard Mrs. Garland saying, "used to sit drumming with his fingers on the table saying: 'Play louder, play louder,' if he heard the thunder. And the louder it thundered, the louder the band had to play. Poor man, he wasn't quite right in the head even then."

"I can't say I like a storm myself," said Mrs. Davis. "I can always feel it in my head; and then one feels so helpless, what with the lightning and all that."

"There were fifty-six people killed by lightning in the Kingdom, exclusive of Ireland, in 1902," Mr. Davis announced.

"And how many in Ireland?" asked Mr. Macausland.

"The figures aren't given, at least not in Whitaker. I happened to read it this morning."

"Very interesting—fifty-six; it seems a great many. I knew an old lady who put on rubber goloshes when there was a thunderstorm. A scientific friend of mine tells me it's the most sensible thing to do—it converts you into a negative pole; I think that's what he said."

"Fancy wanting to be a negative pole," May giggled.

"*You* couldn't be," said Mr. Macausland in a low voice, looking at her. "A question of attraction. Negative poles don't attract the lightning."

May beamed.

"I say, we've been here hours," Hetty broke in. "We can't watch Harry eating any longer." All the ladies got up. Mr. Davis and the vicar stayed with Harry. Harry went on eating mechanically. The room suddenly seemed very quiet: the chairs round the little tables were empty, crumpled napkins lay on the table-cloths, broken pieces of bread, and wine-glasses with small pools of wine at the bottom. Some spirit had died out of the room, leaving it tawdry, melancholy, unpleasant, like a table-cloth with dirty red stains of wine and brown stains of greasy gravy. Upstairs, he knew, Gwen was crying. He wished the other two would talk so that he could listen to them, but they sat silent with legs crossed, one elbow on the table, thoughtful.

"I didn't like to contradict you," said Mr. Davis, "but you weren't right about negative poles, were you? You must have a negative and a positive, so that in a sense the negative pole actually attracts the lightning."

"Yes, of course, you're quite right. Insulate, insulate, that's the word—the goloshes insulate one."

The dull tone, unadorned sentences of male conversation, soothed Harry; he hoped they would go on, but silence began again. Macausland shifted his legs, lit a cigarette, glanced at Harry. Harry had finished; he leaned his arms on the table and covered his eyes with his hands. It was intolerable that Gwen should be crying upstairs. *Could* he marry her? After all, Camilla would never love him. It might be comfortable with Gwen—but God! how tired he would grow of that child's face at the breakfast table, and the lunch table, and the dinner table. And yet it was his fault. She might do anything; she was mad, over the border. Had he believed all that? It seemed to him that he had, that he did still, and yet—and yet—in some curious way not in fact, not in his own body or the bodies of those whom he knew. He became aware that Macausland was speaking to him. He looked up. The vicar was clearly a little embarrassed, rather red in the face, and tapping at his cigarette with his forefinger. Mr. Davis, as usual, was looking at him as he looked at most people, coldly but with interest, as if he were some strange beast stuffed in a museum.

"I'm sure you won't mind—an older man—one with some claim—soon to be one of the family. I've been wanting to speak to you—this seems a good opportunity—about Miss Gwen, the books you lend her, you know. I may be old-fashioned, but they don't seem to me quite—quite the thing for a young girl to read."

A rush of anger passed over Harry as he looked at Macausland's red face, shiny after the long dinner. It was momentary, followed by disgust, depression.

"Why not?"

"It unsettles their minds. They haven't the necessary experience—experience of life—to see clearly. It unsettles their minds."

Harry got up and leant over the table; he was trembling with anger and excitement.

"You're quite right, Mr. Macausland, you're quite right, only you're wrong if you think it's the mind. It's what all the damned old women have been saying since—since I don't know how long. And after all, they're right, and I'm wrong. Only it's not the mind, it's the heart—think of that, Mr. Macausland."

Harry walked out of the room.

"A most uncalled-for exhibition," said the vicar, breathing heavily.

"I ought to apologise. Queer fish, Harry," said Mr. Davis, unmoved. "Something you said must have irritated him."

Mr. Macausland gave two little "kths" through his nose. "Well, after that I suppose we had better join the ladies," he said with dignity.

XIV

THE DEFEAT OF WORDS AND OPINIONS

Gwen was crying upstairs in her room, at first helplessly, like a child, of misery, disappointment, weariness. Harry's words had slashed and gashed her at the time; it was as if now she only felt the dull ache of the wounds that the slashing and gashing had left all over her mind and body. Sitting on the cane-bottomed chair by the open window, with her head in her hands, she was aware of nothing but the rise and fall of this wave of misery within her, the outburst of tears gradually dying down into the hot dry-eyed torpor of wretchedness. And the whole time she was waiting for something, knowing that she would not be left alone, listening for the step outside and the tap at the door that would bring Ethel or her mother with food and hushed inquiries. If only they would leave her alone! For half and hour this was her one thought. She could not be found sitting tear-stained by the window. She undressed and got into bed, and lay there listening. At last the foot-steps came, the noise of the door opening and the rustle of dresses. Ethel was with her mother. She drew down beneath the bedclothes to hide her face.

"Well, dear?" Mrs. Garland's gentle voice was near the bed. "Are you feeling better?"

"I'm all right—only a headache." The tears almost choked Gwen.

"The thundery weather—it's very close to-night. You must have overdone it walking."

Gwen brushed away a tear that trickled down her cheek. "You'll take something now," Ethel said in a hushed voice. "I'll ask them to bring you up a tray. What would you like? A little beef-tea and fish—or chicken? There's sure to be chicken."

"No, I don't want anything."

"But, dear, really you ought to have a little something."

"No, no. Please, please Ethel, don't. If you'll only leave me alone now—I—I'll sleep."

Mrs. Garland nodded to Ethel, who went out of the room. Gwen was difficult. She put her hand on Gwen's hot forehead. It was better to leave her alone. "Good-night, dear," she said, just stroking the forehead. "Get a good night's rest and you'll feel much better to-morrow."

Gwen sat up in bed as she heard the door close softly; she almost called out to her mother to come back. She was frightened, frightened of herself, of the cruel day that had passed, of the long, dark night that was before her. She wanted to feel someone's arms around her, to cry on her mother's shoulder, to tell her everything. She felt like a child again with something threatening, horrible, which could be taken away by someone else's presence— something lurking in the darkness, in dark corners, behind clothes hanging in dark cupboards, ready to spring out of open doors as one passed in shadowy evenings down silent staircases. But something held her back. She waited too long; her mother now must be half-way down the long corridor, on the stairs now, now with the others in the lounge. She sat up, staring into the darkness, motionless with this fear. No one would come to her any more that night to talk to her or to soothe her. Everything frightened her—her loneliness, the vastness of the hotel which made her feel the loneliness, shut away in this one of its innumerable box-like rooms, its silence and muffled sounds.

At last she lay back, stiff and cold. She had to think— think of what had happened and what would happen. Instantly her head became hot, the room was stifling; she threw off her blanket and lay waiting, listening. She could not think connectedly; only broken recollections of what had happened, what she had said and what she had heard up there with Harry on the cliff, drifted across her mind. She tried not to think, but to go to sleep, but at once her mind was full of thoughts, her body hot and uncomfortable. She tossed and turned in her bed. Footsteps passed and repassed down the corridor, doors shut. She lay with open eyes waiting for quiet again and for sleep.

Gradually silence spread over the hotel; she felt that the last step had passed her door, the last pair of boots fallen with a thud on the corridor. Now she was really alone, the time had come for her to think.

She could not think, and she could not make her mind a blank for sleep. Rushes of feeling—physical shock and a kind of irritability—swept over her. Then suddenly she closed her eyes. She was in Harry's arms again, before the shock of his words which showed her. . . She sat up in bed. Her mind had cleared; she was conscious of a sudden rise within her of strength, excitement, determination. She saw now that what she wanted was Harry, only Harry, his presence, his arms round her, his kisses. This flood of joyous strength through her showed that she could not have been wrong to believe him—this was one of the great moments of life, the moment to sacrifice all, and in sacrificing all to gain all. She was his absolutely, and he would, he must take her.

She got up, and without lighting her light opened the door. Two doors off across the corridor was Harry's room. The long passage brightly lit was deserted. She stood a moment looking at the boots which, two by two ranged outside each door, inanimate, and yet with their human look, made everything seem so silent, restful, mysterious. She walked on tiptoe across the passage, opened Harry's door and shut it quickly behind her.

"Who's that?" she heard in a loud voice, and then in

a whisper: "God! You, Gwen! What's the matter?"

Harry's light was on; he was lying in bed, a book open on the pillow. Gwen stood for a moment looking at Harry and smiling, glad to feel that joy in her own strength, the joy of seeing Harry and his surprise.

"I've come to you, Harry. I couldn't sleep—I must see you."

Harry rubbed his eyes with his hand; it seemed unreal. He looked at Gwen. She seemed to him extraordinarily beautiful with her flushed, excited young face, and with the wonderful waves of hair falling around it. A little movement of desire, cruel and brutal, ran through him. It was stifling in the room; his body was damp with sweat. He could see her bare throat through the open nightdress. He turned away his eyes.

"You can't come here," he said huskily. "You don't know what you're doing. Go away, for God's sake."

She still stood by the door, smiling, as if eager to feel the full power of her passion and exaltation.

"Listen to me, Harry," she said in a whisper. "You must listen to me now. I love you, Harry, Harry darling, I love you. And—Harry—all you said was true. You're frightened for me now, because you're so kind—but you know, you know it's true. It's my chance. Oh, you know it's the great thing come to me. How can I live like that again with mother and Ethel? I can't, I won't. I'm yours absolutely. I don't mind if you don't love me; I'll make you. But—but—I can't live without you."

Harry stared at her, motionless; her excitement carried him away. It seemed to him that, somehow or other, even for Gwen his words had been true.

"You—you don't love me, Harry. That's why I won't marry you—I won't. But you'll take me with you to-morrow."

Harry struggled with himself, trying to get back to

reality, to a sense of ordinary life. "Go away," he said brutally. "You don't know what you're saying. We're mad. For God's sake, go—go away."

The next moment he felt her arms around his neck, and her kisses on his face. He caught her in his arms, and pulled her down on to the bed by his side, kissing her hair, her lips, her throat.

"Say it's true, Harry," she panted.

"You darling, darling Gwen," he whispered, kissing her mouth, and pressing her to him.

XV

THE VICTORY OF OPINION

The next morning Harry sat in the dining-room at breakfast by himself; he was so early that he knew none of the others would be down for a good hour. As the dawn crept over the earth the heavy sky had gathered into an immense cloud and broken in rain. He looked out of the dining-room window now upon evergreens and trees glittering wet in the morning sunlight. The trees with their fresh-washed green seemed to be simulating spring; but swaying under the full load of summer leaves, staid, round and jovial, like plump and buxom middle-aged women, they had changed irretrievably the delicate green and grace of spring for that maturity after which the only change is decay. Everything shone and glittered: the yellow road, the grey slate roofs, the great irregular patches of damp on the asphalt of the drying pavements.

It was good to feel the solid old earth again, with its trees and houses, its waiters, and eggs and bacon, after the madness and passion of the night. At the back of his mind he knew that in the bright light of day, with his feet on solid earth among waiters and eggs and bacon, and Mrs. Garland and his mother, he would have again to face the passion of the night. But he did not want to, not yet: it was still too vivid to him. He still felt Gwen in his arms, even the short, deep sleep that came to him after she left him at dawn. The vividness of it was with him now in his exhilaration, his hunger, the mingled lassitude and vigour of his limbs.

After breakfast he refused to face it. It was good to be alive, to feel oneself a man, to feel the freshness of the rain in the sunny air. He went down and bathed in the sea. "Cool me down," he thought with a smile. But it intoxicated him the more; he seemed to be all body as the cold water sent the blood racing and glowing through him. And standing in the bathing-machine afterwards he looked down upon his limbs, ran his hands down the firm flesh, felt and saw the short curves of the muscles, and thought to himself, proud and half-amused: "Thank God, I'm a man!" And again after the bathing he turned away deliberately from the hotel. All that would keep; he wasn't afraid, not even of meeting Gwen; he felt his vigour, and his pride in his vigour, too keenly for that. But—well, it would keep; the morning was too fresh to waste.

He went singing up Beachy Head; he seemed to feel every little muscle moving in him. He walked with the spring of a fresh young mare tossing its head and picking up its feet as if it were brushing the daises off ground that was red-hot. It was a joy even to feel the breeze in his wet hair, and the sun drying the salt on his face. And he chanted aloud to the rhythm and beat of his footsteps:

"On thy bosom though many a kiss be,
  There are none such as knew it of old.
Was it Alciphron once or Arisbe
  Male ringlets or feminine gold?"

He could not think; he could only feel the sensualness of the sun and wind and sea. He lifted his head, threw it back in order to feel the breeze upon his throat and the sun burn his face. And all the while snatches of poetry came into his mind and were shouted aloud, the rhythm of them mingling with the rhythm of his swinging walk, the rhythm of the wind and the rhythm of the dancing seas. As he toiled up the steep places he boomed out in time to his long stride:

"Aeneadum genetrix, hominum divomgue voluptas,

Alma Venus caeli subter labentia signa
Quae mare navigerum, quae terras frugiferentis
Concelebras—"

and then with a rush downhill, he shouted:

"If you were queen of pleasure
And I were king of pain,
We'd hunt down love together,
Pluck out his flying feather,
And teach his feet a measure,
And find his mouth a rein
If you were queen of pleasure
And I were king of pain,
And I were king of pain,
And I were king of pain."

Up on the top, when he came to the wide view of the flat
silver sea, his pace slackened to:

"I am tired of tears and laughter
And men that laugh and weep;
Of what may come hereafter
For men that sow to reap;
I am tired of days and hours—"

He stopped; the freshness had suddenly died out of the
breeze, and with it the vigour out of his limbs. The glare of
the sun on the torpid sea hurt his eyes; the world which a few
moments before had been full of sounds and sights was
vacant, heavy, silent, monotonous, melancholy. He was
extraordinarily tired. He stretched himself full length on
the grass and almost immediately fell asleep.

When he woke up two hours later the earth and sea had
gone grey under an unbroken film of cloud that covered
the sky; a chilly wind was blowing from the land. His
head was burning hot, but he shivered with cold. Suddenly
he thought with horror, terror, of what he had done to
Gwen. He saw his mother, Mrs. Garland, Ethel, the little
houses in the straight, orderly roads at Richstead, Mr.

Macausland and May. It was impossible that he had— He saw Gwen as he had seen her that day on the river, in her white dress and pink-flowered hat and white gloves. What had happened to her down there at the hotel that morning? He began to run back to the hotel, and as he ran he kept on repeating one word to himself: Camilla, Camilla, Camilla.

When he caught his first sight of the hotel he stopped, breathless. He felt sick with anxiety and fear. He only knew that now he must marry Gwen—marry Gwen! He hated her at that moment, hated her soft, childish face and body and mind. In the lounge he stood bewildered. Somehow he had expected to find confusion, excitement, as soon as he entered the hotel. There was no one there; the emptiness and gloomy silence unnerved him still more. What was he to do now?

The hall-porter came up to him.

"The lady, Mrs. Davis, wished to see you, sir, as soon as you came in. She is upstairs in her room, sir."

He walked slowly up the stairs instead of taking the lift. He knew what he was going to do, but he hated the others because they would expect him to do it. He hated them all intensely, his mother, Mrs. Garland, Gwen; the thought of them filled him with loathing and disgust, as though they were something creeping, soiled. The foul, sordid world! There it was in Mrs. Davis, sitting wrapped round in her stale, nasty clothes, soft, peevish, tear-stained. The foul and fetid world!

"They told me you wanted me," he said coldly.

"That any son of mine——" Mrs. Davis began; her lips trembled, the tears rolled down her cheeks.

He turned his head away; it disgusted him too much to see that old tear-stained face. Disgust and cold anger were his only feelings.

"This room's very stuffy," he said. "Beastly wallpaper they always put in hotel bedrooms."

"Haven't you any feeling? Isn't it anything to you that you've disgraced me—d-d-disgraced us all? Mrs. Garland's heart-broken; she's very ill."

"Perhaps you'd tell me what's the matter."

"You know better than anyone what's the matter." Mrs. Davis's anger mastered her tears. "That any son of mine— Oh, I can't talk about it." Another burst of tears. Harry waited silently. "I—it's too horrible. Gwen—she—she's completely broken down."

Harry's heart gave him a kind of spasm; he became cold, almost shivering.

"The disgrace! I can't realise it. You—you've ruined the poor girl. Don't you understand? You must be mad—really you must be mad."

"I think I am," Harry said quietly.

"Oh, I can't believe it. And what are you going to do? Tell me that. What are you going to do?"

"I'm going to marry Gwen." He shuddered. Suddenly he felt sick, faint. He sat down in the cotton-covered armchair, leaned his head back and shut his eyes. His mother was becoming hysterical; her sobs sounded miles away. "Perhaps you'd go to her. I had better see her now—and alone."

"No, no. You can't. You mustn't see her. She's—Mrs. Garland would not—"

"And alone," Harry interrupted her in a low voice.

He heard the rustle of skirts and then the door close; he did not move or open his eyes. He would marry Gwen. He saw a little house in a back street of Richstead with white lace curtains in the window; he saw Gwen's face and un- understanding eyes. He felt as if he had been caught, trapped. He hated the softness of women. He thought of those toy balloons that are sold in the street; you just put your finger on them and you get a peculiar sensation of softness as the smooth skins give to your finger and crinkle round it—the same sensation would come to you if you put your finger on Gwen's bare flesh.

The door opened and his mother came in sobbing. She sat down in a chair and covered her eyes with her handkerchief. "She wants to see you," came in gasps.

He went to her room. He was furious with her; he would tell her that he would marry her, but he would also make her feel what she had done to him—he would make her smart first. She was sitting in a chair between the bed and the window. She was not crying, but the dark rims under her eyes showed that she had been. Her face was quite colourless. He could not misunderstand her feelings—she was afraid, miserably, piteously afraid. She was cowering into her chair, limp, collapsed. He closed his eyes for a moment, hesitating. Then he went to her, knelt by her side and stroked her hand.

"It's all right, Gwen dear," he said. "Don't be frightened. It's all right."

She half fell forward with her forehead on his shoulder. "I wanted you so, Harry. I—I—was so frightened—I was—in the morning when I woke up—and you weren't here. And then mamma came. Oh, Harry, you must despise me."

"No, dearest, no; of course not."

Despise her? He almost laughed. He despised, loathed himself, for not having seen what she was.

"It was so awful. I told her. I—I—was so frightened. Oh, Harry, what am I do do? What am I to do?"

He stroked her hair. A kind of coma began to creep over him: he had to force himself to speak. He listened to himself speaking as if the words came from someone else.

"Don't, Gwen dearest, don't. I came to tell you. I love you, dearest, you must know I love you. It's all right. You will marry me now, won't you?"

Gwen half pushed him away from her, and looked into his face. "But, Harry—oh—"

"You don't really think, dearest, I would have—if I

hadn't loved you. All that—that—that talk—I must have
been mad. Forget it. I—I couldn't live without you, Gwen
darling."

He looked straight into her eyes. It seemed to him that
he was watching coldly what was going on within. He
could have laughed bitterly at himself, at her, at the whole
world. It seemed to him that he saw her soul, her miserable,
weak, frightened soul, forcing itself to believe his lying
words. It knew they were lies, it knew they were lies. It
was turning in there, squirming down there. It believed, it
had shut its eyes. She flushed. It believed—she believed. He
could have taken her by the throat and shaken her.

She dropped her head on his shoulder again and pressed
him to her. "Harry, Harry"—the tears came—"oh, Harry, I
believe it's true. But tell me again, Harry, tell me it's true."

"It's true, Gwen. I love you—I always have really. Of
course it's true."

She sighed. He thought she was going to faint, and half
lifting her so that he could sit in the chair he took her in
his arms.

Gwen lay quietly in his arms with her eyes closed. She
looked as if she were asleep. She was at rest, happy; he
felt it in her body, in the abandonment of herself to him.
There was no passion now, only the security and content-
ment of belief. As he looked at her face, the face of a tired
child that had cried itself to sleep, with its little pink
mouth and its rounded, soft cheeks, his anger and his
hatred left him, left him old and cold, without feeling
except the weight of sadness and the bitterness of regret.
So ended dreams and the romance of life. The brave, wild
words, the revolt of youth, the splendour of love; the
fringe of what he had seen and touched for a few hours,
what he still saw fading away now into another world in
Camilla; hopes and desires and dreams and words. False
hopes and vain desires and absurd dreams and empty

words, how they crumbled before the first touch of this world! How he despised himself, one of the millions of ridiculous little souls, enmeshed, struggling feebly, stuck fast in the intricate sordidness of life.

He sat there brooding over Gwen. Already she was the woman, his wife, trusting, timid, submissive, unseeing, loving. He watched her coldly, saw her already *his*, his chattel, his wife, his dog. He did not hate her; he hated himself.

At last she moved in his arms, sighed, and opened her eyes. He smiled at her mechanically. "Dearest," she said and pressed her cheek against his.

"There's mamma," she said. "She was so—so upset. Hadn't I better—or will you?"

"I think perhaps you had better. I'll see her afterwards."

She got up; she was white and nervous, but with some touch now, he thought, of May's placidity. She kissed him and went to her mother.

XVI

THE EMOTIONS OF HARRY AND CAMILLA

Mrs. Davis recovered; Mrs. Garland recovered; Gwen recovered. Mrs. Garland perhaps was the only one who did not quite recover. After half an hour she dried her tears and kissed Gwen; she received and even kissed Harry. She said: "You—you'll be good to her, Harry?" just as she had said: "You—you'll be good to her, Angus?" in a low voice to Mr. Macausland. That was all she said. She seemed to have become quieter, smaller, whiter even than she had been before. For many days the vague little smile never came over her face. She sat very still with her hands on her lap, an odd, bewildered, frightened look in her eyes. Several times Harry wanted to go up to her and say, "I'm sorry," but he didn't. He pitied her, but what he wanted to say, patting her on the shoulder, was: "Come, come; pull yourself together. These things will happen; they will happen—and why not to you, why not to your daughter?" And of course he did not do that. Something had passed very close to, had touched Mrs. Garland, something which she did not understand—a deadly cold little wind which, sweeping over her, as she sat derelict half-way up the shore of life, made her shiver and very afraid. She recovered when she ceased to remember; and that happened after a week or two and she found that three full meals and tea were eaten daily, and there was Gwen still, just the same as ever, and four walls and a solid floor were still about and below her. So for the most part she ceased to remember, except when a little puff of that cold wind blew over her, and for a moment she shivered and was afraid.

Mrs. Davis recovered almost immediately, because she

forgot so soon. At the first shock her world had fallen
about her ears. These things didn't happen to people in
her class of life. Gwen and Harry! Impossible—impossible
that her son should be a scoundrel, and Mrs. Garland's
daughter a— One of her brothers had gone wrong, of
course, though even he was not a scoundrel. She remembered the scandal of a large red-faced woman in a black
dress standing on the doorstep of her father's house and
crying: "Give me back my daughter." Oscar had taken the
daughter for an afternoon on the river and had succeeded
in missing the last train to town, and then they had gone
to an hotel, and then. . .Well, Oscar was her brother; he
was not a scoundrel, but something had gone wrong with
him, so wrong that at last his fare had been paid to America.
Nothing had gone wrong with Harry; he was honest,
upright, moral. The only thing to complain of was his
discontent, and his habit of making absurd statements—for
instance, that lakes aren't beautiful. And now—and now
Gwen and Harry are in her room, and Gwen is crying on
her shoulder, and Mrs. Davis is crying and kissing Gwen,
and Gwen is going to marry Harry.

After all, that *is* the fact to remember: Harry and Gwen
are to be married. The night was a dream, and the morning
a nightmare; they have passed away, are forgotten. She has
cried with and kissed Mrs. Garland; the real world has
come back again. And now—now of course the *only* thing
is to prevent a scandal. Nobody must know.

"You must be brave, my dear. Hetty suspects nothing—
I sent her out for the whole morning. And Ethel and Janet
and dear May and Mr. Macausland, you must keep it from
them. I am afraid we must stay on till the end of our time
here; it would look too odd to leave suddenly. We had
better announce the engagement to-day. And the wedding,
early autumn, I think, at the same time as May's. That's
early enough. It would look *too* curious to have it before,

and then one can make arrangements, I'm sure. You must be brave for your own sake, for her sake."

The two ladies dried each other's tears, and by tea-time the rumbling of the world's wheels in its old grooves had almost come back to them. Once more, for the thousandth time, they sacrificed themselves for their thankless, graceless children, closed their old eyes and hearts, and presented a bold face to the world. And after all, an engagement is exciting; there was the telling to the others and their surprise; and at dinner Mr. Macausland ordered a bottle of champagne and made a little speech about his being glad to see that his good example was being followed, and nodded over his glass to Gwen and Harry, and drank their health. It was quite a merry party.

And Gwen recovered because she too forgot. Harry watched with amazement and bitterness her face, self-possessed and happy, during Mr. Macausland's little speech. The real world had closed about her again. She loved Harry, and now Harry loved her and there she was engaged. Life was, after all, secure with Mrs. Davis there smiling across the table, and saying, with that air of unruffled certainty which oldish hens and women above the age of forty alone possess, that she never did approve of long engagements. Nothing was left of the past twenty-four hours, except the dark lines under Mrs. Garland's eyes.

So Harry smiled too at the dinner-table, and smiled good-night to Gwen when she went up to bed, and slept soundly through the night. And next morning he found this letter stuck in the green baize rack, waiting for him at breakfast time.

"MY DEAR HARRY,

"I haven't answered your letter, because I've been thinking. I want to tell you the truth. It's certainly true that I want to see you again. Your letter gave me pleasure: it gives me pleasure to know that you love me. Is that just ordinary feminine vanity? Katharine would say it was, but I don't think it's only that. I think it's partly because I like you very much. I write as I think.

"I told Katharine that I am an adventurer; she says I'm an adventuress. Perhaps I'm both. It's the romantic part of life that I want; it's the voyage out that seems to me to matter, the new and wonderful things. I can't, I won't look beyond that. I want them all. I want love, too, and I want freedom. I want children even. But I can't give myself; passion leaves me cold. You'll think I am asking for everything to be given and to give nothing. Perhaps that's true.

"And then there's so much in marriage from which I recoil. It seems to shut women up and out. I won't be tied by the pettinesses and the conventionalities of life. There must be some way out. One must live one's own life, as the novels say.

"If you understand this and don't hate me for it, come and see me when we get back, which will be in ten days now.

"I don't know that I like this country. It's full of trees and lanes and great fields where the cows stand deep in grass and buttercups brush their sides. But it's wonderfully soothing, and we are all as fat as the pastures and the cows. In the evenings at twilight, when there's no wind, it's like being in church.

"Trevor has been staying with us and Arthur for a few days, but now we're alone. I suppose you wouldn't come?

"Yours,
"C.L."

Harry put the letter in his pocket, and—the thought came to him—like a well-conducted person went on eating bread and butter. He thought that he did not think about Camilla. The days passed, the old life returned, and bore him along, submissive, un-understanding through its meaningless, dreamy days. Mr. Macausland still managed expeditions. Harry watched it and himself, outside in some way and aloof. "It works out like a mathematical formula— I: Gwen: : Macausland: May," he thought. He was engaged, and so on expeditions he was left to walk alone with her. They talked of what they would do and where they would live; he would have to make money, he would give up his "art." Mr. Davis had suggested that he should come into his firm, become eventually a partner. He walked through meaningless and dreamy days. He even made love to her and kissed her. He saw that she had forgotten, that she was happy, that she was passionless and secure. He saw his mother and all women in her eyes—the power to believe what they want to believe.

On September 2nd they all returned to Richstead. The wind eddying the dead leaves and dust in the corners of walls was the melancholy wind of a dying summer. Life had stopped for Harry. He had nothing to do; he could not paint. He was waiting, waiting for the month to pass before his marriage. He sat in his room with a book or wandered aimlessly about the streets, or took Gwen for walks or to the theatre or concerts. All the time he was waiting for the moment to come when, he knew, he would go and see Camilla.

It came one Saturday afternoon. He asked for Miss Camilla and the maid showed him into the room with the arm-chairs. Mr. Lawrence, lying back in one of them, said: "Hallo, Davis!" The others too were occupied: Katharine and Camilla and Trevor Trevithick were all there.

"Hallo, Harry!" said Katharine meditatively. Trevor smiled at him, and Camilla opened her lips to speak, but was silent. There they were in their arm-chairs, with books scattered all round them.

"You look as if you've all been here since the last time I saw you," he said bitterly.

"I wish we had," said Mr. Lawrence.

"Why?"

"It might be time for some of us to get up and go. As it is we've only just settled down, and God knows for how long." He yawned.

"We don't yet know where Trevor went to in Italy," said Katharine.

"I told you; I went to Prato."

"Only to Prato? Why did you go there?"

"I wanted to see the Madonna delle Carcini."

"What's that?"

"A church. It was built by Guiliano da Sangallo."

"Never heard of him," said Mr. Lawrence.

"No, he's not much known."

"And that's why you went to see his damned church, I suppose," said Harry.

Trevor smiled at him. "One reason, perhaps."

"And good enough," said Mr. Lawrence. "After all, one only goes to see those appalling Michelangelos and Titians and things because they're well known."

"You're not fair to Michelangelo, I think," said Camilla.

"Oh, well, I expect he's all right. But he's such a bore."

"I met Grainger to-day in Piccadilly," said Mr. Lawrence, smiling, after a few minutes' silence.

"I say, really?" said Katharine.

"I had to speak to him; I ran right into him. He was all in black. 'I've lost my dear Tom. I'm heartbroken, my dear fellow. On the top of all the other trouble.' I almost laughed in his face."

"Good Lord! Tom dead? What did he die of?"

"He walked into a motor car, apparently. If I had been old Lottie's husband I shouldn't have called her running off with somebody else a trouble."

"You think you wouldn't mind your wife running off with anybody, whoever she was, I expect," said Harry.

"Mind? It depends on what you mean by mind."

Mr. Lawrence put the tips of his fingers together and looked judicially at Harry. "I shouldn't mind as old Grainger imagines he minds, who thinks that chastity—where he isn't concerned—is the most important quality in a wife. Yes. *I* think we've got beyond that, and the Victorian view of marriage. Conventions, my dear Davis; I'm afraid you're still what they call hidebound by them."

Suddenly Harry's anger rose as he looked round the placid group—books, books, books, and talk, talk, talk—and Camilla sitting there silent, thoughtful, unpassionate in the midst of it, as he had seen her sitting that first time months ago. He had the same feeling as he had when his mother and Mrs. Garland and Mr. Macausland sat round in a circle and talked, a feeling of uselessness and emptiness and purposelessness. He got up and stood in front of Mr. Lawrence, looking down at him.

"Conventions," he said angrily. "You don't know what conventions are. You think you're open-minded because you call Michelangelo a bore and appreciate Strauss. You're damned intelligent, of course, and cultured, and—and emasculated by it all. You're far more stupid than really stupid people, that's the truth of it; they at any rate don't pretend that they're anything more than they are. They——"

"Nonsense. That's just——"

"Oughtn't I to know? I live with them. They don't. Conventions? Good Lord! You'd call hunger a convention—only it's the one primitive human feeling that your culture can't get rid of without getting rid of you. You——"

Harry stopped. He suddenly saw himself standing there in the middle of the silent figures lying back in their chairs, and Camilla very still, one hand hanging loosely unclasped over the arm of her chair, looking down so that to him her eyes were closed. He turned to Mr. Lawrence and said:

"I retract all that. I apologise."

He went over to Camilla and said to her: "Will you come up to your room, or out? I want to speak to you."

Camilla got up and went to the door, and as he followed her he turned back again and went to Katharine, and shook hands with her.

"Good-bye, Katharine," he said, "I don't expect I shall come back."

"Mad," murmured Mr. Lawrence as the door closed. "The fellow's mad."

Upstairs in Camilla's room, with her sitting just as she had sat the last time that he had been there, Harry hesitated.

"Something's the matter, Harry," she said to him gently. "What is it?"

He leaned his forehead against the mantelpiece and thought. When he spoke it was slowly, as if he were thinking aloud.

"The romantic part of life is what you want—in your letter you said that. I wonder if you mean what I mean by that. To me it's you, ever since I first saw you and your face—it's like a face in a dream to me—in that muddled room. I'm not going to make love to you. I've come to say good-bye altogether, but I can't help telling you now I see you here; and downstairs—that's really what made me flare out at your father. You know, I'm sure you know, it's when one sets out, when one's young; it's romantic, fool-ishly romantic, I daresay—coming from books, novels, and poetry, but coming from something real too, some-thing inside oneself. It's half of one's desires, and all of one's dreams—that's why always your face is like a face in a dream to me. God! what a fool I've been; and now too, to vapour like this about it. But I wanted you to know what—that that's what you'll always be to me."

"But, Harry, after my letter. Is that it? Surely we can go on."

"No, I'm going to be married—two weeks now."

He gave one quick glance at Camilla, and saw a look of pain on her face, and her eyes open wide and little lines on her forehead. She sat almost rigidly still.

"Don't say anything until I've told you," he said, and his voice was uneven from the throbbing of his heart and pulse. "You remember that girl at the garden-party—Gwen, the youngest of the Garlands? I ruined her, or she ruined me—well, we ruined each other, and now we're to marry—in two weeks."

Harry sat forward in his chair, his elbows on his knees, looking straight into her face. She shut her eyes, and, though she made no movement at all, it seemed to him that a shudder passed over her.

"You hate me for it?" he said.

"It makes me afraid."

"Why?"

"It seems so near."

"I wanted you to know. I didn't love her; I don't. I hardly like her."

"Don't, Harry, don't; it seems to touch me. It's something ugly, something cruel."

"Yes; and Grainger and his wife—you could laugh at that, and Tom's death."

She did not answer. It was as if Harry had taken her by the hand and was leading her up to touch something cold and hard.

"Won't you understand?" he said. "It would be some comfort to me. It was all an absurd mistake. I talked to Gwen as you—we all talk down there. She believed, as we don't. It frightened me, just as it frightened you; facts do. I was trapped, I couldn't escape. It was because I loved you."

"And she? Is she——"

"Yes, I suppose so. She was, at any rate."

"You must marry her, Harry?"

"Yes."

She seemed to be nearer to him than she had ever been before. He could hardly keep back his tears.

"You understand, Camilla, I'm done for. But I love you, dearest. After your letter—I had to tell you."

"You can't do it, Harry; you mustn't do it." It was almost a cry.

"Don't, dearest," he said in a low voice. "I must now, you know it."

They sat silent. A sort of fog seemed to gather in the room and a cold silence. It was as if they were waiting for something, without thinking, only feeling each other's presence. Suddenly Harry heard the ticking of the clock, very loud and persistent, as one does late in the afternoon when one has lain ill in bed all day.

"Well, I must go," he said in a dull voice, getting up.

She did not move or speak. She sat back looking at him, her hands on the arms of her chair. He noticed how white her face was. He stood hesitating.

He went to her, and leaned with one hand on the arm of her chair and bent over her, looking into her eyes. Even then she did not move.

"May I kiss you?" he whispered.

He just touched her hair with his hand and then kissed her on the lips without passion, as if it were a symbol, a ceremony, an act to be always remembered. It gave him pleasure even that she did not respond, that she lay back submissive, that, as he left her, she did not move or speak.

XVII

ENDS WITH WORDS

Harry and Gwen were married in church, side by side with May and Mr. Macausland. No questions were asked, and so the Holy Church administered its most holy sacrament to one whom upon a previous page of its prayer-book it condemned to perish everlastingly. Presumably it was all right, for the vicar, who was a minister of God and must have known the material facts, raised no objections; and Harry, who carefully read the marriage service on the evening before the wedding, came to the conclusion that God had "consecrated the state of Matrimony to such an excellent Mystery" that it not only "signified and represented the spiritual marriage and unity betwixt Christ and the Church," but covered still more mysterious anomalies. Mrs. Davis would have preferred a synagogue, but she recognised that certain circumstances made it desirable that the wedding should conform as publicly as possible to the standards of suburban weddings; and it was only natural that if it were possible for a sister to be married on the same day and in the same church as her sister and the vicar of the parish, she should be so married. Every morning and evening Mrs. Davis turned her face to the North Pole, which she thought was the east and the direction in which lay Jerusalem, and said aloud: "Hear, O Israel, the Lord our God, the Lord is one," but in what she called her "heart of hearts" she did feel that a church was better than a registrar's office, and would have more efficacy in casting oblivion over that terrible night and morning at Eastbourne. The matter was really arranged between Mrs. Davis and Mrs. Garland. Not much was said by them on the subject; in their conversations

about Gwen's and Harry's marriage and future their eyes
suddenly met and dropped sometimes, but neither of them
now ever alluded to what had happened before the engagement. The two ladies understood one another.

Harry pitied himself: it seemed to him that he was
watching life close in upon him pitilessly and miserably. So
the days before the wedding day slipped by him. He felt
himself more remote from Gwen than he had ever been
before, and the more so because she was unaware of it.
The presents gave her almost as much pleasure as they did
to Mrs. Davis.

On the day itself he was astonished to find how nervous
he was. It was a damp, warm autumn day when he drove in
a taxi to the church, and through the open window all the
way the smell of dead leaves blew in upon him. The same
smell followed him into the hot, stuffy church. He noticed
it still as he stood shifting nervously from one foot to the
other by Mr. Macausland's side. Even Mr. Macausland was
nervous. They did not speak to one another after the first
greeting, and both kept fingering the rings in their waistcoat pockets.

With the brides and the two bridesmaids, Hetty and
Dolly Lynton, came the smell of flowers. Harry noticed
that Mrs. Garland was very white in the face, and Mrs.
Davis very red. The church seemed to be very full of people,
who shuffled and whispered a good deal. Only Ethel
appeared calm; he saw her in a front pew, half smiling. "A
foolish virgin," he thought to himself, and then immediately he saw Camilla leaning back in her chair, half smiling
too. Someone touched him on the arm. He had to go
forward to the altar; the ceremony was beginning.

He stood and knelt and repeated words, as Macausland
did and May and Gwen. The clergyman had a droning voice,
the place was hot and stuffy; people still shuffled, but an
emotion, not any particular emotion of joy or pity or fear,

but a vague and nameless emotion rose in him, as he felt it
rising in all who stood around him. It made Mrs. Garland
cry, and even Mr. Davis swallow repeatedly. Perhaps it was
the feeling creeping through the church that here was one
of the great moments, the crises of life, materialising before
their eyes. Births, marriages, and deaths—Harry thought of
the first column of newspapers; to be born, to marry and to
die—there seemed to be something solemn, something noble
almost tragic connected with these three operations of
humanity, which was stirring him and the black-coated,
besilked and besatined and beribboned people around him.
The words which the priest droned at first sounded absurd
and out of place, but every now and then some phrase
seemed to fit in with and raise the emotion. "Who giveth
this Woman to be married to this Man?" A curious hush fell
upon them; something old, out of date and forgotten,
stirred in the words. Then the incongruity of the words
began again; they were singing hideously about happiness
and praise of God. There was a great shuffling, and everyone knelt. A silence fell, and then:

> "Lord, have mercy upon us."

A pause.

> "Christ, have mercy upon us."

Another pause.

> "Lord, have mercy upon us."

The emotion surged back over them. Something terrible
was happening; they were crying out in terror.

> "O Lord, save thy servant and thy handmaid,"

groaned the clergyman, and the congregation moaned:

> "Who put their trust in thee."
> "O Lord, send them help from thy holy place,"

groaned the clergyman, and the congregation moaned:

"And evermore defend them."

"Be unto them a tower of strength,"

groaned the clergyman, and the congregation muttered:

"From the face of their enemy."

"O Lord, hear our prayer,"

moaned the clergyman, and the congregation whispered:

"And let our cry come unto thee."

"O God of Abraham, God of Isaac, God of Jacob," gabbled the clergyman, and the spell was broken.

Harry almost smiled: Mrs. Davis must be feeling that she was practically in synagogue. Abraham, Isaac, and Jacob! So those long-white-bearded old patriarchs of his childhood were presiding over his marriage with Gwen, and their God, old Jehovah! Shemang Yisrael adonai elohainu adonai echad! he could remember it still: "Hear, O Israel, the Lord our God the Lord is one." And God, the Father, and the Lord Jesus Christ, and the fellowship of the Holy Ghost! "This woman," droned the clergyman, "may be loving and amiable, faithful and obedient to her husband; and in all quietness, sobriety, and peace, be a follower of the holy and godly matrons." Poor Gwen! A follower of holy and godly matrons! "And live together in holy love unto your lives' end. Amen."

A sort of sight of relief went round. Well, that was over. Everyone turned half to the right or to the left to show that it was over, and met the eyes of someone else and smiled. Mrs. Davis squeezed Harry's hand; she was crying. Mrs. Garland was crying. They herded together into the vestry to sign the register. Everyone seemed to be crying, and kissing somebody. In the end Harry kissed even May.

He was sitting in a hired brougham with Gwen, driving back to St. Catherine's Avenue. Again the smell of dead leaves blew in and overpowered the heavy, sensual smell of Gwen's flowers. "There's the bride," he heard people say. Gwen was crying; he took her hand in his. He had nothing to say to her, so he said: "Don't cry, Gwen dear," and she answered: "I'm so happy, Harry."

The remainder of the day passed for him intolerably slowly. There was a large meal at which he drank a great deal of champagne. Mr. Macausland's speech was a great success. He said: "Although I cannot pretend to have an unbiassed opinion as to the respective merits of the two brides, it seems to me that everyone will agree on the wisdom of the two bridegrooms in marrying one of them." Ethel joined in the laughter: Gwen and May had been very gentle and kind to her all day.

In the afternoon he went home and packed his box. His head was hot and ached. Then he returned to the Garlands' house, where Mrs. Garland was "at home" from 4.30 to 7.30. He was congratulated by fifty or sixty people, and for an hour and a half edged despondently round crowded rooms. Late in the afternoon he found himself standing in a corner by Ethel's side.

"Wish me luck," he said to her.

"I do, Harry."

They shook hands.

"No oil in your lamp, Ethel. But who knows which is wise and which is foolish?" She did not understand what he meant, but she smiled at him, because he said such funny things. He shook hands with her again.

Later he found himself in another corner with Janet. To-day her frank grey eyes made him feel nervous and uncomfortable. In the crowded drawing-room among the gay and flimsy young women she, planted firmly on her large feet, seemed like a great sheaf of wild, sweet-smelling gorse that had by some whim or mistake of the gardener grown up among the exotic, delicate flowers in a greenhouse.

"I don't think you've ever congratulated me," he

said tentatively.

Her eyes were steady; the lips, sensitive like those of a child rather than of a woman of thirty, tightened for a moment.

"I wish you luck," she said reticently, but not unkindly.

"I wish I knew what you really think about."

"Golf." There was a trace of contempt for him in her voice. It roused him.

"You despise me. I expect you're right."

She laughed. "My good fellow, don't let's get sentimental. I think: 'Poor Gwen,' if you want to know."

"Poor Gwen? Well—I daresay you're right."

"You're a man, Harry. You ask for the truth, and pull a long face when you get it. But I always made up my mind I'd tell it to you if you asked me for it. I shall like you better afterwards."

It hurt him, and yet he could be impersonal enough to realise that he thought her charming. "I can bear it," he said, smiling.

"I don't think you're a cad, but I believe you behaved like one," she went on in the matter-of-fact voice in which one school-boy gives his opinion of the character of another. "You're a jolly sight too clever, Harry, that's what's wrong with you. You're one of those people who are always quite sure they can get down in three; they have a safe four, they go for the three, and take six. You think I've never thought about anything but golf. Oh, yes, you do. But I have. When I was eighteen I thought a jolly good deal too much about myself and what people thought of me. Then I suddenly found I was twenty-six and I thought an awful lot about what was going to happen to me. I'd rather be out of doors than in this"—she looked quietly round the drawing-room—"anyway. And to tell you the honest truth, I had rather be playin' golf this time next year than nursin' babies. I can't exactly explain what I mean, but you're so jolly clever I dare say you'll twig it."

Mr. Davis came up to Harry. "It's about time you went, isn't it? Your train's at 5.30."

Harry looked at his father's large blank eyes; he shuddered to see so little understanding there. And it wasn't his father's fault, it was just as much his own. It suddenly appeared to him and shocked him that he was responsible for those blank eyes and for the lack of any bond of humanity, let alone filial feeling, between himself and his father. He turned his own eyes to the crowd of people surrounding him. A great hubbub of words and laughter was going up from them. He tried to hear what was being said; he could only catch disjointed sentences.

"Oh, I say, not really!"

"My dear, you really must talk to——"

"Good for you, good for——"

"Poor old Macausland!"

They were waiting, with blank eyes, too, waiting to watch him and Macausland and Gwen and May go out to—to what did they picture it? It was for him they were there, to see him begin his life with Gwen. Did that call up anything before their blank eyes, their blank imaginations? He tried to remember what he had thought at other people's weddings. Some stray prurient thought and joke about the first night—that was all that it meant to them.

He made his way slowly to the door. As he passed, a young man whom he did not know said something in a whisper to another young man, and they both laughed in a half-bold, half-repressed way. In the hall Hetty, rather flushed, met him.

"Oh, I've been looking for you. Gwen's just ready. Come and say good-bye to mamma."

He was in a trance now; he obeyed Hetty mechanically, and went into the small room which was known as the study. There he found his mother and Mrs. Garland, both again tear-stained, and Mr. and Mrs. Macausland. He smiled at them. His mother came and put her hands on his shoulders and looked up into his face. "This is a great day in your life," she said. He looked into her eyes, wondering whether the words meant anything at all to her.

It was a relief to him that Gwen and Ethel came into the room at that moment.

"You ought to be going, Harry," Mr. Davis called from the passage.

"You go first," said May, majestic now in a new fawn tailor-made costume and a new hat with a straight feather in it.

"Good-bye, mother," said Harry, kissing Mrs. Davis.

"Good-bye, my boy," said Mrs. Davis, kissing him and feeling that something ought to be said to mark the occasion, but that there was nothing to say.

"You'll be good to her, Harry?" said Mrs. Garland, kissing him and crying.

Mr. Macausland shook his hand. "Good luck and God bless you," he said in a hearty, manly, priestly voice.

"You'll be late," Mr. Davis called from the passage.

"Did you put the hair-brushes in?" Gwen asked Ethel suddenly.

"Good-bye, Ethel, good-bye." Harry kissed Ethel, to her astonishment. "You've been very nice to me," he went on in a low voice, "and you're wise."

He was in the crowded, noisy hall. People already began to pelt him with rice. Even then he seemed somewhere at the back of his mind to be trying to find—as he had been all day and for many days—some explanation for all this. It was only half-real, half-dream, these things happening around him. He pushed his way through, smiling; he felt Gwen close behind him and heard her laugh.

His father was on the pavement to shut the door of the taxi. He shook Harry's hand through the window and said:

"Good luck." Harry looked into those blank eyes again as they drove off.

He held Gwen's hand, but he could not think of or attend to her. There was still some thought, something like an answer to a problem, which he felt eluding him continually. He was not even putting the problem to himself. He sat back looking out as it were over life, letting thoughts come and go passively, waiting for what he almost felt would be a revelation or sign. It was the same in the bustle and turmoil of the station, it was the same when at last he sat opposite to Gwen in the corner of the railway carriage.

He watched out of the window the country flash by, dim and silver and shadowy under the light of the moon. He was not unhappy, though he felt sad. Again the smell of dead leaves blew in. Lights flashed by, clustered together in towns and villages, or twinkling far off in twos and threes, or solitary and romantic, calling up visions of men and women sitting in lonely houses around the table and the lighted lamp. It pleased him to think of them there in their soft, warm rooms, and yet it made him feel lonely and homeless, rushing on with the roar and rattle of the train through the night. Suddenly the train seemed to run out softly into a new and open country, that stretched far away without trees or hedges or lights to the pale sky. A line of dim lights appeared, and a river coiling like a great silver snake. Something of the profound peace of the hills and the river and the water meadows, softened by the light of the moon, came to him—and then suddenly a stab of pain. He knew the gentle curve of that hill; it was there that he had sat with Arthur, there that he had walked with Camilla. He looked at Gwen, saw her childish face, her eyes blank as his father's, and then he saw Camilla. He had failed, failed, failed.

He looked up again at the curve of the hill; it was fading away as the train rattled on. As it disappeared it seemed to him that the answer came to him. A kind of wave of happiness passed over him. He had known Camilla: he had loved her.

"Nothing matters," he cried to himself.

The train slowed down, stopped. There was turmoil again as they left the train for the boat.

Half an hour later he stood on deck with Gwen. There was no wind, but the air was keenly cold. The sea lay without a wave or ripple, smoothed out to a sheet of silver by the moon. Gwen put her arm through his and drew him close to her.

"Dearest," she whispered.

He looked down at her face so close to him, and, shutting his eyes, kissed her.

THE END